Dear Reader,

When you're only five years old, the world can be a confusing and frightening place. Powerful superheroes may be comforting to think about, but flesh-and-blood heroes are even better insurance against being scared. In *Sparks*, a fatherless little boy named Denny desperately needs such a hero, and a fireman steps up to the challenge.

If you're looking for a knight in shining armor, Jeb Stratton's your guy. He's the one with the ax, the forcible-entry man, or as Denny calls him, "the force-ball entry man." Like knights of old, Jeb suits up and rides out to meet and slay the dragon. In the process, he rescues damsels (and other vulnerable creatures) in distress. He understands the danger of his task, and he does it anyway, which is my definition of courage.

Best of all, he doesn't take himself seriously. In my opinion, a man who can make jokes when his life is on the line is positively irresistible. Obviously I couldn't resist Jeb. Here's hoping you won't be able to, either.

Warmly,

Vicki Lewis Thompson

VICKI LEWIS THOMPSON

loves writing hot stories. She is the author of over fifty novels for Harlequin Books, and with more than fifteen million of her sizzling books in print worldwide, it's a cinch she's contributed to global warming, and she's proud of it.

A Waldenbooks bestseller, she's a seven-time finalist for Romance Writers of America's RITA Award and has been honored by both *Romantic Times Magazine* and *Affaire de Coeur.*

Vicki has been married for an astonishing number of years and has two grown children.

& BACHELORS USA

Vicki Lewis Thompson
Sparks

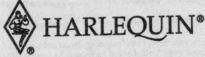

TORONTO • NEW YORK • LONDON
AMSTERDAM • PARIS • SYDNEY • HAMBURG
STOCKHOLM • ATHENS • TOKYO • MILAN • MADRID
PRAGUE • WARSAW • BUDAPEST • AUCKLAND

To Jeff Peto and Lee Rau
for their generous help and advice,
and to firefighters everywhere
who risk their lives
for their fellow human beings.

HARLEQUIN BOOKS
225 Duncan Mill Road, Don Mills,
Ontario, Canada M3B 3K9

ISBN 0-373-82261-8

SPARKS

Copyright © 1988 by Vicki Lewis Thompson

PROLOGUE

To Jeff Peto and Lee Rau
for their generous help and advice,
and to fire fighters everywhere
who risk their lives
for their fellow human beings.

WHEN THE ALARM CAME IN at midnight for the old Madison Hotel, Jeb Stratton knew what to expect. An abandoned building surrendered to fire like a willing lover, as if choosing the drama of flames over the indignity of the wrecking ball. While it burned, the Madison would test the mettle and challenge the endurance of every man running across the apparatus floor. The Melwood Park Fire Department had a working fire.

Jeb shoved his arms into his turnout coat and swung up on the ladder truck beside his best friend, Kevin McWade. They exchanged a glance, both acknowledging without words what they would risk tonight, both knowing they wouldn't have it any other way.

While Jeb searched for the fire's heart and anyone caught in the blaze, Kevin would give the smoke and flames an escape route. The fire fighters had nicknamed him "Catman" for his agility as he vented the fire from above, chopping or sawing holes in the roof to release the monster's superheated breath. Kevin's friends claimed that he had nine lives, which was fortunate, because the roof man had the deadliest job of all.

Jeb tried not to think about the condition of the Madison's roof as the ladder truck and the pumper sped through the muggy summer night toward the fire. In less than three minutes they reached the old hotel, and seconds later the ladder swiveled into position. Jeb spared only one more glance at Kevin climbing the aluminum rungs in the glare from the spotlights before he fastened his mask and headed toward the main entrance. Kevin would make it. He always had.

The fire was on the top floor. The search for anyone trapped in the hotel had to start there, at the source of danger, where a vagrant might have fallen asleep while smoking. Abandoned didn't always mean uninhabited, and the fire had started somehow. Once the search for life was over, the engine company could bring the hose in and put water on the fire.

Jeb and Steve, the other inside man that night, took the narrow stairs steadily, not wanting to be out of breath when they got to the fire, not wanting to use up too much of the precious oxygen seeping into their masks. Sweat soaked their uniforms under the heavy canvas turnouts.

At the top of the four flights they veered left, toward the heat. Mustard-colored smoke drifted from under a door, and Jeb tried the knob. Locked. He motioned to Steve, who pried the door open with his halligan tool. Smoke poured out of the opening, and both men dropped to all fours. The fire crackled just beyond, in the next room. Jeb heard the faint chopping as Kevin worked to open a hole above it, to keep the blaze going up instead of spreading out.

Then the chopping stopped. There was a crack, and then a ripping sound, and Jeb pictured Kevin leaping back as the roof gave way beneath him. But something didn't fit the picture. A muffled scream. Kevin? Jeb hurtled into the blazing room in time to see his friend hit the floor with a sickening thud.

Thank God it was a short way, Jeb thought, fighting across the stove-top heat of the floor to Kevin's motionless body. *Have to get him out of here. Something's probably broken.* Even before he reached him, Jeb knew what was broken. Kevin's neck was twisted at an impossible angle. His eyes were open, unseeing. His nine lives were gone. He was dead.

Later, after the fire was out and the men of the engine company were taking up the lengths of hose, Jeb walked wearily out of the blackened building. Steve was still inside, finishing up the job by overhauling the ceilings and walls, pulling down anything suspicious to check for sparks.

Jeb slumped on the ladder truck's running board and buried his face in his hands. The other fire fighters didn't acknowledge his sobs except for an occasional hand on his shoulder. The old-timers had lost at least one buddy in the line of duty and they understood. The new recruits were sobered by a glimpse of their own mortality and kept their distance from the man on the running board.

At last Jeb lifted his head, too exhausted even to cry. He stared at the smoldering shell that had killed his friend. They'd found no one in the building. Chances were it had been deliberately torched. Gradually Jeb's sorrow curdled into rage. The building hadn't killed Kevin—people had.

Chief Gregorio, looking years older than fifty-four, walked over and stood beside Jeb. Together they gazed at the gutted hotel until finally the chief uttered an obscenity and glanced away.

"We'll get them, Chief."

"We can try."

"Anything to go on?"

The chief turned a soot-blackened face toward Jeb. "Not much. We think it's kids again," he said.

CHAPTER ONE

DENNY BURROWED UNDER his Mickey Mouse quilt, and his toes touched the cool plastic of the lighter. "Do I *have* to go to bed, Mommy?"

"Yes, you do." His mommy smoothed his hair. "It's late, and you have school tomorrow."

"So what? They make us take naps." Denny snuggled deeper and rubbed his toes against the lighter, his secret. "I'm too big for naps."

"I know. Next year they won't make you do that."

"Can I stay home tomorrow and ride around with you? I'll be real good while you tune pianos. I promise."

"Afraid not, sweetheart."

"Aw, no fair. Come on, please?"

"No, Denny."

"Mommy, my throat's all scratchy. I think I'm getting sick."

She smiled. "And I think you're stalling, trying to keep me from turning out the light. You didn't say anything about a scratchy throat when you ate those cookies a little while ago."

Denny gazed into her face. His friend Eric said she looked like a movie star, and that made Denny feel real good. But even if Eric's mommy wasn't as pretty, she was home more. And Eric had a daddy, too. And a dog and a pet rabbit. "Eric's lucky, Mommy." Sometimes when he said that he got his way.

His mommy sighed. "Oh, Denny." She gathered him into her arms and hugged him. "Someday we'll have a house like Eric's and you can have a puppy, and your own swing set, and maybe a sandbox, and—"

"Let me stay up, Mommy. Let me watch you and Bill practice. Bill said I could. He said I was a good audience."

His mommy laughed and made him lie down again. "Sometimes I think I have two kids, you and Bill."

"Bill's not a kid. He's almost as old as you. He told me so."

"Okay, he's not a kid, but he doesn't get to vote on whether or not you stay up. I'm still the boss in that department, and you need your sleep." She kissed him on the cheek. "Good night, punkin."

He grabbed her around the neck once more, loving the softness of her hair, which was nicer to touch than Eric's rabbit. His mommy's eyes were a chocolate kind of brown, and he liked looking into them and seeing his own face reflected there. "Please, Mommy, I—"

"Good night, Denny." She unhooked his arms from around her neck and stood up. "It's time to go to sleep." She smiled and turned off his teddy bear lamp. "See you in the morning."

Denny rolled over, turning his back on her. He couldn't get his way anymore, ever since his mommy started working on this new act with Bill. She was always busy, busy, busy.

After the door closed and Denny heard the piano and banjo playing again, he reached under the covers and pulled out the lighter. It was bright red, his favorite color, and about as big around as one of his Lincoln Logs. The top part had the fire in it. He pushed the tiny pedal with his thumb and the light jumped up, making his shadow like a giant on the wall.

Denny made the flame go out and held the lighter up to his nose. It had a sharp, grown-up kind of smell. He was glad he'd seen it first instead of Eric so that he could keep it. Holding the lighter, Denny slid out of bed and tiptoed to the door. He put his ear against the wood to listen to his mother and Bill practicing.

He didn't know the song. Probably one of the new ones Bill was making up. Bill was real good at making up songs. He'd said that someday he would go to New York and be famous.

Lots of keys on the piano crashed all at once, and Denny clapped a hand over his mouth so they wouldn't hear him giggle. He knew just what his mother had done—flopped both arms down on the piano and put her head down, too. She looked funny when she did that, and it always made Denny laugh.

"Ease up, Liza," Bill coaxed. "It's not that hard."

"Yes, it is, Bill. This is a complicated little ditty you wrote."

There was a long silence as Denny waited to hear what Bill would say next.

"You haven't practiced it, have you?"

"Sort of."

"You're playing this for the first time, aren't you?"

"Well, yes." Denny heard his mommy sigh real loud, the way she did when he forgot to make his bed. "I meant to find time over the weekend," his mommy continued, "but Denny wanted me to help him build this thing with his Legos, and between that and catching up on the wash... Listen to me with my excuses. You don't want to hear excuses."

"Liza, I know it must be tough, raising Denny by yourself. Maybe you should ask your parents to baby-sit once in a while.''

''They announced before Denny was born that they didn't consider that their function. No way would I ask them.''

''Yeah, but it doesn't seem fair that you're stuck all alone in this thing. No contact from Denny's father, your parents pretty much out of the picture....''

''That's the way it has to be. And I can balance everything okay. This weekend just got away from me, that's all. I'll practice more. I promise.''

Denny's shoulders slumped, and he turned away from the door. It sounded like his mommy would still be busy all the time. Holding the lighter, he padded over to his desk and stooped down next to his Mickey Mouse wastebasket. He took out a crumpled piece of paper from school, one the teacher had said was too sloppy, and held it in his hand. He pushed the tiny pedal on the lighter and held the paper over it.

In the living room of the small apartment, Bill lifted the strap of the banjo over his head and laid the instrument on the couch. ''Maybe we've been working too hard, anyway. Want to knock off for tonight?''

Liza gazed at him sadly. ''I feel as if I'm holding you back. I wonder if you'd be better off with a different partner, one who didn't have my responsibilities.''

''Are you crazy?'' Bill sat down on the piano bench beside her and put his arm around her shoulders. ''After four years you want to split up the act? We're just getting it right! Besides, do you think for one minute that Dulcie would let me up on that stage with someone else?''

''If she knows what's good for the club she probably should.''

''Hey.'' He squeezed her shoulder. ''No more of that

talk. We'll bring Rags and Riches out of the red, the three of us together.''

"Or we'll sink like a rock together."

"Hey, what're you talking?" Bill stood up and spread his arms like a sideshow barker. "We're a natural team, you, me and Dulcie," he announced. "We have Liza Gayle from the suburbs to keep us in tune with middle-class respectability, Billy Bach from the city to give us sophisticated flair, and Dulcie Middleton from— Where is Dulcie from, anyway?"

She laughed at his good-natured rambling. "I don't know for sure. A farm in Wisconsin, I think."

"There you go. Dulcie behind the bar to give us down-home warmth and friendliness," Bill finished. "How can we lose? Within a few weeks we'll have Chicago—" he bowed and swept his hand downward "—at our feet."

"I sure hope you're right. I can't bear to think of Dulcie losing the place. She'd be a mess. And without that extra paycheck from Rags and Riches, I can forget trying to buy a house for Denny and me. We'll never qualify for the loan."

"I still think you're crazy to sink money into a house. And here in the suburbs, yet."

"Not very bohemian, is it, Bill? Sorry, but I can't see taking Denny into the heart of the city where you and Sharon live."

"Okay, don't do that, but this place seems big enough for two of you."

"Not when one of us is a five-year-old boy. Denny needs more. He should have—" Liza paused and sniffed. "Could I have left something on the stove?"

"Better check. I can smell it, too."

Liza hurried into the kitchen, but the oven and burners were turned off. "The smell's getting worse," she said, her gaze darting around as she walked back into the living room. "It seems to be coming from—my God!" She raced to Denny's bedroom door and threw it open. "Denny!" Snatching him away from the smoldering rug, she dashed into the living room. "His rug's on fire! Get something to smother it!"

Bill hurtled into the bedroom just as the smoke reached the alarm on the living room wall and a raucous buzzing began.

"Mommy, I'm scared!"

"Me, too." Liza's heart pounded as she turned her son every which way, looking for burned places anywhere on his pajamas. "Does anything hurt, Denny?"

"No," he whimpered.

Liza took her attention away from him for a brief second. "You doing okay in there, Bill?"

"I think it's out," Bill called back. "We found it early enough."

Someone pounded on the front door of the apartment, and Liza sat Denny on the couch. "Don't move. That's probably one of the neighbors. I suppose we've roused the whole building." She answered the door and found Mr. Peters standing in the hall in his robe and slippers, his eyes wide with concern behind his glasses.

"I heard your smoke alarm, Liza. At first I thought you were testing it, but the noise kept up, so I came over."

Liza tried to smile. "I think everything's under control, Mr. Peters. I'm sorry we disturbed you." She noticed other heads poking out of doors. The landlady was two floors below her, but she'd be up soon for sure.

"Lots of smoke in there," Mr. Peters said. "I guess we all get a little nervous with smoke around."

"Yes, well, the trouble's taken care of. I'll open a win-

dow so we can stop the noise. Good night." She closed
the door quietly. They mustn't see that she was upset.

She crossed to a window and opened it before returning
to Denny who sat quivering on the couch. The smoke
alarm stopped its grating buzz, and Liza examined Denny
inch by inch once more. She began to shake when she
discovered little spots on his arms where the hair had been
singed. "I can't believe this. How could a fire start in
your bedroom?"

His lower lip trembled. "I'm...I'm sorry, Mommy."

Cold air seeped in through the open window along with
the sound of traffic passing on the street. Liza stared at
her son. "You're sorry? What do you mean you're
sorry?" When he didn't answer, Liza clutched his shoulders in a fierce grip. "Did you do this?"

"Eric and I f-found a l-lighter."

Her throat almost closed over the words. "You had a
cigarette lighter in your room?"

"Ow, Mommy, you're hurting me!"

"Denny, how could you?" Liza's heart hammered in
her chest. "What were you thinking?"

"I just wanted to see if it worked. And then I dropped
the paper, and—"

"Do you realize what almost happened? Do you?" She
shook him, hard.

"Mommy," he begged, "don't be mad."

"I can't believe you did this."

"Please don't cry."

"I'm not crying." Liza let go of him with one hand
and swiped at her eyes.

"You are so crying," Denny said in a small voice.

Liza put her face close to his pale one. His pupils were
wide with fright. "Listen very carefully," she said, deliv-
ering each word like a slap. "If I ever, and I mean *ever*,

catch you playing with fire again, there will be no house, and no dog, and no swing set—no anything! Is that clear?''

Denny nodded as tears dribbled down his cheeks.

''Oh, Denny.'' Liza put both arms around him and held him tight as her own tears dripped on his flannel pajamas. Were they flameproof? She thought all kids' night wear was these days, but she'd never worried about it much. What if she and Bill hadn't been practicing and she'd gone to bed? Would the smoke alarm have awakened her before it was too late?

Liza felt light-headed as she pictured what could have happened. ''Denny, you scared Mommy something awful. Please don't ever try to light something again.''

''Okay.''

''I mean it. You could have been burned up. I love you more than anyone or anything in the world, Denny. I couldn't stand to lose you.''

''I won't do it again, Mommy.''

Bill walked back into the room. ''Fire's out, I think. But if you have an extinguisher, we could spray the rug to be sure.''

''It's in the broom closet in the kitchen. Thanks, Bill.''

''Oh, and I found this.'' Bill held out a red cigarette lighter.

''I'll take it.'' Liza shoved the lighter deep into her pocket and took a moment to despise the nameless person who had dropped it where a child, her child, could find it.

''Is Denny okay?''

''He seems to be.''

''How about you?''

''I'm...I'm fine.''

''Hey, most kids experiment with fire once. They scare

themselves to death, and that's the end of it. Denny's not going to try this again, right, buddy?"

Denny looked up at Bill and shook his head.

"There, see? He's learned his lesson."

Liza lifted Denny from her lap. "He'd darn well better have." She took him by the hand. "Come on, kid. Let's see what happened to your rug. I'll have some fancy explaining to do with the landlady over this."

When they walked into the room Denny held his nose. "Phew, it stinks in here. Hey, my Mickey Mouse quilt is all black!"

"Bill probably used it to smother the fire. Let's open a window in here, too."

"Mommy, my quilt's all yucky. I want a new quilt!"

Liza turned and looked at her son. "I'll have enough trouble paying for new carpeting in here, Denny. It'll probably take some of the house money. I can't afford a new quilt."

"But, Mommy!" Denny began to sob.

Bill appeared in the bedroom doorway. "I found the extinguisher, and your landlady's at the front door."

"Oh, great. Hold off on spraying the rug, then." Liza walked reluctantly into the living room. "Hello, Mrs. Applebaum."

Her landlady was also in a robe and slippers, with a nylon net over her hair. "One of the tenants called me," she said sharply. "Have you had a fire in here?"

"A...a small one, yes. But it's out now."

"Where?"

"In a bedroom."

"You'd better let me see. Which one?"

"Denny's." Liza stood aside and followed her landlady into the bedroom. "It's only a small part of the rug, Mrs. Applebaum. I'll be glad to pay for a new—"

"Did you do this?" Mrs. Applebaum peered at Denny. "Did you start this fire?"

Denny shrank back against his rumpled bed, and Liza put a protective arm around her son. "I'm sure he didn't mean to start a fire, Mrs. Applebaum. He found a discarded lighter that still worked. You know how kids are. They experiment once, and then it's over." Liza prayed that Bill's words would soothe her landlady.

Mrs. Applebaum put both hands on her hips. "How about twice? I saw him and that other boy, Eric, trying to light a pile of leaves last Saturday. But they were too wet, I guess."

Liza glanced sharply at Denny, but he kept his gaze on the floor. She thought quickly. "That's what I was talking about. The boys tried to experiment with the leaves, but they wouldn't light, so Denny had to keep trying to light something. Now that he's done it, and knows how dangerous it is, he won't play with fire anymore."

"I don't want an arsonist in this building."

Liza gasped and pulled Denny tight against her. "He is not an arsonist!"

"He started a fire, didn't he? Tried to start one last Saturday, too."

Liza began to quiver with anger. "That doesn't mean he's an arsonist, and I won't have you calling him one."

"Maybe you won't, but I have a building and people to protect." Her gaze narrowed. "And I believe your lease is up next month."

"You would throw us out?"

"I may be forced to, if this kid's a danger to my other tenants. Let's just say I'd give it a lot of thought before I renewed your lease."

"Well, well…fine! Don't renew it!"

Bill touched Liza's arm. "Could I talk with you in the kitchen for a minute?"

"Sure, but Denny's coming, too." Liza glared at her landlady before guiding Denny out of the room.

When they reached the safety of the kitchen, Bill spoke in a low, urgent voice. "Tell me to mind my own business if you want, but I'd advise you to find a way to stay here for at least another six months."

"But you heard what she said! I don't want to live here if she believes that Denny would—"

"I know. Just remember that the rent isn't very high, considering the space you have, and besides, moving will take all kinds of time, time you don't have if we're going to polish the act for Rags and Riches."

"You're right, but dammit, Bill— Whoops. Sorry, Denny, Mommy forgot about using naughty words."

"I have an idea," Bill said. "I saw this Melwood Park fireman on TV. The Chicago station picked up the story because the guy's donating his off-duty time to start a program for kids who may have a problem with fire."

"One accident with a lighter doesn't make Denny a pyromaniac."

"I know, but what if you told Mrs. Applebaum that you'll get this guy to talk with Denny? That should impress her."

"But we're not sure that Denny needs some program, Bill. I don't like the idea of rushing into something like that, with total strangers possibly trying to take charge."

"You can stay with him all the time. You can control it. Which is better—that or moving? It'll cost you to get that baby grand down from a third floor apartment, not to mention the time spent packing, looking for a new place, unpacking. Talk about no time to practice!"

"Mommy, will the fireman give me a ride on his truck?"

"I don't know, Denny. Why, would you like that?"

"Yeah. Fire trucks go fast. Zoom, zoom!"

"Give it a try, Liza," Bill urged.

"I'm not happy about this, but maybe the idea makes sense." Liza gritted her teeth. "Even if Mrs. Applebaum goes for it, though, I'm not allowing any self-righteous fireman to intimidate my kid just because he found somebody's lighter and played with it."

Denny snuggled against his mother. Everything was much better than before. When the paper had gotten too hot to hold and he'd dropped it on the rug, he'd been a little scared. But then his mother had hugged him tight and told him how much she loved him. And if a fireman came to visit, he might get to ride on a fire truck.

JEB STRATTON THOUGHT about the job ahead as he rang the doorbell of apartment 301. He didn't much like having the appointment set up by the landlady instead of the boy's mother. "To make sure it gets done," Mrs. Applebaum had said over the phone. If the boy's mother was antagonistic to the idea, that wouldn't help his cause any.

From behind the door he heard rollicking piano music. Whoever was playing wasn't worried about disturbing the neighbors. Maybe the landlady didn't like loud piano playing or little kids. Maybe her irritation had made her exaggerate when she claimed that Denny Galloway had tried to burn the apartment house to the ground.

Denny was Jeb's first case since the TV interview, and sure enough, the call had come from a disgruntled outside party who might have an ax to grind, just as the chief had predicted. If all the calls were like that, Jeb knew he'd have a devil of a time getting funding next year. The chief wanted to beef up the existing fire prevention talks in the schools, where the department could reach lots of children at once. He didn't think Jeb's idea of fire fighters making friends with individual kids was cost-effective.

The cheerful music stopped for a second, and Jeb rang the bell again. He heard voices and then footsteps before the door opened.

He towered over the woman standing there—would have towered even if she'd been wearing shoes, which she wasn't. Her chestnut hair was caught up in a haphazard ponytail, and her shirt hung out over her jeans. She looked about fifteen, except for her eyes. No fifteen-year-old looked at a man the way she was looking at him, with knowledge and a touch of arrogance in that brown gaze. And defiance. She didn't want him here.

He swallowed. "Mrs. Galloway? I'm Jeb Stratton from the Melwood Park Fire Department."

"Is that the modern uniform, jeans and a sweatshirt? I expected at least one of those hats with the shiny emblem on the front."

"Sorry to disappoint you. I have a helmet with a flashing red light on the top, but I thought that might be overdoing it, especially since I'm off duty."

She started to smile and stopped, as if she couldn't allow herself to lower her guard.

A boy with hair a shade lighter than hers poked his head under her arm. Like most five-year-olds, his eyes looked too big for his face. "Are you the fireman?"

"Yes, I'm with Ladder Company Three."

"Where's your spotted dog?"

Jeb laughed. "Apparently I haven't brought the right equipment, Denny. It is Denny, right?"

The boy nodded.

"I just wanted to talk to you and your mother for a

little while, if that's okay. Another time you can visit the station, if you want."

"Did you leave the dog down there?"

"I'm sorry, Denny. There's no dog at our station right now."

"Aw, gee."

"Do you like dogs?"

"Sure do, but we can't have one here, 'cause old Mrs. Applebaum—"

Liza opened the door a little wider. "Maybe before we discuss the subject of my landlady you'd better come inside, Mr. Stratton."

"Could you call me Jeb?"

"I don't think so, under the circumstances. I agreed to this charade because Mrs. Applebaum threatened to put me out on the street next month." She gestured to the baby grand piano. "And moving isn't an easy proposition, Mr. Stratton."

"I see." He stepped carefully over a plastic spaceship and a three-inch-high armored tank.

"Good. I hope you also see that my son is a normal, healthy five-year-old with a natural curiosity about the world around him. He learned his lesson about fire this week, and we'll have no more problems."

"I hope not, Mrs. Galloway."

"It's *Ms* Galloway."

"Oh."

"Why don't you sit down?" She motioned to an overstuffed chair with a red throw carefully arranged over the upholstery.

Jeb picked a toy dump truck out of the chair and settled himself in before glancing around the room. The couch where this intriguing pixie sat with her arm around Denny also was covered with a throw, but in bright yellow and red flowers. The low table in front of the couch was freshly painted the same lemon color of the flowered throw. Jeb admired her attempts to disguise poverty with paint and bright colors.

The room was definitely child centered. Dr. Seuss books were scattered on the coffee table, and the floor held a sizable population of the small barrel-shaped people that fit into Fisher-Price toys. Jeb had bought sets containing the same round little folks for his sisters' kids.

Jeb's gaze returned to the woman seated on the couch with one foot tucked underneath her. She looked so young. "Do you work outside the home, Ms Galloway?"

"You mean like sweeping the walk or trimming the bushes?"

"You know what I mean."

"Yes, but the question still isn't polite, don't you see? Would you ask a man if he worked outside the home?"

"I guess not."

"That's my point."

"Point taken. Okay, how's this? Do you work for pay?"

"I play for pay."

Jeb rolled his eyes. "I have the feeling you're trying to be difficult."

"Maybe I resent the twenty-question approach, Mr. Stratton. Why don't you give us the lecture about children playing with matches, and we'll listen, and then you can leave. Isn't that what you're here for?"

"No, it's not. Denny could hear that sort of thing in school. In fact, he will next month. October is Fire Prevention Month, and we'll have a big push in the schools."

"Great. Then why don't we save a lot of time and let you proceed with your day? Denny will get what he needs from school."

Why not indeed? Jeb thought. He half rose from his chair before remembering that he'd have to write up a report on this visit. How would he describe his encounter with Liza Galloway? *Subject's mother baited me until I finally left?*

He took a deep breath and shook his head. "Whether you like it or not, Ms Galloway, Denny started a fire in his room. That puts him in a different category from most of the other children in his school. If you resent my questions concerning you, perhaps you'd rather leave Denny and me alone?"

"Not a chance."

Jeb sighed. He had to separate them somehow and try to talk some sense into her. "Denny, I notice that you have a lot of toys."

The boy shrugged. "Some, I guess."

"I bet you have a favorite."

"Sure! It's—"

"Don't tell me yet. Let's play a game and see if I can guess. Take ten of your toys and line them up on your bed. I'll come in pretty soon and see if I can figure out your favorite, and your second favorite, all the way down to ten. You can count to ten, right?"

"Course I can." Denny swaggered across the room. "Even twenty."

"Then do twenty, and make it really hard, okay?"

"Okay!" Denny scurried around the room gathering toys as he went. "You'll never guess this."

"And Denny, close your bedroom door, so I can't peek."

Denny laughed. "I'll close it real tight."

When he was gone, Liza folded her arms and stared at him. "Smooth move."

Jeb turned to her and held out both hands in an appeal

for understanding. "Listen, I don't know if Denny has a problem with fire or not, but—"

"Mr. Stratton, I've handled the situation. The lighter is gone, and I've cleaned his room from top to bottom. There are no matches or lighters in there, and none in the rest of the house, either."

"None?"

"I don't smoke or give candlelight dinners, so that's right. None."

"Okay, but Denny could find matches or a lighter somewhere."

"I've talked to him very carefully about the dangers, Mr. Stratton. He's not a stupid child."

"Of course he's not. That's the point, in fact. Are you aware that Denny fits all the criteria for being a potential fire starter? He's the right age, he's very bright, and there's no father figure in the house."

"I resent that!" Liza stood and faced him. "Why does everyone assume that a boy without a father around will be a troublemaker? Denny doesn't need a father. He has me, and we're doing just fine, thank you. Before the year's over I plan to buy a house, and Denny will have a yard, and a dog, and—"

"Whoa, there. I can see how much you're doing for Denny. And I can imagine how hard you must have to work to pay for everything. I'm only trying to—"

"To what? Make me feel guilty? Tell me I'm not a fit mother? Denny had an accident with a lighter. Lots of kids do—even ones with fathers! I have taken care of everything, and it won't happen again. You can be sure of that, because I— Oh, damn." Liza turned away, but it was too late. Jeb had seen her tears.

"Hey, don't..." Jeb crossed to her without thinking and put both hands on her shoulders.

She shrugged him away angrily and wiped her eyes with the back of her hand. "Okay, Mr. Jeb Stratton, so I'm crying. That doesn't mean you've won some advantage over the situation. Do whatever you have to do to satisfy Mrs. Applebaum, and then leave. The only reason you're here is that I have to placate her."

"Mr. Stratton, I'm ready!" Denny called through a crack in his bedroom door.

Jeb stood looking down at Liza. He wanted to wrap her in his arms and let her cry until all the hurt, all the frustration was washed away. But he didn't dare touch her again. "Do you want to come into Denny's room with me?" he asked gently.

She sniffed. "I guess not."

Her decision not to follow him around was a small victory, and he decided to take it. At least she now trusted him alone with her kid. Come to think of it, knowing how she felt about Denny, he'd scored a major victory. Jeb decided that he might have two strikes against him, but he wasn't out yet.

CHAPTER TWO

LIZA WATCHED JEB WALK into Denny's bedroom. *Okay, you blond clean-cut, all-American type. Can you imagine, even slightly, what it's like to be pregnant when the man you love doesn't love you, and your parents' only suggestion is to give the baby away?*

Kyle, of course, had been in favor of adoption, too, once he'd realized that she wouldn't have an abortion. He'd kept talking about "our little accident," as if a child were something to be cleaned up like a spilled glass of beer. For more than a year she'd believed herself in love with Kyle, but his attitude about the pregnancy convinced her that she wanted nothing more from him.

At first she'd thought she could do what her parents wanted and give up the baby. She'd had two years left on her musical scholarship at the University of Illinois, and her parents had quickly pointed out that she'd lose it if she quit school or took a lighter load in order to care for a child. The solution had been so neat: the baby was due in July, so Liza could finish the spring semester, have her child and put it up for adoption, and continue with her studies in the fall.

Except that by June, Liza had known that she couldn't say goodbye to this wonderful human being taking shape inside her. With the first kick the bonding had begun, and the logic of her parents' arguments had crumbled in the face of Liza's growing mother love. Her announcement that she would keep her child ended the tolerant support she'd received from her parents. They'd never been so angry with her before, and the memory still brought a queasy sensation to her stomach. If she'd made this decision, they said, then she was ready to face the world alone.

Perhaps this strapping, big fire fighter would have agreed with her parents and recommended that Denny be put up for adoption so that he could have two parents instead of one. With two parents Denny might be living in a house of his own by now instead of a rented apartment. Then if he had accidentally burned his rug there would be no landlady to deal with, no need to call in a man with a probing blue gaze and a square and determined chin.

Liza didn't want to like this intruder. Unfortunately he was likeable, with his open, honest expression and his casual approach. Except for the remark about fatherless boys, he'd made a favorable impression on her as she'd put him through his paces.

He wasn't so bad to look at, either. He possessed the solid physique demanded by his job, and he carried himself with easy confidence. Liza wasn't happy about noticing the physical attributes of Jeb Stratton, but there it was. Apparently she was changing from the asexual being who had taken her baby home from the hospital five years ago and had sworn to have nothing more to do with men.

She admitted to herself, although to no one else, that recently her dreams had taken on an erotic cast. If it weren't for Denny, she would probably date again. Yet she knew how disruptive such a move could be for him, how confused he might become dealing with the temporary nature of the dating game.

In the last five years Liza had refused offers of dinner

and movies. Bill, who was a far cry from a father figure, had been Denny's only close contact with a man. Jeb had been right. Denny had no male role model, but Liza was determined to prove that he didn't need one at the moment. Later he'd get into Scouts, or Little League, and that would do the trick.

Attractive or not, this fire fighter could only cause trouble in her already complicated life. He'd already made her cry by probing the most sensitive area of her life: her stewardship of Denny. On top of that he appealed to her as a man, and the fewer temptations of that sort she had around, the better.

She could hear Jeb and Denny murmuring and laughing in the bedroom, and the sound was far too pleasant to her ears. She wanted to stay angry and belligerent. That way, she could keep Jeb at a safe distance. To drown out the friendly cadence of Denny's childish voice and Jeb's deeper baritone, Liza sat on the piano bench and began banging the keys energetically.

In Denny's bedroom, Jeb paused in the guessing game as the vibrant music erupted from the other side of the door. The sharply struck notes displayed resentment, but lots of spirit, as well. He smiled and glanced at Denny. "She's upset because I'm here."

"Yeah." Denny marched one of his Masters of the Universe figures across the quilt toward where Jeb sat on the end of the bed. "She's been getting mad a lot. And she practices all the time for that dumb show."

Jeb felt slightly underhanded for asking, but he couldn't help himself. "What show is that?"

"The new one. The one with Bill."

"Who's Bill?"

"The banjo player where Mommy works."

"And where's that?"

"Oh, at Rags and Riches. I never get to go there." Denny pushed two of his figures together in an animated battle.

"What do you do while your mommy's playing at Rags and Riches?"

"Go to bed. I have to have a *baby-sitter*, and I'm not a baby."

"You're certainly not."

"Babies sleep in cribs, but I have a big bed. Did you see my quilt?" Denny patted the Mickey Mouse pattern beside him.

"Very nice. Matches your wastebasket, I see."

"Yeah. So did my other one, but it got all black. Mommy buyed me a new one."

"All black from the fire?"

"No, all black because Bill smashed the fire with it. Dumb guy."

"No, smart guy, Denny. You have to smother a fire or it will burn everything, including you." Jeb paused until Denny looked up at him. He wanted eye contact with the boy. "Fires can kill people, you know."

Denny glanced away. "Not all the time."

"If they don't, it's because someone stops the fire before it gets too big, like Bill did. In fact, that's what my job is, stopping little fires before they get big. If I don't find a fire in time, one match or one lighter like the one you had can burn down a whole building. Do you understand how that could happen?"

Denny sighed. "My mommy told me all that," he said wearily.

"All what?"

Denny repeated his mother's words with the cadence of a memorized speech. "Don't pick up lighters or matches. Don't play with them. Don't start fires. Can we play our guessing game now?''

"In a minute. Denny, you don't sound as if you believe those things you just said.''

"Well, sure I do.''

Jeb didn't buy it. The kid needed more reinforcement. At the station they had a video of some big fires—nothing gruesome, but footage dramatic enough to grab Denny's attention. "Say, Denny, would you like to come down to the station sometime?'' Jeb suggested. "I could show you around.''

"Can I sit in the fire engine?''

"Sure.''

"Can I spray the hose?''

"I'm afraid not. That costs money, and the fire department doesn't have a lot to spare.''

"We don't have too much to spare, either. That's what Mommy says.''

"You sure have a lot of nice toys, though. Does your mommy buy all those?''

"Mommy, and Santa Claus, and Grandma and Grandpa.''

Jeb assumed from the way Denny said it that he only had contact with one set of grandparents, probably Liza's folks. "Do you see them much? Your grandparents?''

"Nope. I've never been in their house.''

"Then they live far away.''

"Nope.'' Denny flipped one of his plastic figures in the air. "I just never go there.''

"Hmm.'' Jeb wondered what the problem was. Denny was a cute kid, one most grandparents would be delighted to claim.

"What do you do at the fire station?'' Denny asked, losing interest in the subject of his grandparents.

"Lots of things. Clean the apparatus, wash the—"

"What's an apparatus?"

"That's what we call the ladder truck, and the pumper, and the emergency vehicle."

"You mean the fire engines?"

"Right."

"What do you do at the fires?"

"Most of the time I'm the forcible entry man."

Denny's brown eyes grew wide. "What's that?"

"I'm the first guy in the door. If it's locked, I pry it open with something called a halligan tool or I use an ax."

"You chop it down?"

"Sometimes."

Denny regarded him with awe and then motioned to the little figures on his bed. "You're like these guys, huh?"

"No, I'm not a superhero."

"Seems like it to me."

"I'm just a man. When I get burned I hurt, like anyone else."

"Not me." Denny puffed out his chest. "I'm tough."

"Fire's tougher, Denny. I've seen really strong guys cry because of fire."

Denny looked at him suspiciously. "Did you ever do that?"

"Yes. When one of my best friends was killed in a fire."

Denny accepted the knowledge with a moment of silence. "I cry sometimes, but mostly not, because I'm a big boy."

"I can see that you are. So how about it? Have we got a deal that you'll come down to the station?"

"I have to ask my mommy."

Jeb smiled. Big boy, indeed. "Then let's go ask her."

"You didn't finish guessing my toys."

"You're right. Okay, I think they go in this order." Jeb arranged the rest of the toys in a line on the bed.

"Wrong!" Denny giggled. "Like *this*, silly guy."

"Boy, you got me on that one."

"I knew I would."

"You were right. Shall we go ask your mom about the trip to the station?"

"Yep, let's ask her." Denny bounced out the door.

Jeb followed, thinking hard. Denny had loved all the personal attention Jeb had just given him, had gobbled it up the way lonely children often did. But Denny wasn't seriously neglected, and his mother probably gave him all the time she could.

Perhaps the situation had become more critical recently. She had this new show on her mind, and maybe Denny felt left out. That wasn't necessarily bad; the boy needed to learn a little independence. But learning to be independent could be frustrating, and fire might have been his method of expressing hostility, as a psychologist had explained to Jeb not long ago. Then again, maybe the boy had only been curious. The truth was probably somewhere in between, and Jeb had enough unanswered questions to make him uneasy about Denny.

Liza stopped playing the piano as Denny bounded over to the bench where she sat.

"Can I go see the fire station, Mommy? Mr. Stratton said I could sit in the fire engine, and see everything, but I can't spray the hose because it costs too much money." Denny paused to take a breath.

"Then you'd like to go?"

"I sure would."

Jeb stepped toward the piano. "I can pick him up some afternoon, if you don't have time to—"

"I'll bring him down, Mr. Stratton. When would be convenient?"

"You name it. Anytime next week. We can plan this for when I'm on duty or when I'm not. Doesn't matter, except that if I'm on duty I might have to leave suddenly."

Denny patted Liza's arm. "Mommy, Mr. Stratton is the *force-ball entry man*. He cuts holes in doors with axes, Mommy!"

Liza looked up at Jeb. "How macho. Is that what you've been telling my son? No wonder he wants to visit the station."

"No, I ha—" Jeb stuck both hands in the back pockets of his jeans and looked up at the ceiling. He must not get into another argument with this woman. "When can you bring Denny down, Ms Galloway?"

Liza watched him standing there controlling his temper, and she felt a stir of admiration. He was quite handsome with his jaw clenched like that. She hated to admit it, but she was awed, just like Denny, with anyone who axed down doorways in the line of duty. "I have appointments all day Monday, but on Tuesday I have a spare hour in the afternoon."

Jeb looked confused. "Appointments?"

"Mommy tunes pianos for people," Denny announced as he plunked on the piano keys in front of him.

"So you have two jobs," Jeb murmured and shook his head. "I don't see how you manage."

"I manage," Liza said with an icy smile. "Denny and I will be at the station by four o'clock on Tuesday, if that suits you."

"Right down to the ground," Jeb returned with a deliberately cheerful tone. He gave Denny a little salute and turned to leave. "See you on Tuesday."

"Don't forget," Denny warned.

Jeb stopped with his hand on the doorknob and glanced back at them. Deliberately he repeated a phrase she'd used earlier. "Not a chance."

After he closed the door Liza got up to write the fire station visit on her kitchen calendar, but as she penciled in the memo she knew that the reminder was unnecessary. She'd led Jeb Stratton to believe that she'd bring Denny because she didn't trust him to escort her son to the station and back. Liza tried to convince herself of the same thing, but underneath her righteousness lurked the suspicion that she wanted to see the fire fighter again.

Whatever the reason for her taking Denny next Tuesday, Liza knew she wouldn't forget the appointment at the station, or the look in Jeb Stratton's blue eyes when he paused at the door before leaving. His gaze seemed to say that, despite what he'd endured from her, he'd like to stay a little longer. Liza didn't want Jeb Stratton around, not really, but she treasured the look in his eyes all the same.

THE SMOKY INTERIOR of Rags and Riches was sprinkled with customers—the usual Thursday night quota. Liza only remembered once when all of the twenty or so round mahogany tables had been full, and that was during the evening wedding reception for Dulcie's son. Dulcie had tended bar that night, too, just as she had every night of the year, including Christmas.

With an apron spanning her large bosom, a silk gardenia tucked in her dyed-blond hair and a welcoming smile on her face, Dulcie looked completely at home behind the curved length of the bar. The mirrored wall behind her and the shelves of sparkling glasses attested to her pride in the establishment. She moved at a leisurely pace that helped her customers relax even before they took their first drink.

On Tuesday night when Bill had asked Liza where Dulcie had come from, Liza hadn't remembered the name of the little town in Wisconsin, but she had remembered that Dulcie had grown up on a farm. Her rural urge toward hospitality had been stifled, however, when she'd met and married a city man. Then, weeks before collapsing with a massive coronary, her husband had bought a bar on Rush Street named Rags and Riches.

After he died, Dulcie had thrown herself into running the place, which she had insisted on calling a nightclub once she introduced entertainment. None of the musical groups she'd hired had lasted long until Bill and Liza had applied for the job four years ago. Using the stage names of Billy Bach and Liza Gayle, they'd created an act based largely on sing-along tunes and had built a small but loyal following.

The combination of their entertainment and Dulcie's hospitality had worked fine until the landlord had raised the rent. Rags and Riches needed more customers now, and Bill's answer was to change the entertainment format to something more sophisticated and original by weaving songs that he'd written into the sing-along program.

As Liza would have expected, Dulcie had been all for the change, especially if it gave Bill a chance to perform his own material. Dulcie had always treated Bill and Liza as if they were her children, and at times Liza had thought of Dulcie as a substitute mother, which was ironic considering how much Liza's real mother disapproved of her daughter working at the nightclub.

Tonight, after the first set ended, Liza planned to tell Dulcie about Jeb Stratton and the unsettling effect he was having on her life. Liza always liked to get Dulcie's opinion about the major events that happened to her. She couldn't shake the feeling that meeting Jeb Stratton was one of them.

Bill's fingers tripped over the banjo strings in tune with Liza's boisterous rendition of "The Yellow Rose of Texas." The words to the song were projected on the wall above them, and the crowd belted out the final chorus as if they all had sweethearts in Texas. Bill responded by escalating the pace and pushing the range of the banjo's strings upward until Liza worried that he'd start breaking glasses.

The crowd loved it. When the number ended, Bill mopped his brow and waited for the stomping and clapping to die down. His dark hair curled riotously around his head from the heat and exertion, and the back of his shirt was damp. Slowly he leaned toward the microphone. "Liza and I are going to take a little break."

The customers groaned their disapproval at having to make do with music from the jukebox.

Bill chuckled. "You folks are insatiable, and we appreciate it, but I need a beer."

A man back in one corner waved his arm in the air. "Come on back, Bill. I'm buying."

"Thanks, Eddie. I'll be right there." He turned off the microphone and lifted the strap for the banjo over his head. "About ten minutes?" he asked Liza as he hopped down from his stool and laid the instrument on top of the old upright piano.

"Take fifteen," Liza said. "You really outdid yourself on that last one."

"It's fun." Bill grinned. "I'm glad we decided to work the new act in around the sing-alongs, rather than ditching them altogether. I must be into audience participation or something."

"You're a certified ham is what you are."

"You, too. That's why we're going to knock this town on its ear, Liza baby." Bill stepped from the platform and wound his way through the tables to his buddies.

"I hope you're right," Liza muttered as she too left the platform and wandered over to the bar.

"The usual?" Dulcie asked, polishing an already clean spot in front of Liza.

"The usual. Although I could probably use a stiff drink right now."

"Problems?" Dulcie poured a chilled mineral water into an ice-filled glass and added a twist of lemon.

"Sort of, I guess."

"No more fires, I hope?"

"No. Just a fireman."

"So today was the day." Dulcie took an order from the club's only waitress and began measuring bourbon into glasses. "Was he rough on Denny?"

"No, I can't say that he was." Liza poked her lemon peel with one finger and waited for the waitress, whom she didn't know very well, to leave.

Dulcie leaned her plump elbows on the bar and gazed at Liza. "Then what gives, honey?"

"He's very good-looking, Dulcie."

"Aha! A *good-looking* fireman. Now that's a different story."

"I'm not supposed to be noticing that right now, you know."

"That's what you keep on saying, honey, and I keep on telling you that a twenty-five-year-old woman has to be dead not to notice. I'm still noticing at my age."

"Yes, but there's more to it than that. He wants to spend time with Denny, and that means I'll have to spend more time with him, and he's very good-looking."

"I believe you mentioned that. Is he single?"

"I don't know, but even if he is, I can't let myself become involved with a man right now. I have the new act to think about, which is important to you, too. And the house. I want to get that house for Denny. I can't lose my focus, Dulcie."

"Oh, focus my hocus-pocus. Tell me, is he interested in you?"

"I don't know. Yes, maybe. I'm not sure."

"Let me try and get a fix on this man. You say he's handsome, but how handsome?"

Liza sipped her mineral water. "Well, not movie-star handsome, like Denny's father was. Kyle was almost pretty. Denny looks a lot like his father, with those long eyelashes that make women bite their knuckles in envy."

"Will I ever see that little boy of yours, Liza? He's liable to be of drinking age before you let me have a peek at him."

"I'd love you to meet him. You know that. But I can't very well bring him down here, and you and I are both so busy during the day."

"Maybe some Sunday. You could bring him to my place."

"Maybe." Liza glanced down at her drink to avoid, as she usually did, making definite dates to socialize. She didn't really have the time for it, and besides, on Sundays she and Denny often did things alone, just the two of them.

"Well, there's no rush," Dulcie said, as if sensing Liza's reluctance. "Tell me about this fireman."

"As I said, he's nothing like Denny's father. When I think of Kyle I think of those colorful hot air balloons, beauty without substance."

"Thank God you didn't marry that jerk."

Liza smiled. "I probably would have if he'd asked me, but he didn't."

"No, he wasn't that much of a gentleman."

"You're so loyal, Dulcie. You don't know anything about Kyle except what I tell you, and you're ready to roast him at the least opportunity."

"I may not have known him, but I know you. You could never have been happy with a man whose idea of fun was getting blotto and then having belching contests."

"He was very young, only twenty-one. I was even younger, but I really thought I was in love."

"I don't care. He wasn't right for you." Dulcie paused to draw two beers from the draft kegs behind her and take them to the men at the other end of the bar. Then she returned, wiping her hands on her apron. "Let's get back to the fireman. If Kyle was a hot air balloon, what's this new fellow?"

"More like a Boeing 747."

"Well, all right!"

"No, not all right. All wrong. For one thing, he thinks Denny is a prime candidate for his new prevention program for juvenile fire starters. I can't become involved with a man who thinks my son might be an arsonist. I get furious every time I think of Jeb Stratton and his assumptions about Denny."

"Well, of course you do." Dulcie patted Liza's hand.

"Just who does he think he's dealing with? I put him in his place right away."

"And haven't stopped thinking about him since."

"No," Liza admitted miserably.

"Couldn't you talk him out of this thing with Denny? Sugar works better than vinegar any day. Then maybe you could both relax and concentrate on something else besides kids and fires."

"Even if I could do that, I'm still breaking my own rule about getting involved with a man before I have everything I want for Denny."

"Some rules are meant to be broken. I worry about you, honey. There's more to life than being the mother of a five-year-old. You're too much of a loner."

"I really can't help it, Dulcie, with working two jobs and housework and finding time for Denny. Even if I had a nice man in my life I wouldn't know where to put him."

"And if you don't come out of your shell a little, you might wake up one day and realize that Denny's gone and you're all alone. Come on, Liza. You wouldn't be talking to me about this fireman if you weren't interested."

Liza glanced at Dulcie. "I thought you might talk some sense into me."

"No, you didn't. You're looking for permission to indulge yourself." She reached across the bar and patted Liza's cheek. "So do it. Call this Jeb Stratton and invite him to the club. Watching you perform should warm him up. Then between sets you can convince him to forget about the big program with Denny. Let him find some other kid to practice his theories on, and the two of you can advance to other topics."

"Aren't you worried that I might not spend enough time on the new act, Dulcie? A lot rides on whether Bill and I can bring in more customers in the next couple of months."

"The new act will be fine. A bit of romance in your life might be good for the new act—give it more zest."

Liza sipped on her drink and thought about her boss's suggestion. "All right, Dulcie. I'll see if he can come by the club tomorrow night."

"Good girl."

Liza wasn't sure that she was a good girl. But Dulcie's

suggestion had merit. When Liza had first confronted Jeb she had reacted with anger and that wasn't the best tactic; she could see that now.

Maybe the following evening she and Jeb could talk about the matter like two adults and Jeb would realize he had evaluated Denny's situation incorrectly. Once he acknowledged that Denny didn't really belong in his fire prevention program, Liza would decide whether to allow the relationship to develop further, assuming that Jeb was single. The idea made her smile with anticipation. Maybe Dulcie was right. Maybe it was time.

CHAPTER THREE

JEB KNEW EXACTLY WHERE Rags and Riches was. He'd cruised past it several times on Thursday night as he had tried to decide whether or not to go in. In the end he'd driven back to Melwood Park.

The next morning, when the chief called him at home and told him to contact Liza Galloway, Jeb had expected her to cancel Tuesday's fire station tour. Instead she'd invited him to the club. The rest of the day had been slow going as he waited impatiently for evening to come. Finally he decided it was late enough to head for downtown Chicago.

Liza had said the entertainment started at eight-thirty. Jeb glanced at his watch and decided to take another turn around the block. He wanted to saunter in about a quarter to nine, as if he hadn't been clock-watching for the last ten hours.

He wasn't sure why Liza had called after her obvious antagonism, but he wanted to find out. She'd been on his mind a lot and not just because her kid was a potential fire starter.

From what she'd said, and what she hadn't, he'd pieced together a picture of a woman alone, financially and emotionally, yet determined to raise her child to the best of her ability. She displayed fierce loyalty to her son, and Jeb didn't blame her for that. He'd always admired loyalty and responsibility. The fact that they were qualities belonging to a woman who was nice to look at didn't hurt, either.

At last Jeb parked his small pickup and headed for the entrance of Rags and Riches. On the landing just inside the door he paused and out of habit checked for a rear exit. Experience had taught him the fire danger of basements, especially ones like this, where people might be careless with cigarettes. He located the red neon exit sign at the top of a flight of steps at the back of the club.

The arrangement of the room was straightforward, bar and kitchen on the right, platform stage on the left, tables in between. The decor leaned toward nostalgia, with antique beer signs and sepia-toned photos lining the walls. Because the landing was a terrific vantage point for watching Liza, Jeb stayed there a moment longer and gazed at the pair of musicians on the small stage.

She shared the spotlight with a young banjo player, and the two of them filled the small club with their exuberant music making. The tune was "Bicycle Built for Two," and Liza was adding all sorts of tinkling notes Jeb had never heard as part of the old song.

Her playing danced around him, distinct to his ears from the accompanying banjo music and the cheerful singing of the crowd. The illumination from the spotlight glistened in a silver circle on the top of her head. Gone were the ponytail and the oversize shirt that had made her seem so young. Her rich brown hair fell in soft curls to her shoulders, and she wore a cherry-red sweater over a brightly patterned skirt.

There was no point in kidding himself. Liza Galloway, or Liza Gayle as she'd been billed on the poster beside the entrance, had captured his imagination. He wanted to get to know her better—a lot better. His roving gaze spotted a table near the stage, and he headed for it. Tonight could be the start of something good.

When the song ended Jeb clapped so loud that the waitress had to clear her throat before he realized she was standing next to the table waiting for his order. He quickly asked for a beer and returned his attention to the stage as Liza and Bill launched into another number.

From his seat Jeb had a view of Liza's profile and her fingers on the keys. He wondered if she knew he was there. If so, she'd given no indication of it between songs. Her face was animated as she played, her lips parted in a soft smile. He recognized a familiar energy, one he shared, of love for one's work.

Briefly Jeb glanced at Liza's partner. The poster named him as Bill Bach, but Jeb suspected his real last name was something besides Bach. Bill and Liza liked each other, Jeb concluded. Their mutual respect was obvious. Was there anything more to the relationship? Jeb couldn't tell for sure, but something about the way Bill looked at Liza tipped him off that they were simply good friends.

Jeb was more sensitive to how a man's eyes gave away his intentions ever since Connie. He'd misread that situation for sure. When she gave him an ultimatum to choose her or the fire department, he'd never dreamed that her boss was waiting, hoping that he'd make the wrong choice and set Connie free.

Not the wrong choice. Even if Connie had given in and married him despite his job with the department, she'd have been miserable as a fire fighter's wife. She'd never have understood his dedication to his work. Jeb glanced up at the stage. Liza wouldn't have that problem.

Of course, there could definitely be other problems. She'd been very suspicious of him yesterday afternoon and then had called the very next morning and invited him to the club where she performed. Well, he was here to find out why. He was concentrating so hard on her that he barely tasted the cool bite of the beer or smelled the acrid smoke that usually bothered him tremendously in an enclosed space like this.

As she played, he studied her carefully from the anonymity of the surrounding crowd. Mentally he traced the straight bridge of her nose and touched the shadowed hollow under her high cheekbones. She wore no jewelry of any kind, and that alone made her different. Nearly every woman he'd known at least wore earrings, but the delicate lobes of her ears were bare. Jeb found that sexy.

Neither was she hooked on the totally natural look. She wore makeup to counteract the bleaching effect of the spotlight, but she wore it well, with her cheeks only showing a faint blush and her lips tinged the color of ripe nectarines. Her fingernails were short but polished with the same color. Jeb was fascinated with her hands, the supple way they scampered over the black and white keys. He fantasized what her touch might be like on his skin.

Jeb could have sworn he'd been sitting at the table only a few minutes when Bill announced the first break of the evening. But two empty beer glasses in front of him indicated otherwise. He wondered if he should stand up so that Liza would find him, but she turned and walked directly toward his table. She'd known he was there all along.

"So you made it," she said with a smile. "Are you enjoying the show?"

"Very much." Jeb got up and pulled out a chair for her. "What can I get you to drink?"

"Dulcie knows. She'll have it sent over." Liza discovered she was shaking, not enough for Jeb to notice, but enough to make her fold both hands in her lap.

"You're very talented, Ms Galloway."

She laughed nervously. "Okay, we can drop that miss and mister stuff if you're willing to."

"I always was."

"I know, and I made everything difficult yesterday afternoon. I had the manners of a bee in a bottle, and I apologize."

"Apology accepted."

She looked fully into his eyes for the first time since she'd sat down. The effect was like jumping off a high dive. She'd told Dulcie this man was good-looking, but that didn't quite cover it. His face was lean and tanned, with lines of experience lending sincerity to the brilliant blue of his eyes and the generous curve of his mouth. Frantically she tried to concentrate on what he was saying.

"...and I can understand why you were upset. No one likes to have someone else dictate what they'll do. I wasn't happy that the call came from your landlady and that my being there was a condition of you keeping your lease. People who are forced into things usually aren't very cooperative."

Then Liza remembered her mission tonight: to extract Denny from Jeb's program. In her admiration of him she'd almost forgotten why they were sitting at the table together. "That's exactly what I wanted to talk with you about," she began, taking a drink of the mineral water the waitress had placed in front of her.

"Oh?" Jeb wrapped one large hand around his beer glass.

"I... How long have you been working on this project to help kids who start fires?"

"Let me explain. The MPFD has had fire prevention programs for children for years, but they always dealt with kids in large groups, like schools, for instance. My idea is to follow up on individuals, sort of a big brother or big sister approach. That's what's new.''

"How new?''

"We just got started.''

Liza was encouraged. If the program was new, Jeb was still inexperienced. That should make it easier to talk him out of including Denny in his plan. "When a potential fire starter is reported to you, what's the procedure?''

"We make the first visit, like yesterday, and start a file. If possible we maintain contact with the child, give him or her a tour of the station and make follow-up visits. We also investigate suspicious fires in the child's neighborhood or school.''

Liza tried to hide her dismay. A file? He had a file on her son? "How many, ah, files have you accumulated?'' She pictured Denny's folder tucked in with those of hardened young delinquents who had dropped out of school and hung around in alleys looking for thrills. At the age of five her son had a record. She had to change that.

Jeb took a drink of his beer and put the glass down. "I may as well end this fishing and tell you straight out. Denny's my first case.''

Liza felt relieved. How natural that Jeb would make a mistake on his first case. She could forgive him, as long as he'd agree to tear up the file. "Your first case?'' she said with a sympathetic smile.

"And now you're assuming that I've been overzealous with my first live one—that I want to make Denny into something he's not, to justify my ideas.''

"Jeb, now that I know you're just beginning with this thing, I'm not surprised at all about what happened. And believe me, I don't want to sabotage your program. It sounds like a great idea for kids with problems. But really, I don't think Denny's little accident warrants starting a file on him, do you? Aren't you wasting time that could be spent on more needy children?'' Liza congratulated herself on an excellent point.

"Not necessarily. Melwood Park does have other kids with problems, and I hope to find them. But don't think a five-year-old, middle-class kid with a lighted match can't be just as dangerous as a twelve-year-old from the wrong side of the tracks. In fact, middle-class boys like Denny are statistically more likely to set fires than poorer children.''

Liza couldn't believe his stubbornness. "We're not discussing statistics. We're talking about my little boy, who accidentally started one fire. He's hardly a menace to society.''

"I didn't say that. Listen…'' Jeb put his hand on her arm and then drew it away again when she flinched. "You may be right. That one fire could be the end of the situation. But I think you and I have an obligation to talk with Denny, educate him, watch him carefully to make sure he doesn't do this again.''

"I *do* watch him, Jeb, like a hawk, and I've alerted his baby-sitter, too. I've also talked with him about all of this. You're free to handle your other cases, because this one is closed.''

"I'm…I'm not so sure.''

Her patience was nearly gone. "What do you mean?''

"I'd like to keep an eye on Denny awhile longer until I'm convinced that he was motivated by curiosity and not something else.''

Liza felt as if someone had just dropped an ice cube down her back. "Like what? Lack of a father figure, Mr. Stratton?''

Jeb sighed and leaned back in his chair. "So we're back to formalities, are we?''

"I'm afraid we are, unless you're willing to stop playing amateur psychologist and tear up that file."

"If I tore up the file, I wouldn't be doing my job."

Liza shoved her chair back. "Then I guess we'll have to agree to disagree."

"What about Tuesday?"

Liza wanted so much to tell him what he could do with his tour of the fire station, but for all she knew, that information would end up in Denny's file, too. "We'll be there, Mr. Stratton. After all, I gave my word that we would, and I wouldn't want to be labeled uncooperative. Besides, Denny will enjoy it. He doesn't understand that he's under suspicion."

"Liza, that's not—"

"Good night, Mr. Stratton." Liza turned and walked back to the platform. After she and Bill began playing once more, she glanced quickly at the table where Jeb had been sitting. He was gone.

ON TUESDAY AFTERNOON Liza made certain that Denny had belted himself securely into the front seat of her old Mustang before they drove to the fire station. He was so excited that she imagined the seat belt was all that kept him from floating around in the car like a helium balloon.

She was probably as highly charged as Denny, she admitted to herself. Seeing Jeb again aroused such conflicting emotions in her that she couldn't decide what to think. Dammit, she liked him and admired his dedication to his cause. If only he hadn't gotten his hooks into Denny! But if he hadn't, she wouldn't have met him in the first place. Maybe today Jeb would finally see the light and recognize Denny as a normal, curious little boy.

Her heart was pounding by the time she walked into the main office of the station. She held tightly to Denny's hand, lest he run straight out to the garage where the gleaming red fire engines sat waiting.

"Hello, you two." Jeb met them just inside the door, before Liza had a chance to catch her breath and compose herself. "You're right on time."

"Hello, Mr. Stratton," Liza said, not looking at him as she took off Denny's red jacket.

When she was finished Denny pulled away from her. "Hi there, Jeb." He gazed happily up at the tall fire fighter and pointed to the light blue shirt and darker slacks that he wore. "Is that your uniform?"

"Part of it," he answered, scooping Denny up in his arms. "Ready to sit in a fire engine, sport?"

"Yeah! Can Mommy sit in it, too?"

"If she wants." Jeb's glance slid over her face in quick assessment. "How about it, Mommy? By the way, you can hang his coat and yours on those hooks by the door."

Liza wanted to shout at him to put Denny down immediately. Jeb had no right to hold her child with such easy familiarity. And what was this "mommy" stuff? Was that how he planned to avoid calling her by her last name?

"Thank you," she said, sounding as stiff as she felt. She hung her trench coat on the same hook with Denny's jacket so they'd take up less room. When she turned she caught Jeb looking at her with unmistakable interest, and her blood pressure shot up another notch.

She'd dressed carefully for this meeting, choosing gray slacks and a white bulky sweater. She wanted to impress Jeb and any of his cohorts with her respectability, and Denny's. She usually allowed her son to choose what he wore, but today she'd insisted on the Izod shirt and his new jeans.

"Let's get started," Jeb said abruptly and headed down

a hallway. "But first I want you to meet the chief." He stepped through an open door. "John Gregorio, I'd like to introduce Liza Galloway and her son, Denny."

The white-haired man looked exactly the way Liza imagined a fire chief should look, distinguished and filled with authority. She stepped forward as he rose from his desk chair. "I'm glad to meet you," she said, shaking his outstretched hand firmly.

She assumed this man knew Jeb's suspicions about Denny. After all, wasn't there a file to tell anyone anything they wanted to know about Denny, about her? She looked for surprise in the older man's eyes, as if he hadn't expected such conservative-looking people to be the object of Jeb Stratton's investigations. But Chief Gregorio didn't seem surprised.

"We're going to start with the apparatus floor," Jeb told his chief, "and then move to the living quarters."

"Don't disrupt Jerry in the kitchen," the chief warned. "He's concocting Hungarian goulash, and I've never met such a temperamental cook. I asked for a taste and he nearly took my head off."

Liza was intrigued. "You cook here?"

"Yep." The chief grinned. "Everyone has a specialty. Jeb's is macaroni and cheese from a box."

"But I toss a mean salad," Jeb argued. "Not everyone was meant to slave over a hot stove."

"Sometimes we give Jeb a pass on his night to cook," the chief confided.

"I see." Liza took secret satisfaction in finding a flaw in this man who appeared to be so perfect. Not that she was a gourmet cook herself, but she could do better than boxed macaroni and cheese.

"I'm going to take these folks out of here before you

tarnish my reputation any further," Jeb said, heading for the door. "Come on, troops."

Liza decided his description was apt. She felt like some sort of recruit as she followed Jeb meekly toward the garage—what had he called it?—the apparatus floor? Apparently she would learn something today along with Denny.

"This is the apparatus I ride on," Jeb said to Denny as they approached an enormous red giant. "I'm part of Ladder Company Three."

"Wow. It's huge!"

The shiny red door of the truck acted like a mirror, reflecting back to Liza the image of her son standing with his head tilted back and his mouth open. Her eyes misted as she thought of the danger he'd so narrowly escaped last week. If this tour prevented that from ever happening again, she'd be very grateful to Jeb Stratton. But he still didn't need that file.

"Do you drive this apparatus?" Denny asked, grinning as he used the big word.

"Sometimes. Not usually."

"I want to sit in that seat up there," Denny announced.

"And I promised you could. Here we go." Jeb opened the door and lifted Denny up to the leather upholstery.

"Mommy, you should see all the stuff in here! Boy!"

Liza's curiosity was getting the best of her attempt at disinterest, and she peered around the open door into the truck's cab.

Jeb touched her elbow. "Come on, you can sit in the other seat." He guided her around the front of the vehicle and steadied her hand as she climbed up. His touch communicated a sense of controlled power that she couldn't ignore. She responded to that touch no matter how much she tried not to. Could he see the warmth rising to her cheeks? She looked away.

As she and Denny sat and stared at the complicated instrument panel, Jeb pointed out some of the functions of the dials and buttons. His explanation required that he lean into the cab on Liza's side, and his arm brushed more than once across her lap.

Liza sat very still. Their closeness was innocent enough, wasn't it? After all, Denny was very curious about everything, and Jeb had to indicate what he was talking about. Liza tried to pay attention, too, but instead she kept focusing on the pattern of Jeb's sandy hair at the nape of his neck and the smooth-shaven curve of his jaw. He smelled good—like soap lather. Liza wondered how her proximity to him could make her feel both languid and excited at the same time.

"But how do the hoses squirt?" Denny asked.

"The hoses are on a different apparatus, called a pumper. That's one next to you, over there." Jeb pointed to the engine on Denny's left.

"A pumper." Denny nodded. "That name is in one of my books. Remember, Mommy?"

Liza cleared her throat. "Yes, I do, Denny." It was a miracle she remembered anything, so lulled and distracted was she by Jeb's presence and the steady rhythm of his voice.

Jeb glanced up at her, his own expression relaxed and open. "I hope you're not too bored."

"No, I... This is very interesting, Jeb."

His blue eyes sparkled but he said nothing.

Liza realized that she'd forgotten to use his last name and flushed.

Jeb winked at her in response. "Thanks, Liza."

"I didn't mean to—"

"Let it go. Life's too short."

"Maybe so." Liza gauged the depth of emotion in his eyes. She knew the answer to Dulcie's question now. Jeb was definitely interested in her. And who was she kidding? She found him pretty damned interesting, too.

Beside her, Denny began to squirm. "Are you going to show us where you sleep, Jeb? I want to slide down the pole like a real fireman."

"You bet." Jeb glanced at his watch. "And after that it will be close to dinnertime. Could I interest both of you in a hamburger or a pizza or something when we get finished here?"

Liza was surprised by the offer. "Aren't you on duty?"

"Actually, no. I traded with a buddy of mine so that I'd be free to show you around. If I'd been on duty and an alarm had come in, I'd have had to leave you both in the lurch."

"But you wore your uniform," she said, still confused.

"The chief suggested that. He thought I'd carry more authority for...you know."

"I understand."

"So how about that meal?"

"I'm sorry, but I can't." Liza found that she was indeed very sorry. "Bill is due over at my place in about half an hour for a practice session. We'd planned to grab a sandwich while we worked."

Jeb nodded. "Then how about Denny? Would it be okay if I took him?"

Liza stiffened. "Oh, I don't think—"

"Please, Mommy? Can I, please?" Denny bounced on the seat of the ladder truck.

She put a calming hand on his shoulder. "I don't think that would be a good idea, Denny."

"Aw, Mommy!"

"Maybe another time, sweetheart."

"You *always* say that and I never get to go anywhere."
He crossed his arms and stuck out his lower lip.

"Liza." Jeb touched her arm and spoke in a low voice.
"I don't want to interfere, but is this really such a terrible
idea? I'll have him home long before bedtime, and my
chief will vouch for my character."

"It's not that. It's..." She paused, unable to admit to
him that Denny had never been on an outing with anyone
but her, and the thought of Jeb taking him for pizza without her was frightening. Yet she knew that Denny was
aching to have supper with his new friend, the "force-
ball entry man." And maybe, after Jeb had spent another
couple of hours with Denny, he'd realize that this particular little boy didn't belong in his program.

She glanced at Jeb. "His bedtime is eight-thirty."

"Oh, boy!" Denny shouted. "I can go!"

"I'll take good care of him, Liza."

She gave him a level gaze. "I expect you to."

"I will." He held out his hand to help her down from
the cab. "We'll finish up this little tour, and you can be
on your way."

Liza placed her hand in his and sensed the firm strength
of his body in the way he supported her whole weight
with the muscles of one arm. She had never known a man
who probably could carry her across the room as easily
as he'd hoisted Denny into his arms earlier.

He released her hand at the exact moment he should
have to avoid any suspicion that he had enjoyed touching
her. But Liza felt the extra pressure of his grip just before
he let go. It was almost, if not quite, a squeeze.

Then he rounded the front of the big fire engine and
swung Denny to the cement floor. "Time to see the rest

of the place. This is our emergency vehicle," he said, pointing.

"It's an ambulance," Denny announced, pleased with himself for knowing.

"That's right. And last but not least, over here is our antique. This old apparatus is fifty-five years old, Denny. Can you imagine that?"

"Fifty-five years? Then why's it so shiny?"

"Because we fixed it up. It was a broken-down rig when we brought it in here. With the cab open like that, you can imagine what the weather had done to it. And those big fenders were rusted, and the running board had to be rechromed."

"Well, it's beautiful now," Liza said, running a hand over the leather seat. "The interior looks as plush as those expensive roadsters from the thirties."

"Yeah, well, Steve, one of my buddies, loves doing this sort of restoration. He donated his time and scrounged materials so it didn't cost us too much."

"Who paid for it?"

"The guys. We... It was fun, I guess. Every time any of us look at this antique or take her into a parade, we have a sense of pride that we rescued her from the junk heap. I'm sure she saved plenty of lives in her day, so it's only right that we saved her."

Liza smiled gently as she wandered the length of the gleaming truck. "A sentimental lot, aren't you?"

"Yeah, I suppose so."

"Hey, Jeb, are we going upstairs?" Denny asked. "I want to see where you sleep and then slide down that pole."

"Sure, sport. Right this way."

Liza followed Denny and Jeb up the narrow stairs.

"I hope I remembered to make my bed," Jeb said over his shoulder.

Denny giggled. "Know what my mommy does if I don't make my bed?"

"No, what?"

"First she gets mad because I forgot, and then she gives me a kiss because she knows I'll remember next time."

"And do you remember?"

"Yep."

"I think I might, too, with motivation like that."

Denny laughed, but Liza figured he was reacting to Jeb's tone more than his words. She decided not to react at all.

"Here we are." Jeb waved his arm around the room as they reached the second floor.

"So this is where you sleep," Denny said. "Which bed is yours?"

"That one." Jeb pointed to one of the metal cots lined with military precision along the wall. "But I rarely sleep in it. I'd rather stay down in the kitchen when I'm on duty. I don't like waking up to the sound of an alarm coming in."

The realities of his job were beginning to make an impression on Liza. This wasn't exactly an electronics plant here, or a bottling company or a real estate office. The people who accepted this job did so knowing that every workday involved risking their lives. She wanted to ask Jeb why he'd chosen to be a fire fighter, but the question would expose her interest in him, and she hesitated.

"Then you don't get to slide down the pole, if you don't sleep here," Denny said, reasoning it out.

"That's true. I don't do that often."

Denny walked toward the shiny brass pole. "I would

stay up here all the time, so that when a fire happened, I could slide down, and jump on the truck, and—''

Liza rushed forward. ''Not so close, Denny. Jeb has to help you.'' She glanced at Jeb. ''Are you sure this is a good idea?''

''He'll be fine. I'll go first and then catch him at the bottom.'' He stepped toward the pole. ''Watch me carefully, Denny. You grab the pole in both hands, like this, wrap one leg around it, push off and go!'' Jeb disappeared through the hole in the floor.

''My turn! My turn!'' Denny jumped up and down.

Liza had grave misgivings, but there was no turning back at this point.

''Send Recruit Galloway on down,'' Jeb called.

Liza shivered. She hoped Denny never considered a career with the fire department.

''Aye, aye, sir!'' Denny chortled.

''I'll tell you when he's coming,'' Liza said as she guided Denny's small hands around the pole and held him while he wrapped both legs around it, too. ''Now *hang* on,'' Liza instructed. ''Ready, Jeb?''

''Ready below.''

''Okay, here he comes. On three. One, two, three!''

''Bombs away!'' shrieked Denny as he whisked down the pole and was caught in Jeb's arms at the bottom. ''Wow!'' he cried. ''Can I do it again? Can I?''

''I think it's your mother's turn,'' Jeb said. ''Want to give it a shot, Liza?''

''I don't think so,'' she called down. ''I'll take the stairs.''

''You can manage. Come on. You might never have another chance. Poles are being phased out of fire stations. This is one of the few left.''

"Do it, Mommy!" Denny called from below her. "Don't be scared. It's fun!"

Liza studied the gleaming pole. She'd always wanted to try sliding down one. Before she could change her mind, she grasped the pole in both hands and wound her leg around it. "Geronimo!" she yelled and pushed off. Once gravity took over she was terrified and knew she would break both legs. What had possessed her to try this stupid stunt?

Then it was over, and strong hands caught and steadied her descent. Jeb held her until she was standing firmly on the floor again. For the barest moment she had the dizzy sensation of being in his arms.

"Now, wasn't that fun?" he asked, grinning at her.

"Yes, fun," she said through the clenched teeth of her determined smile. "And I never want to do it again."

"I do! I do!" Denny hopped on one foot. "Can we slide down again, Jeb?"

Liza put her hand on Denny's shoulder. "Once is enough."

"But the firemen do it all the time, Mommy."

"It's part of their job." She took a deep breath. "I think it's about time for me to go."

"Denny and I will walk you out, and then he and I can cover any of the areas we missed." Jeb took Denny's hand.

"But you covered the pole sliding, right?" She gave Jeb a meaningful look.

"Uh, sure. We covered that. Right."

Liza shook her head. "Boys will be boys." But she kind of liked the fact that Denny had been fearless with the pole and related well to Jeb. She'd never wanted him to be a clinging momma's boy just because he hadn't had a father to be rough and tough with him. It was good for

Denny to be around a man like Jeb, she decided. Reluctant to leave for many reasons, Liza paused at the door. "Thanks for the tour, and for taking Denny out to dinner."

"You're welcome. You know that."

Liza looked at Denny. "You be a good boy, okay?"

"I will."

"I'll be a good boy, too," Jeb promised solemnly.

Her smile was wry. "Glad to hear it." Liza started out the door but turned back at the last moment. "Jeb, about the other night..."

He shook his head. "Don't worry about it. I think we're in the process of fixing that."

Liza allowed herself one last look into his blue eyes. "I guess...I guess maybe we are."

CHAPTER FOUR

"HOW MUCH PIZZA CAN YOU EAT, Denny?" Jeb surveyed four sizes of round aluminum pans nailed to the wall behind the order counter.

"Let me see up there." Denny held his arms out to Jeb.

Jeb picked him up, amazed at how familiar Denny felt in his arms already. With Liza gone Jeb had paraded Denny around the remainder of the station house as if the boy belonged to him. Denny hadn't seemed to mind. And now, when Jeb held him up to see the different sizes of pizza pans, he leaned easily against Jeb's chest and wrapped one arm around Jeb's neck in a gesture of complete acceptance.

At moments such as this he couldn't believe that a boy like Denny could possibly be responsible for destruction of property, even death. That was the paradox, of course—youthful innocence paired with deadly power.

Denny shifted in his arms and pointed to the largest metal circle, a pan designed to hold a pizza the size of a truck tire. "That one, with pepperoni, and olives, and sausage, and lots of cheese."

The young girl behind the counter glanced at Jeb. "Are you a policeman?"

"Fireman."

"Oh. Are you having a party for disadvantaged kids or something?"

"No." Jeb frowned and hoped Denny hadn't understood the word *disadvantaged*. "This is a small party for one kid, and I think that's more pizza than we need."

"No, it's not," Denny insisted. "I can eat all that. What's she mean by *disadvantaged*?"

"Hungry, I guess," Jeb said, figuring that was close enough for now.

"That's me. I could eat that whole thing."

Jeb doubted it, but what did he know? Maybe Denny ate like a horse. Besides, the food wouldn't go to waste, even if Denny's eyes were bigger than his stomach. They could take the leftovers home to Liza, and if she didn't want any, Jeb would cart the rest to the station.

"Give us the jumbo, please," Jeb said to the girl.

"If you say so." She smiled and shook her head as she wrote down the order. "But that's a big pizza for such a little boy."

"I'm not so little," Denny muttered.

The girl glanced up. "Drinks?"

"A pitcher of orange," Denny said immediately.

Jeb wondered if he should order milk for Denny instead. It dawned on him that he'd never been in charge of a five-year-old's meal before.

The girl tapped her pencil impatiently. "A pitcher of orange, then?"

"Uh, I guess. Is that what you usually have with pizza, sport?"

"Yep."

"Okay." Jeb nodded to the girl. "A pitcher of orange."

For a moment Jeb considered ordering a mug of beer for himself, but then he canceled the idea. He didn't want liquor on his breath when he brought Denny home. He couldn't afford to give Liza an opening to start slinging moral accusations around.

The girl behind the counter reached for a plastic pitcher and shoved it under a tap that spewed forth orange drink. "If you'll give me your name, I'll call you when the pizza's done," she said, scooping ice into glasses.

In a flash of inspiration, Jeb gave her Denny's name instead of his and noticed the pleased look on the boy's face.

"You can put me down now," he announced to Jeb, who complied immediately.

The girl handed Jeb the pitcher and glasses. "Okay, Mr. Denny. Your pizza will be ready in about fifteen minutes."

From below him Jeb heard Denny's giggle. "She thinks you're me," he said in a stage whisper.

"That's fine with me, sport. You're a great guy. Want to carry the glasses over to that booth?"

"You carry the glasses. I'll carry the *pitcher*."

"Uh, okay." Reluctantly Jeb lowered the pitcher of orange to Denny. "Walk slowly, now."

Jeb remained by the counter and held his breath while Denny navigated a meandering path through the tables to the booth Jeb had pointed out. The tip of Denny's tongue stuck out from the tight line of his mouth as he concentrated on the sloshing orange drink.

When he made it to the table and set the pitcher on it, he turned to Jeb with a grin as bright as that of any triumphant Olympic star. Jeb smiled back and made a circle of his thumb and forefinger. So far, so good. The psychologist had mentioned giving problem kids a sense of accomplishment. Improving their self-worth always helped, the guy had said.

Jeb carried the glasses to the booth where Denny was already kneeling on the seat and drawing pictures on the frosty sides of the pitcher.

He glanced up when Jeb sat down. "Can I pour it in the glasses, Jeb? Can I?"

"Why not?" Jeb congratulated himself on the success of his approach. "Do it slowly," he added to be on the safe side.

Denny spilled very little as he poured orange over the ice in each glass. Then he gulped his down in five seconds, giving himself a bright orange mustache. "I think I'll have some more," he announced, and was pouring before Jeb could utter a sound. The boy was having such a great time that Jeb couldn't deny him a third glass, either.

Finally Denny plopped the empty glass to the table with a satisfied sigh. "Thanks. I needed that."

Jeb chuckled. "I guess the tour made you thirsty."

"Yep. 'Specially sliding down the pole all those times."

"Now remember, we aren't telling your mother about that."

"Right." Denny swiped at his mouth with his hand and removed about half of the orange mustache.

"What did you think of the fire movies we watched?"

"Scary."

"Good. You should be scared of what fire can do, Denny. Fire is dangerous."

Denny fidgeted in his seat. "Well, gotta go to the bathroom now." He slid out of the booth and headed for the back of the pizza parlor.

"Uh, me, too," Jeb called, striding after him.

"I can take care of myself."

"Oh, I'm sure you can." Jeb kept walking. Probably nothing would happen to a kid in the rest room of this friendly neighborhood pizza place, but he wasn't taking any chances.

He could tell that Denny didn't appreciate being accompanied to the rest room and back, and as they returned to the booth Jeb vowed to give him another opportunity to be grown-up soon. His last move, letting Denny pour the drinks, hadn't worked out so hot. Jeb worried that the kid wouldn't eat any pizza with all that sugary junk in his stomach. Something told Jeb that Liza wouldn't have allowed her son to drink so much.

Liza. A smile of pleasure curved his mouth as he remembered catching her at the bottom of the fireman's pole. He loved being near her, and today she'd shown some indication that she enjoyed his company, too. If only they could discuss Denny's problem reasonably and work together on a solution, then the way would be cleared for other feelings to develop between them.

But Jeb sensed that Liza wasn't ready to discuss Denny's problem with him. The more he pushed, the more she'd back away. Jeb sipped on the orange drink, forgetting that he didn't like the taste, while he tried to figure out a nonthreatening way to bring Liza and Denny closer to him.

Denny waved a hand in front of his face. "Wake up! They just called my name."

"Did they?" Jeb started guiltily. "I must have been sleeping on the job."

"That's okay. I'll get the pizza."

"It'll be hot, Denny. Maybe I should—" Jeb saw Denny's expectant expression fade. "Maybe I should get some napkins ready, so we don't burn our fingers," he finished, pulling them from the metal dispenser on the table.

Jeb sat poised and ready to rush to Denny's aid if necessary. Mentally he prepared himself to pay for an entire pizza that ended up on the floor of the restaurant. If Denny burned himself on the pizza, he'd never forgive himself, but he was gambling against that happening. If he remembered correctly, the pizza was placed in a Styrofoam container before it was given to the customers, anyway. He'd never paid attention before, but then he'd never had to worry about a little boy carrying a huge pizza, either.

Denny was too short to see over the counter and get anyone's attention, so he called out instead. Jeb hid a smile behind his hand as Denny's voice rose on the second try and became quite loud on the third. At last the young girl who had taken their order peered over the counter and saw him.

"I'm Denny," Jeb heard him announce proudly. He pointed across the room. "*He's* Jeb."

The girl's lips formed a round O. With her next action she earned Jeb's forgiveness for earlier calling Denny "such a little boy." She carried the pizza around the counter, rather than trying to hand it over and down, and presented it with deferential respect to Denny. "Enjoy your pizza, sir," she said clearly.

"I will," Denny replied, his chest puffed out with pride. Then he marched over to Jeb bearing his gigantic trophy. "Here's our pizza, Jeb," he said, placing it on the table with a flourish.

"Great. I'm starved. How about you?"

"Yeah!" Denny scurried into his side of the booth.

"But let's wait until it cools a little. I hate hot pizza."

"Me, too." Denny looked grateful not to be required to stuff a piece in his mouth immediately.

"I've been wondering," Jeb began, trying out his first idea. "How do you like football?"

"It's okay."

"Ever see any pro games?"

"Nope."

"Want to?"

"Nope."

Jeb refused to be daunted. "Then how about basketball?"

"Eric and I play sometimes. He has a hoop in his backyard. It's down lower so we can make baskets."

"Then how would you like to watch the big guys play—the Chicago Bulls?"

"I don't think so."

"Oh."

"Jeb, when do you think you'll get a dog at your station?" Denny asked.

"Oh, I don't know, we..." He paused and looked at the boy. "You like dogs a lot, don't you?"

"Yep. Someday I'm gonna have one. Mommy promised."

"I'm sure you'll enjoy that."

"Yeah. Wish I could have one now."

It was a cheap shot, but Jeb was desperate. "I'm thinking of getting a dog."

"You are?" Denny's brown eyes grew wide. "When?"

"Soon." He wasn't lying, he told himself. He had wanted a dalmatian for a long time. Why not get it now?

"Big or little?"

"Little, but he'll grow big. I think it's better to start with a puppy, so you can train him yourself."

"Me, too!" Denny bounced up and down on his knees. "Can I help you train him, Jeb? I'm real good with puppies. They like me."

"If it's okay with your mother, sure."

"Can we ask her tonight? Can we?"

"If she's not too busy with her practice session."

Denny slumped down in the booth. "Practice. That's all she ever does."

"But she's trying to earn more money so you can buy a house, so you can have a dog."

"But it takes so long. I've *already* waited so long."

Jeb had no answer for him. A month was a long time when you were only five years old. A year was an eternity. The more he thought about it, the more Jeb became convinced that a dog might be the very thing to turn Denny away from his preoccupation with fire. But the dog couldn't be Jeb's; it had to be Denny's. Slowly an idea formed.

"What color dog are you gonna get, Jeb?"

"I don't know. What color do you like?"

"All colors." Denny giggled. "I'd even take a *purple* dog." He laughed at his own joke.

"Well, then, how about a spotted dog?"

"*Purple* spots?" Denny laughed harder.

"No, black spots. A white dog with black spots."

Denny stopped laughing and cocked his head to one side. "You mean like a dog that rides on fire engines?"

"Right. A dalmatian."

"Cool!" Denny began bouncing again. "Yeah, that would be great! A fire station dog. I'd love one like that."

"Then it's settled. I'll start looking tomorrow." Jeb eased a wedge of pizza out of the Styrofoam container and held it out to Denny. "Want some?"

Denny's expression was repentant. "I'm…kinda full, Jeb."

He looked so stricken that Jeb couldn't bear to make a point of it. "Me, too," he said, replacing the wedge and making the circle complete once more. "Let's get a lid for this and take it home to your mother."

"Yeah! She likes pizza." Denny brightened as he saw a way out of his blunder of ordering too much food.

Denny chattered about dogs, and movies about dogs and friends who had dogs for most of the trip home. Jeb listened enough to make appropriate comments, but his mind was elsewhere.

As he drove his red pickup with the pizza smelling up the cab on the seat between him and Denny, Jeb anticipated the cozy scene coming up. He, Liza and Denny would sit around Liza's kitchen table eating pizza and discussing dogs some more.

Jeb supposed he'd have to invite Liza's partner Bill to join them, but maybe Bill would decline. Maybe Bill would leave. Then after a while it would be Denny's bedtime, but Liza would ask Jeb to stay until after she'd put Denny to bed. Then...

From that point on he'd better stop fantasizing, he decided. Liza had been nicer to him today than the first time they met, but he couldn't expect her to—to what? Let him hold her? He'd wanted to do that from the beginning, when she'd broken down and cried that day in her apartment.

But he wanted more than holding. He wanted kissing, touching, melting together until there was no—

"Jeb! You passed it."

"Oh. So I did. Guess we'll go around the block."

"You're a goofy guy. That's two times I've had to tell you stuff."

"Good thing I've got you around, huh, sport?"

"Sure is. Without me around you might get a purple dog." Denny started laughing again.

"Then you'd better stick close."

"I will."

Jeb beamed at him. Everything seemed so simple now.

The way to the kid was through a dog. The way to the mother was through the kid. They'd form a strong unit—man, woman, kid and dog—and banish the evils of smoke and fire, of loneliness and frustration. It would be so easy.

Denny burst through the door of the apartment shouting about the dog at the top of his lungs. Bill and Liza stopped their playing and stared at him, then at Jeb who stood in the open doorway holding the jumbo pizza and smiling benevolently.

He held the carton aloft. "Pizza, anyone?"

"Mommy! Mommy!" Denny tugged on Liza's sleeve. "Jeb's getting a spotted dog, and I'm going to help him!"

"Yes, dear, just a minute. By the way, Bill, this is Jeb Stratton. Jeb, my partner Bill Buckhalter."

The two men nodded at each other.

"Excuse me if I misunderstood," Liza said, glancing back at Jeb. "But I thought you were taking him *out* for pizza?"

"I was. I mean, we did, but we were both full so we brought the pizza back here."

"Full?"

"Mommy, I poured the orange drink all by myself, and I had *three* glasses."

Liza frowned at Jeb. "And how much pizza did he eat?"

"Well, none, but I thought we could all have some here, now that the orange drink's had a chance to…"

Liza sighed and stood up. "Could I talk to you a minute in the kitchen, Jeb?"

"Sure," he said uneasily. This wasn't going quite as he'd planned it.

When they were inside the kitchen Liza closed the door and faced him. "Jeb, I realize your intentions were good, but you've filled my kid full of orange drink and brought him back at eight o'clock at night without feeding him. If we give him pizza now he'll need more to drink with it, and he'll be up half the night, if he doesn't wet the bed.''

"Yeah, I know that wasn't good, but he was so proud of himself, pouring that big pitcher, and I think it's important for his self-esteem if he—"

"You think *what*?"

"Sometimes if a kid misbehaves he's seeking power over his—"

She lifted her gaze to the ceiling. "I see. And how many children have you raised, Jeb?"

"Well, none, but..." Jeb felt at a distinct disadvantage standing before her holding the pizza carton like a delivery boy. "Do you mind if I set this down?"

"Go ahead. And what's this business about a dog? What are you trying to do, getting him all excited like that about a dog when he wants one of his own so much?"

"I have this idea. If we could sit down, have a little pizza and discuss it, maybe you'd—"

"Bill and I are practicing, Jeb. My time is limited, and I already spent a large portion of it with you this afternoon. If I don't get this act worked out with Bill, we have no chance of bringing more customers in. If we don't bring in more customers, Dulcie will lose the nightclub, and I'll lose income and the chance to buy a house."

Jeb rubbed the back of his neck. "I know that, and this discussion won't take up much of your time. It's just that Denny needs—"

She kept her voice low but there was no mistaking her irritation. "Darn it, Jeb, you're in no position to decide what Denny needs. You've been with him a few hours and you're behaving as if you were his father, and an inexperienced one, at that."

"Liza, please listen to me."

"No. The orange drink and pizza fiasco is temporary, but if Denny becomes involved with your dog, I can imagine a lot of problems. I'm sorry, Jeb."

"You're going to make Denny one unhappy kid."

"I am? Listen, whatever you've said to him without checking with me first is your problem, not mine." She picked up the pizza carton. "And please take that with you. Under the circumstances Denny will be better off with a bowl of chicken noodle soup than something as spicy as pizza right before he goes to bed."

"Liza, you're making a mistake. Maybe I've handled this wrong. You're probably right that I should have checked with you first, but don't let that detail spoil something wonderful for your son."

"Good-bye, Jeb." She pushed the carton against his chest. "Thank you for the tour this afternoon. That should be enough to satisfy Mrs. Applebaum."

Jeb took the pizza but didn't move from his spot. He had bungled this, and he was losing his chance to help this boy, besides losing a chance to know Liza Galloway better. He couldn't believe how rotten that was making him feel. "I want to see you again—see Denny again." He could hear the desperation in his plea and was a little ashamed of it. But an irrational sort of need was taking over his usual calm acceptance of rejection.

"I think we should call it quits right now and simplify everything."

"Liza, please."

For an answer she opened the kitchen door and walked into the living room. "Jeb just realized he has to get back to the station, so I convinced him to take the pizza and feed it to all those hungry fire fighters."

Bill smiled at Jeb. "Well, thanks for the thought."

"Yeah," Jeb muttered. Denny was watching him with a worried frown. "So long, sport."

"Did you tell her about the dog, Jeb?"

"Not exactly, sport. Maybe you can do that." He shot one last glance at Liza to confirm that she was indeed glaring at him like a wary mother tiger. He had no more tricks up his sleeve, so he waved nonchalantly and headed out the door. Dammit, dammit, dammit. But this wouldn't be the end, he decided as he stuffed the pizza in the nearest trash dumpster. Liza Galloway hadn't seen the last of him.

Inside the apartment Liza glanced from Bill to Denny. "That takes care of Mr. Stratton."

"Mommy, what about the dog?" Denny looked ready to cry. "We didn't decide anything about the dog."

Liza walked over to Denny and put her hands on his shoulders. "You can tell me about it in a minute. Right now I'll fix you a bowl of chicken noodle soup while you hop into your pajamas."

"I don't want any soup."

"Then how about oatmeal with raisins?"

"I don't want oatmeal. I wanted some of that pizza, but you let Jeb take it all away."

"That seemed like the best thing, Denny. If you're not hungry, then get ready for bed and I'll be in soon to say good-night."

"And talk about the dog?"

She sighed. "Yes, and talk about the dog."

After Denny left the room Liza collapsed on the piano bench. "I should never have left him alone with Denny. It was against my better judgment, but like a fool I let myself be swayed by Denny's positive reaction to him." *And mine,* she admitted silently, remembering the warmth of his arms when he had caught her at the bottom of the fireman's pole.

"He seems like a nice enough guy," Bill commented.

"Oh, he's nice, all right, but he doesn't understand anything about my life."

"Insensitive, huh?"

Liza hesitated. "Maybe that's too harsh. After all, why should he understand? He's single with few responsibilities. Anyway, it doesn't matter. I've put an end to the whole business."

"Denny seems to like him a lot. How are you going to handle that?"

"I'm not sure. That's the part that really irritates me, the way he's tried to win Denny over to his side."

"Why's he so determined?"

"I don't know." Liza combed her hair back from her face with her fingers. "Maybe because he's out to save the world. Maybe because he thinks Denny's a potential delinquent or something."

"Maybe because he's attracted to Liza Gayle?"

Liza glanced quickly at Bill. "What makes you think that?"

Bill shrugged. "Intuition. Observation. You could do worse than a big, strong fireman, Liza. And Denny likes him."

"Who says I'm in the market for any man, big and strong or small and helpless? I have a show to prepare, a job to do and a son to raise. I don't have time for anything else."

"That's the point. If you had a man around to help with some of those things, you'd have more time. Sharon and I split the housework, and we each have less to do than before we moved in together. I have two jobs, just like you, don't forget. And Sharon's modeling and auditions for modeling take up a good fifty or sixty hours a week. But we still have time to relax now and then because we share the dumb chores that have to be done."

"You don't have any kids, though."

"Having a kid would be even more reason."

Liza groaned. "Not you, too? Doesn't anybody think I can raise this kid by myself?"

"Now, Liza, don't be getting on your high horse. I only said—"

"Mommy," Denny called from the bedroom. "I'm ready."

"Bill, I'm really not in the mood to discuss this. I'd better go tuck Denny in."

Bill put a hand on her arm. "You're one terrific lady, but nobody can be superwoman."

"Mommy, are you coming?" Denny called again.

"Yes," Liza called back. Then she turned to Bill. "I'm doing just fine. Once we have this show in hand I'll be doing even better. Somebody like Jeb Stratton would only throw me off my pace."

"If you say so."

"I do. But thanks for caring." Liza walked back to Denny's bedroom while she thought about what Bill had said. Bill liked Jeb. Denny liked him, too. She was the only one who saw him as an unwanted complication. But she also was the only one who knew that the real issue wasn't the pizza dinner or Jeb's dog. The problem was far more basic. She'd given in to her attraction to Kyle, and it had changed her life forever. Liza feared the crippling power of her own desires.

CHAPTER FIVE

DENNY WAS HUNKERED DOWN under his new quilt with only his eyes and the top of his head showing. Liza still wondered if she'd done the right thing in replacing the quilt, but a new one helped put the fire incident behind them. That was exactly what Liza wanted to do. Jeb reminded her of the fire, which was another strike against him.

Denny's voice emerged from beneath the covers. "Mommy, can we talk about the dog now?"

Dreading the approaching conversation, Liza sat on the bed. "Okay. Tell me about it."

Denny pushed back the covers and bounced to a sitting position. "Jeb's getting a dog, Mommy." His brown eyes sparkled with delight. "A dalma—dalma—"

"Dalmatian?"

"Yeah! A fire station dog. Except it won't be one yet, because it will be a puppy, but Jeb says I can help train it, and pet it, and brush it, and everything."

Fresh anger washed over Liza at the eager hope written on Denny's face. Jeb had enticed him with a dog, except that it wouldn't be Denny's dog, it would be Jeb's. That puppy wouldn't be as accessible as Eric's old collie, and Denny didn't consider Eric's dog even partly his.

Jeb couldn't possibly expect to have Denny around enough for the boy to feel a part of the puppy's training.

Even if Jeb did imagine that close a relationship, Liza wouldn't allow it.

She looked into Denny's bright eyes and searched for a way to explain the situation to him. "Denny, Jeb is a busy man."

"I know," Denny responded proudly. "He's the force-ball entry man. He fights fires."

"Yes, and that means he doesn't have much time for puppies and little boys."

"Mommy, I am *not* little. How many times do I have to tell you?"

"I'm sorry, Denny. I meant to say *young men*. Is that better?"

Denny folded his arms across his chest. "Yes."

"Anyway, I'm afraid it won't work out for you to help train Jeb's puppy, if he even gets one. I can't take you over to his house every day, and he certainly can't come and get you all the time."

"Maybe I can walk."

"Honey, we don't even know where Jeb lives."

"I bet he lives close. I bet I can walk."

"Denny, you'll have to forget about Jeb's dog. Having your own will be so much better, and after Bill and I get this act going, we'll soon have enough money for the house."

"You keep saying that, but we never buy it."

"Things like this take time, but we're getting closer every day."

"So when will I get *my* dog?" Denny scowled at her. "Tomorrow?"

"Of course you won't get your dog tomorrow, Denny, but very soon."

"How soon? The next day after tomorrow?"

"You're being silly. A few months. Maybe by the time the weather gets warm again. When you're six."

"Six?" Denny wailed. "That's too long!"

"It's the best I can do. I'm trying very hard, sweet-heart."

"Then let me help with Jeb's dog. Please, Mommy."

"No. That would only cause problems for us."

"Mommy!" Denny began to cry.

At that moment Liza could have strangled Jeb Stratton. If he hadn't opened his big mouth she wouldn't be dealing with a sobbing boy who jerked away from her when she tried to comfort him. At last she gave up, kissed the top of his head and turned out the light.

For the next hour Liza pounded the keys on her piano with a vengeance as she practiced with Bill. After he left, she took a long, hot shower and climbed into bed while she continued to imagine exquisite tortures worthy to be inflicted on a certain broad-shouldered fireman.

"I BLEW IT, STEVE. She hates me." Jeb polished the hood of the antique ladder truck until he could see his own disgruntled face reflected in it. He and Steve usually volunteered for the job of spit-shining the old apparatus. It was one of the few maintenance chores they welcomed.

Steve was into nostalgia and tradition, with his handle-bar mustache and red suspenders. After hanging around him for the past two years, Jeb was hooked on traditional things, too. He figured that explained his decision to get a dalmatian instead of some other kind of dog.

Steve sprayed a fine mist of cleaner on his side of the windshield. "You should have checked with her before you brought up the dog. I'll agree on that one." He wiped the windshield clean again and glanced at Jeb. "But hey, we all make mistakes. If she's the woman you say, she can forgive a little mistake.''

"She won't have the chance if I never see her again.''

"Don't you have to check up on the kid?''

"I already asked the chief about that, and he said no. The boy's behavior was minor stuff, and the people down at juvenile have given me the names of two other kids I'll be working with. They live near the Madison.''

"Oh.'' Steve frowned. "Any chance that they're the ones who torched it?''

"Maybe. They're quite a bit older than Denny, about twelve or thirteen, I think the chief said.''

"If there's any chance they're the ones who started that fire, or they know who did, I'd concentrate on them, buddy. For the Catman's sake. Hell, for all our sakes. Any one of us could end up that way, just because some bored kid decides to play with matches. I've had it with that garbage. Let me know if you need any help with those boys.''

"I will.'' Jeb spread wax over the front fender. "I miss that guy like hell,'' he said without looking up.

"Yeah,'' Steve responded quietly.

"I keep expecting him to show up for his shift.''

"I know what you mean.''

"Dammit, Steve.'' Jeb tossed the rag onto the fender and looked at his friend. "I got into this business to fight fires. Kevin did, too. When we were kids together, we thought of what big heroes we'd be, saving people from horrible, accidental fires. But when someone deliberately sets a fire...''

"Arson's a part of the job, too, buddy.''

"Maybe, but that's the part that stinks, you know?''

"I know.''

They worked in silence for a few minutes, each knowing there was no answer. A certain percentage of fires wouldn't be accidents, but they'd have to risk their lives to fight them, no matter how they'd started.

"Anyway," Jeb said at last, "the chief and I agree I've done enough for Denny for the time being. I've given him a tour of the station and taken him out for pizza. Or I should say, out for orange drink."

"And that was your biggest mistake."

"The orange drink?" Jeb grimaced. "I know."

"I don't mean that. I mean throwing away an entire, perfectly edible pizza. I sure would have enjoyed pizza Tuesday night instead of that mess Jerry calls Hungarian goulash."

"Too bad. I couldn't stand to look at the thing."

"Which shows just how far gone you are on that lady, buddy-boy. A man who tosses an uneaten pizza in the nearest dumpster has either stomach problems or heart problems. Besides, you're no fun to live with these days, so I'd appreciate it if you'd find some way to patch things up with her. Apologize or something. Send flowers. I'll even pitch in for them if it'll improve your mood."

"Flowers aren't my style. They die too quick."

"Have you called her, at least?" Steve moved to the other side of the windshield. The chief had taken the old pumper out for a publicity run and had annihilated several bugs in the process.

"She won't talk to me."

"You know, that might be a good sign. At least she's not indifferent. I think you'd better see her face-to-face."

"She won't let me in the door."

"Then pick someplace where she has no choice, like that nightclub where she works."

"I thought of that, but it's too crowded and noisy. I need more privacy if I'm going to get anywhere."

"Okay, doesn't she have two jobs? I read that report you wrote on her, but I can't remember what the other job was."

"No help there. She tunes pianos."

"And last time I was at your place I didn't notice a piano hanging around." Steve refolded his rag to a cleaner side. "I suppose buying yourself one is a little extravagant."

"Not to mention useless. Even if I had a piano she wouldn't accept the job of tuning it. She really wants me out of her life, Steve."

"Well, maybe. Maybe not. I think we owe it to ourselves to find out for sure."

"We do, do we?"

"Yeah. So we'll have her tune Mo's piano."

"Mo's piano? What good's that?"

"Mo could talk to her, tell her what a nice guy you are."

"No way. I won't have your wife doing a commercial for me while Liza's tuning Mo's upright. That idea's worse than the flowers."

"Okay, maybe it is. Let's expand on that theme a little. Picture this." Steve put down his rag and spread both hands as if he were smoothing the air in front of him. "Mo makes an appointment to have the piano tuned when you and I are off duty. Let's say next Wednesday afternoon. I invite you over for a beer. We sit in the kitchen while Liza tunes Mo's piano."

Jeb groaned.

"No, wait, this is good. Suddenly Mo and I have an urgent errand to run, and we leave you in charge of the house while we're gone." Steve beamed at Jeb.

"Sure. Liza would take off like a scalded dog. In fact, she might disappear the minute she sees me."

"I don't think so. Unprofessional. Besides, she doesn't have to know you're there when she arrives. That can be a surprise later."

"Steve, Liza will hate this."

"Maybe at first, but you can convince her to stay and listen. And to make doubly sure she doesn't cut out, Mo can pay her in advance so she has to finish the job or give back the check."

"She'll be furious that she's been set up."

"At least she's been set up with imagination. Admit it, the idea has style."

"It's a hell of a lot better than flowers," Jeb agreed.

"Then let's do it. I'll call Mo right now and have her try for next Wednesday. She's going to love this."

"I'll pay for the tuning job, Steve."

"Forget it. That beautiful old piano deserves to be tuned right. Mo and I keep saying we'll call somebody, now that we're settled in the house, and we keep procrastinating. I should mention that the piano is an heirloom. Your lady can be trusted with it, I hope?"

"She can be trusted with it."

"Good. I like her already. Everything's falling into place, buddy. It's fate. It's kismet. It's serendipity. It's—"

"Getting pretty deep in here," Jeb finished, but he was grinning for the first time in forty-eight hours. All he wanted was one more chance to talk with Liza alone, and if this plan worked, he'd have that chance.

As LIZA DROVE TO her newest customer's home the following Wednesday she felt encouraged that her business was finally branching out. Maureen Talbot had apparently gotten her name from the yellow pages, which meant that a good job today might result in referrals to Maureen's piano-playing friends.

More money was always welcome, especially considering Denny's increasingly urgent demands for a house and a dog of his own. She had Jeb to thank for that, of course, and she was still irritated with him, but her feelings had mellowed.

Every time she heard the wail of a siren she thought of Jeb and wondered whether he was on duty. She wished some way existed for her to know that he was okay. After all, his intentions toward Denny had been good, and Liza knew he was a kind, if somewhat pushy, man.

She felt sorry for the way she'd treated him, now that she had time to think about their final confrontation. He'd stopped calling, so she supposed he'd given up his efforts at reconciliation. That was for the best, naturally, but she missed the tingle of excitement that had filled her life for the few days that Jeb was a part of it.

The Talbots lived in a bungalow a few blocks away from the small house that Liza hoped to buy someday soon. She promised herself a drive past the house after this tuning job. The For Sale sign had appeared in the front yard about six months ago, and fortunately for Liza no buyer had made a reasonable offer. The real estate agent knew that Liza was interested, but the bank required a larger down payment than she could provide right now.

She parked the Mustang at the curb and took her case of tools from the front seat. Piano tuning had served her well, she thought as she approached the house. Each appointment paid her the equivalent of a day's earnings at some minimum-wage job.

Thank heavens she'd had the foresight to get some training before Denny was born, even if she'd had to borrow the money to do it. The flexibility of the job had saved her during bouts of croup and chicken pox, school holidays and blizzards. Through it she'd met Bill, when she'd tuned his parents' piano, and they'd mentioned that their son was looking for a partner. And eventually this business she was building would buy a house for her and Denny.

Liza rang the bell and a young blonde who introduced herself as Mo Talbot answered the door. "The piano's in the living room," she said, taking Liza's coat. "In a house this small there's nowhere else to put it."

Men's voices drifted out from the kitchen, and Liza glanced at Mo. "You have company?"

"Just my husband and a friend from work."

"I hope they don't mind the noise. Most people rank listening to a piano tuning session right up there with a trip to the dentist."

Mo laughed. "They won't mind."

"Just so they've been warned." Liza appraised the room as she put down her case. The serenity of the decorating scheme, with its crocheted afghans and refinished antiques, inspired a moment of envy. "I like your house," she said. "And you have a lovely side yard." She gazed longingly out the window at a large tree with a rope swing hanging from it. "Do you have children?"

"Not yet. Steve and I bought the house only a year ago, and we wanted to settle in a bit before starting a family. Then, too, we wanted to see how soon the department would give him a raise."

Liza wondered why the name Steve sounded familiar. Where had she just heard it? "What department is that?" she asked politely.

The question destroyed the woman's former composure, and immediately she glanced away from Liza and muttered something under her breath.

"Pardon me?"

"Uh, nothing. I just—I think something's burning on

the stove, if you'll excuse me a minute. And here's your check. I have it all made out for you.''

"Thank you, but that's not necessary. You might want to wait until I've tuned the piano. Maybe you'll be dissatisfied.'' Liza wondered why her innocent question had made this woman so nervous. Was her husband with some secret agency of the government? Maybe at this moment he was having a clandestine meeting in the kitchen, in which case his dopey wife shouldn't have invited a piano tuner into the house.

"I'm sure you'll do a fine job with the piano,'' Maureen said, backing toward the kitchen. "Just have at it.''

"Okay.'' Liza shook her head in puzzlement after the woman left. She was even more confused when she heard raucous male laughter coming from the kitchen. She'd encountered some strange situations in the four years she'd been tuning pianos, but this one might turn out to be the oddest of all. With a shrug she unpacked her instruments and lifted the top of the old upright.

Within a short time she'd forgotten about the people in the other room as she adjusted the hammers and the strings of the ancient piano and tested each adjustment carefully against the other keys. It was a Baldwin and reminded Liza of the one her first piano teacher had owned, worth its weight in gold in today's market.

Once Liza had been foolish enough to think an upright piano was beneath her and had begged her parents for a baby grand, the piano she now had in her apartment. After tuning hundreds of pianos over the years she'd learned that the baby grands seldom rivaled the old uprights for quality of sound. The Talbots owned a real gem, and Liza wondered if they knew it.

Halfway through the tuning process, Liza glanced up and saw Maureen standing near the piano. "You have a beautiful instrument here, Mrs. Talbot," she said. "If you ever want to sell it, let me know."

"Thank you, but I couldn't ever part with it. This piano has been in my family for years. And call me Mo. Everyone does."

"Okay, Mo. And you're a lucky pianist to have inherited this beauty."

"Yes, I am, and I should have kept it in better tune. Next time I won't wait a whole year."

"That'll be good for my pocketbook." Liza smiled and returned to her work.

"Um, excuse me, but I'm afraid Steve and I have an errand to run."

"Oh." Liza put down her tools. "I'll be finished in another fifteen or twenty minutes, if you can wait, or—"

"We have to leave right away, but our friend will be here, so you don't have to worry about locking up or anything."

Liza narrowed her eyes. This woman was acting very suspiciously. Something was going on, and Liza had the feeling she was part of it. "I guess that will be okay."

"He's back in the kitchen finishing his beer, if you need anything. Ready, Steve?"

"Sure thing, honey," said a burly man with a handlebar mustache who emerged from the kitchen. "I'll get our coats."

Liza returned to her work, determined to finish this job quickly and leave. The Talbots might look like an average middle-class couple, but for all she knew they were foreign spies or part of a crime syndicate. She didn't need business that much that she had to risk becoming involved with shady characters.

The front door closed behind the Talbots, leaving her alone in the house with their "friend." Liza hoped he wasn't wanted by the police and that he would stay in the kitchen with his beer.

She was struggling with the lower register of the piano when she heard footsteps coming out of the kitchen and heading for the living room. *Wonderful,* she thought. *He wants to be sociable.* She kept her eyes focused on the keys and worked faster.

"Liza, we need to talk."

She almost fell off the piano bench. Then she whirled around and stared at him. "Jeb Stratton?"

"I'm sorry if I scared you."

Her heartbeat thundered in her ears. "That's...an understatement."

"I wanted to see you, and Steve suggested this. I—" He rubbed the back of his neck. "Hell, it was a lousy idea. But I was so desperate to—"

"Steve," Liza mumbled. "Of course. The department. Steve is the one who restored the antique engine."

"Yes. We're in the same ladder company."

She looked at him in disbelief. "You arranged this, having me tune their piano, so that you could see me? You tricked me into talking to you?"

"Well, yes, but Steve said the piano needed tuning, and they are paying you, so it's not as if—"

"As if what?" She stood up. "As if I'd been manipulated like a pawn in a chess game? Jeb, it's just this kind of attitude that I object to about you."

"I'm sorry. I couldn't think of any other way to be alone so that we could talk and get some things straightened out."

"I'd say they're straight as the furrows of an Illinois cornfield. I'd suggest you return to the kitchen and have another beer while I finish tuning this piano. Then I'll leave, and we can both forget this little stunt ever took place."

"No."

"Suit yourself. I have a piano to tune." She returned to her bench and began banging on low C as she adjusted the pitch.

"Liza, please listen to me."

She felt the warmth of his body just behind her. She kept hitting the C note and ignored him.

"For heaven's sake, stop that terrible noise."

"Sorry, it's my job."

He sat beside her on the bench with his back to the piano keys. "Listen for ten seconds, will you?"

"No." She kept hitting the C note until the small house reverberated with the monotonous sound.

"Liza, stop it!" Jeb threw his right arm across the keys in a discordant jangle of notes.

"Move your arm, please."

"All right." He kept his right arm where it was and circled her shoulders with his left. "Better?"

Liza stared at him. "How dare you?"

"I dare," he said quietly, "because I have nothing to lose. You've rejected every effort I've made to get close to you."

"So you'll force yourself on me, big macho man?" She found it hard to breathe, hard to think with him so near.

He shook his head. "All I want is your full attention, and now I have it."

"I could scream, you know," she said without much conviction. "The neighbors aren't that far away."

"Don't scream, Liza. Just listen. When I first met you, I was there as a fire fighter concerned with a little boy who'd burned his rug."

"You hardly have to remind me of that."

"The point is, that's all changed."

"What do you mean?"

"I'm no longer just a guy doing his job. It's gone beyond that now. Liza, I can't get you out of my mind."

Her heart lurched as she looked into the blue of his eyes. Then he smiled and she caught her breath. His nearness made her forget exactly what she had to be angry about.

"I've wanted to hold you ever since that first day," he said softly as his arm tightened around her.

"This is a mistake," she choked out.

"Don't push me away."

Her heart thudded in her chest. She wanted this, yet she didn't. Timidly she touched his cheek, and he closed his eyes. His skin, chafed by the weather he was forced to work in, had a rough texture that excited her. "I'm afraid of you."

He opened his eyes. "Don't be. I won't hurt you."

"How can you promise that? You don't even know me."

"And you don't know me. My whole life is dedicated to keeping people from harm. I'm the last person in the world you should be afraid of."

"But I don't even want a man in my life, let alone a fireman. Your work is dangerous, your schedule is crazy and you're bossy to boot."

"All true. And your work is demanding, your schedule is crazy and you've got a giant chip on your shoulder."

"Thanks a lot!" She pulled her hand away, but he caught it and brought it to his lips. "Jeb, don't."

He turned her hand over and circled her palm with the tip of his tongue. Then he glanced at her and smiled before pressing his lips against the pulse point of her wrist.

"You're taking advantage of me." Her resistance was disappearing fast.

"Am I?" His breath was hot against her skin.

"Yes."

"And do you like it?" He pushed the sleeve of her sweater up and kissed the inside of her elbow.

"No. Yes. I don't know." She closed her eyes as he sought the hollow of her throat with velvet lips that felt so good against her skin. She moaned, giving herself away.

"You smell like cinnamon," he murmured, pulling her closer. "God, how I've wanted to do this."

"Jeb…" She clutched his shoulders as he nibbled his way up the column of her throat. He took his time, kissing the line of her jaw, the curve of her cheek, her closed eyelids, until she thought she'd go mad if he didn't reward her waiting lips.

At last he hovered near her mouth. "Liza." Her name was a sigh that trailed away as he kissed her.

The moment shimmered, as if she were hearing a beautiful song for the first time and yet recognized, somehow, a heartbreakingly familiar refrain. And as with a beloved song, she never wanted it to end. She moaned softly when he lifted his lips from hers.

"I knew it would be like that." He was trembling.

Slowly she nodded. "I think I did, too. That's why I was afraid."

His gaze searched hers, and the expression on his face was luminous. "Surely this isn't something to be afraid of."

"Not for you, maybe, but I have…things to consider."

"Such as Denny?" he suggested gently.

"Yes."

"Let's talk about it."

"I'm...supposed to be working."

"You can finish tuning the piano first, if you want to."

Her answering smile wobbled. "It would help if you weren't so close. In fact, it would help if you left the room."

"Okay." He kissed her lightly on the nose. "I'll have another beer in the kitchen while you finish. Then we'll talk."

She took a long, steadying breath. "I'll finish tuning the piano, but I'm not sure about the talk. I'm very confused."

"Don't worry about that now." Slowly he released her. "Are you all right?"

"I'm, uh, fine, I guess." She ran quivering fingers through her hair.

"I'll be in the kitchen when you're ready to talk."

She nodded. "When do you expect your friends back?"

"They're sitting down at a little tavern about two blocks away, waiting for my call."

"Oh."

After he left the room she used all the self-discipline she possessed to finish her tuning job. When it was done, she closed up the piano and put away her tools before walking into the kitchen.

He glanced up immediately. "Hi."

"Hi."

"Want a beer? Steve and Mo wouldn't mind."

"I have another job in fifteen minutes."

"That's too bad."

"No, it's probably just as well." She sat down across from him and folded her hands on the table. "We have to get one point settled. The most important thing in the world to me, despite what just happened in there, is Denny's welfare."

"I respect that."

"I've avoided any emotional entanglements because I was afraid that might affect him adversely."

"I can understand that, too, but please don't close the door on us, Liza."

"What about your official relationship with Denny? Isn't becoming involved with me some sort of conflict of interest?"

"Even if he were part of the active file, I don't think so, but he's not. That's something I wanted to tell you. His case is considered inactive now."

"Did you arrange that because of me?"

"No. The chief decided Denny's case didn't warrant any more time, especially considering some other boys I'll be working with who are of more immediate concern."

Liza sighed. "I've tried to tell you that all along."

"You were my first case, and perhaps I got a little possessive." He shrugged. "Besides, from the beginning I liked the idea of keeping tabs on Denny so that I could be near you."

"But now you don't have to 'keep tabs' on him anymore?"

"Nope." He reached over and took her hand. "I have to come clean and admit that lately I've become more interested in the mother than the son."

She allowed her hand to rest in his, just for a moment. "My life is so complicated, Jeb. I wonder if you realize how little free time I have for...for anything."

"I think I do. We'll work it out."

She shivered with the temptation of it. For years she'd willingly denied herself the pleasure of a man's arms. She'd been able to do that because no one she'd met seemed worth the risk until now, until Jeb. "Denny's such a big part of my life," she said, emphasizing it again. "I can't do anything that would shut him out."

"I wouldn't expect you to. And speaking of Denny, would you let me tell you my idea about the dog?"

"Oh, Jeb, don't. Don't bring up the confounded dog."

"Why not? It makes even more sense now. We can spend more time together, all three of us, and the dog idea works right in there."

"I don't think it will help Denny to have a part-time dog, Jeb."

"I agree, so I have a better idea. We'll look for two puppies, one for me and one for Denny. I'll only be keeping it for him temporarily."

"I don't know, Jeb. My life is bananas enough without adding something like that."

"That's the beauty of it! Denny can have his dog now, when he really wants one, and I'll bear the brunt of the work. Just think, by the time you take the dog he'll be house-trained and maybe even leash-trained, too."

"I don't think that's fair, saddling you with two dogs to take care of."

He stroked the inside of her wrist. "Let me decide what's fair. I want so much to make you happy, both you and Denny. You know a puppy would thrill him to death."

"Yes, it would." She gazed at him silently and knew from his expression that he wasn't thinking about Denny and the puppies anymore.

"Just give me a few hours of your free time, Liza."

She began to tremble. "I'll try."

"How soon?"

"Soon."

CHAPTER SIX

AS SHE DROVE AWAY FROM the Talbot's house Liza wondered if she looked as disarrayed as she felt. She was crazy, plain crazy. This wonderful, bossy fireman would turn her world topsy-turvy, no doubt about it. She didn't have time for this. So why was she anxiously waiting for Saturday, when they could be together again?

They had tried to find an earlier time, but Liza's prediction of schedule conflicts was proving to be true. She was practicing with Bill tonight, as she did every Tuesday and Wednesday night, and Jeb worked a twenty-four-hour shift beginning at eight Thursday morning. On Friday he began his forty-eight-hour break, but Liza had tuning appointments all day on Friday. Even Saturday didn't promise to be very romantic. Denny would be home from school and would be included in their activities.

Liza planned to tell Denny about the puppies tonight, and Jeb would scout for a litter immediately. On Saturday they'd look at puppies if he'd found any prospects. If not, they'd have a barbecue in Jeb's backyard so that Denny could see where his puppy would be staying.

The extra time Liza had spent with Jeb at the Talbots had thrown her off schedule, and she gave up her earlier idea of driving past the house she hoped to buy. The house didn't consume her interest at the moment, anyway. For the first time in years, the present held more excitement than the future, and she wasn't thinking beyond Saturday.

That night, still in a jubilant mood, she took Denny out for hamburgers.

"But you always say this is too expensive," Denny said as they headed for McDonald's.

"I feel like celebrating tonight. Later on Bill and I have to practice, but in the meantime you and I can do the town a little, can't we?"

"What's that mean, *do the town*?"

"It means to party, have a good time."

"Yeah, I'd like to do that. Can I have a chocolate milk shake?"

"Sure. I'm having one, too."

"Boy, you're happy today, huh?"

"Yes, I am."

"You look pretty, too."

"Why, thank you, Denny."

Liza savored the news she was about to share with him. She wished now that she'd asked Jeb to have dinner with them, so he could be part of this moment, but it was too late for that. Besides, she'd have had to send him home when Bill arrived for their scheduled practice, and that would have been awkward.

The bright reds and yellows of the restaurant and the smiling face of Ronald McDonald molded in plastic on the wall exactly complemented Liza's frame of mind. She wondered how many months, or even years, had passed since she'd experienced this sort of giddiness.

Denny basked in her goodwill, turning his face up to her like a flower to the sun. With a pang of guilt she pictured the times recently when the pressure of her responsibilities had made her cross with him. In the past few weeks they hadn't taken as many walks, either, or read as many of Denny's storybooks. How long had it been since they'd baked a batch of cookies together?

Denny's kindergarten and day-care teachers had complained about his irritable behavior, and Liza could imagine why, although she'd hated to acknowledge the worsening situation. Things would be different now, Liza decided.

Denny chattered about school and his friend Eric through most of the meal, and Liza waited impatiently for him to finish his shake and Big Mac. Once he learned about the puppy, he wouldn't be able to eat another bite. Finally he started slurping the last of his shake from the bottom of the cup with his straw.

"Denny, I—"

"I know, I'm not supposed to make that noise. But I can't get it all out, Mommy."

"I wasn't going to say anything about that. I have something exciting to tell you."

"What?" Immediately he lost interest in the last drops of shake.

"I saw Jeb Stratton today, and he—"

"Jeb?" Denny's brown eyes grew bright. "Does he have that puppy yet?"

"No, but—"

"Oh." He slumped in the plastic chair. "I thought it was about the puppy."

"It is." She leaned toward him. "Jeb has decided to get two puppies, one for him and one for you."

His mouth dropped open and he stared at her.

"Would you like that? Jeb would keep your puppy until we have a place for it. I found out that you can't walk to his house, but I'll drive you over there as often as I can, and sometimes Jeb can come and get you."

"My puppy?" he whispered.

Liza nodded.

His words came faster and louder. "My very own, that I can name, and play with and teach him tricks?"

"Yes." A lump formed in her throat. Jeb had been right about the dog.

"Oh, Mommy!" He leaped from his chair and threw himself into her lap with the fiercest hug he'd ever given her. "When, Mommy, when?"

"Jeb has to find a litter," she said, holding him close and fighting tears of happiness. "You two had decided on dalmatians, right?"

"Yeah, dalmatians!" Denny hopped from her lap and began jumping from one foot to the other. "Can we get it tomorrow? Can we?"

"Now, Denny, you'll have to be a little patient. Jeb has to work tomorrow, but maybe by Saturday he'll know of some puppies. Then again, maybe not. When you're looking for a certain kind of dog it can take longer."

"Jeb will find some," Denny said as he continued to jump around. "I know he will."

"I'm sure he'll try hard, but if he hasn't found a litter by Saturday, we're going over to his house anyway for a cookout in the backyard. That way you can see where your puppy will be staying."

"Mommy, do you think I could sleep over at Jeb's house sometimes? I'd love to sleep with that puppy."

Liza smiled. "I don't know, Denny. We'll have to wait and see." She considered the irony of the situation. It would be easy to arrange for Denny to spend time alone with Jeb, but practically impossible for Denny's mother.

All the way home Denny discussed his dog—what to name him, what to feed him, what to teach him. He was so full of the news that Liza delayed the beginning of her practice session with Bill so that Denny could tell him about his puppy.

"That's one happy kid," Bill commented after Denny was tucked in for the night.

"I hope it works out."

"Sounds like an ideal situation to me. You don't have to housebreak the little sucker or lose your best pair of slippers when he's teething."

"But Denny will ask to go over there every minute, and I'll have to transport him a lot."

Bill scrutinized her. "You don't sound too unhappy about that. Do I detect a note of interest in the fireman?"

"Maybe." Liza ran her finger down the piano keys. "Although heaven knows I haven't got time to be interested. And this puppy business means I'll have more to worry about."

"You look great, though, and you've needed something to brighten your life for a long time. I'm glad for you."

"Thanks, Bill. I thought you might be worried about the act."

"Ah, the act. That brings up another subject, although I hate to with you in such a good mood."

She glanced up sharply. "What?"

"I stopped in the club for a beer this afternoon after work and talked a little with Dulcie. She admitted that she might be late with our checks."

"Late? She's never done that before."

"She's never had to pay this kind of rent before, either. She'll do well to cover that. She, ah, told me we were free to look for another gig if we wanted to."

"Leave Dulcie? Without entertainment she'd be closed in a month!"

Bill grinned. "That's my humble opinion, too. We make a big difference."

"But not big enough, apparently." Liza touched the piano keys in a soft version of Bill's newest melody.

"Not at the moment. Are you solvent enough to make it without a paycheck for a few weeks?"

"I'll just dip into the savings account again." Liza's shoulders slumped. "Damn, that money for the house is hard to come by."

"Sharon got a good check this month, so we'll be okay, but next month's another story."

"Why is it that the minute the landlord raised the rent business started dropping off?"

"It's been dropping off for a long time, babe. We haven't wanted to face the fact, that's all. We've got to open with the new act as soon as possible."

"I guess you're right."

"Listen... Sharon already has the flyers printed." He hesitated. "Can you handle it by next weekend?"

Liza winced. She'd been afraid he was leading up to that. Why right now? Sure, there were openings in her tuning schedule next week where she could work in some extra practice, but she'd been hoping that maybe...

What a silly idea, she thought. Why should she be entitled to a love life? "Uh, sure, Billy-boy." She sighed with longing at the golden hours she would have to sacrifice to be ready for the new show next Thursday night. "Have Sharon turn her crew loose with those flyers."

ON FRIDAY NIGHT LIZA arrived home and learned from Sue-Ann, Denny's sitter, that Jeb had called. He'd talked to Denny, and from what Sue-Ann could understand Jeb hadn't been able to locate any dalmatian litters. He'd promised Denny a trip to the pet store on Saturday, though, to buy dishes, food and collars for the puppies.

Liza wished she'd been with Denny to help cushion the blow of not getting his puppy right away. Maybe Jeb's suggestion of shopping for accessories had done the trick, however, because Sue-Ann didn't seem to think Denny was upset.

Still, Liza wrestled with the familiar unease that always hit her when other people seemed to have more to do with her son than she did. Such a thing couldn't be helped—she had to work and Denny was in the best hands that she could find. The kindergarten and day-care center were both excellent, and Sue-Ann was very conscientious for a nineteen-year-old. Denny liked her, and that was important. Yet Liza sometimes wondered how Sue-Ann would react in an emergency.

Her fears were stronger, she admitted reluctantly, ever since Denny had pulled his little trick in the bedroom. She'd told Sue-Ann about the incident, and Sue-Ann's reaction had been similar to Bill's; she couldn't imagine that Denny would repeat his experiment. Liza hoped that Bill and Sue-Ann were right. In any case, the puppy would be a distraction, if not the solution to her problems with Denny.

The next morning Liza and Denny were both in high spirits as they got ready for the cookout. They packed up the makings for potato salad, which Liza had told Jeb she would bring, and drove over to Jeb's house in the Mustang.

Denny had hoped for a ride in Jeb's pickup, but Liza and Jeb had agreed beforehand not to take a chance with three in the front seat and only two seat belts. Whatever else she thought about Jeb's behavior toward Denny, Liza knew that he was concerned about her son's safety, and a part of her relaxed with that knowledge.

Jeb lived on the ground floor of a red brick duplex. From the tall, narrow windows and the pillars of the front porch Liza guessed it to be at least sixty years old, far more ancient than her apartment building. Even so, Jeb's rent had to be higher than hers. He had what she yearned for—a fenced backyard.

Jeb met them at the front door. "Hey, sport!" he called out as he opened the screen, but his gaze met Liza's, not Denny's.

"Hi, Jeb," Denny said, sauntering through the door as if he owned the place. "Ready to go shopping?"

"Let's get you in the front door first, sport. Here, Liza, I'll take that stuff." As he lifted the paper bag out of her arms, the back of his hand grazed her breast.

She guessed that he hadn't meant to be so bold, but the flare of desire in his blue eyes told her that he acknowledged the contact, nevertheless. Her heart raced. Even through three layers of clothing she responded to that brief touch with as much charged energy as if he'd ripped her blouse open.

In one casual gesture he'd ignited the emotions she'd been working to control ever since she'd seen him framed in the doorway in his typical off-duty outfit—jeans that had learned his exact shape and a soft, chest-hugging sweatshirt. Two days of thinking about Jeb and their blossoming relationship had sent her fantasies into overdrive.

"Hey, are we going shopping?" Denny tugged on the flap of her trench coat. "Or are you going to stare at each other all day?"

They both glanced down at the boy's upturned face, but Jeb was the first to answer. "We'll go shopping as soon as I put this food away."

Liza followed him toward the kitchen. "Maybe...maybe I should get started on that potato salad."

"No hurry," Jeb said over his shoulder. "It's only a little after ten, and we won't eat until about one this afternoon. I think Denny's right. We should go shopping."

Liza took a deep breath. "Yes. Shopping."

"Jeb!" Denny called from the living room. "What're these things on the wall?"

"Oh, just some awards," Jeb called back as he opened the refrigerator and transferred the contents of Liza's sack into it.

"Will you read them to me?"

"Sure, later."

Liza stuck her hands in the pockets of her trench coat to keep from reaching for him. "Awards, huh? Are you some kind of hero?"

"Absolutely." He shut the refrigerator door and turned to her. "I was hoping you or Denny would notice those certificates so I wouldn't have to point them out. I'm trying to impress you."

"Oh?" She tried to sound carefree, in control enough to tease him. "Why would you do that?"

His steady gaze made her weak. He lowered his voice. "I haven't thought about anything but you, but us, for two solid days. How does next week look?"

"Bill wants the new act to open on Thursday. That means I've got to practice extra hours."

"Damn. Couldn't you—"

"I don't know, Jeb. We'll see."

"God, you're beautiful."

His comment left her speechless and trembling. No man had wooed her for a long time, and she felt vulnerable to every significant glance, every murmured word of praise.

"Mommy, aren't you done in there yet? I'm tired of standing here in my coat."

Jeb touched her arm. "I suppose we'd better go."

"Yes." She was incapable of moving away from the sweet connection of his hand on her sleeve.

He tightened his grip. "Liza, I—"

"Are you guys ready *yet*?" Denny's exasperated voice was much closer this time. He'd gotten bored with the living room and had come in search of them. "I've never seen people *stare* at each other so much."

Jeb smiled apologetically at Liza and released her. "I'll get my coat, sport."

Denny's shoulders sagged in an exaggerated sigh. "Well, *finally*."

At the pet store Denny headed straight for the rows of small cages housing the puppies for sale while Jeb and Liza talked to the owner about different brands of puppy food.

Within seconds Denny was back beside them, hopping up and down. "Jeb, Jeb! They have spotted puppies here! We could get them today!"

Jeb glanced at Liza in dismay. "I forgot about that. Of course they have dalmatians, but with pedigrees as long as your arm."

"Expensive?"

"Very." He hunkered down in front of Denny. "I'm afraid those puppies are out of my price range, sport."

"Price range?" Denny frowned.

"Yes. You see, those are purebred dogs, and even one puppy costs a lot of money. We're planning to get two. I can't afford those puppies."

"But you said we'd get spotted dogs. Aren't we going to?" Denny's eyes filled with tears.

"Yes, we are, but I'm looking for some that don't have a pedigree. They'll look like these puppies, but they won't have papers."

Denny sniffed. "You mean they just hafta go on the floor?"

Jeb stifled a smile. This was no laughing matter, especially to Denny. "I'm not talking about newspapers,

Denny," he said gently. "The puppies in this store have a record of who their parents and grandparents, and great-grandparents were. All those dogs have to be dalmatians, so the puppies can be called purebreds." Jeb felt like a louse. He hadn't thought carefully enough about this trip to the pet shop, and now Denny was miserable because what he wanted was just out of reach.

"That's right, Denny." Liza crouched down beside Jeb, and he sent her a look of gratitude for helping out. "The people who sell these dogs give you a piece of paper with all those dogs' names on it. That's what we mean by 'papers.'"

"You mean like an award, like Jeb has on his wall?"

Liza nodded. "Something like that."

"Wow. These puppies must be special, huh?"

"Our puppies will be just as special," Jeb said. "Just because their great-grandfather was a doberman doesn't mean they won't be terrific dogs."

"They'll still have spots?"

"Yes, or we won't get them."

"Jeb," Denny began and took a long quivering breath. "How soon can we get our puppies?"

"I'm going to spend next week looking as hard as I can, Denny."

"That's good," Denny said fervently, "because I sure do want to get them fast."

"I'll try. Right now, how about those collars and food dishes they'll need? What color should we get?"

"Spotty's going to have red everything," Denny announced as he raced toward the pegboard display of collars.

"Spotty?" Jeb lifted an eyebrow in Liza's direction as they both stood.

"Denny wants to name his dog Spotty," she said. "So

you see, purebred or not, I'm afraid the dog has to have spots."

"He will," Jeb vowed, "even if I have to paint them on myself. Liza, I'm sorry about this."

"Never mind. He has to learn about disappointments. It's part of growing up."

"I have to work tomorrow, but first thing Monday I'll scour the *Tribune* and any of the local papers I've missed. Somebody has to have dalmatians with a slightly screwed up family tree. I wish I could just buy two from this shop, but..."

"Don't even think it. You're doing plenty as it is, and besides, I'll pay for Denny's dog."

"No, I can't let you do that. You're scrimping to buy the house to put the dog in. That's enough. Let me buy the dog and the paraphernalia."

Liza chuckled as Denny ran toward them, his arms full of plastic food and water dishes, a collar, a leash and numerous doggy toys. "I'm going to give you a chance to back out of that generous offer."

"No, no, it's okay. This stuff I can handle, as long as we don't go looking at show-quality puppies."

Denny beamed at them over the mound of red items he carried. "Spotty's all set, Jeb. What color will you get for your dog?"

"I think Freckles should have blue."

"Then come on. I'll show you where I got most of this stuff."

Liza glanced at Jeb in amusement as they followed Denny to the back of the store. "Freckles? Couldn't you come up with something a little more original?"

"Not in five minutes, and I figured we needed to name both dogs. Makes them more real, you know."

"Ah. Perhaps you're right. Spotty and Freckles. I see what you mean. A name does make a difference."

His tone was deliberate. "You bet it does, lover."

She started at his choice of words and glanced into his eyes to see if he was teasing her. He wasn't.

"Makes it more real, doesn't it?" he said softly.

CHAPTER SEVEN

THEY RETURNED TO JEB'S PLACE with their loot. Jeb was relieved that Denny seemed to have forgotten about the expensive pet store puppies that he couldn't have and instead was concentrating on the dogs Jeb would surely find for him next week.

"Where shall we put these bowls?" Denny asked as soon as they got inside the door, and he'd shed his coat and tossed it onto a chair.

"On the counter for now, I guess," Jeb replied, putting his jacket on the same chair.

"No, I mean when the puppies are here. Where will the bowls go then?"

"I hadn't thought about it."

"Well, I think we should put them right where they're supposed to go."

Jeb paused to look at Denny. Finally by reaching back into his own childhood, Jeb figured out what Denny wanted. "Would you like to pretend the puppies are here and make believe that you're feeding them?" he asked.

"Yeah!"

"But not with real food. That's too expensive to waste."

"No. Pretend food."

"Okay, then I think the bowls should go—let's see—right here." He pointed to a spot in the middle of the floor and glanced at Liza. She looked so right standing in the kitchen doorway with an approving smile on her face as she watched him play with her son.

Denny laughed. "In the middle of the kitchen? You crazy guy. They have to go beside the back door, like this." Denny positioned the bowls carefully. "Now I'm going to call the dogs."

"First you have to unlock the back door. They're out there chasing each other in the backyard. They always do that until their tongues hang out a mile."

Denny giggled. "They sure do. Silly puppies." Denny twisted the lock and turned the knob. Then he opened the door a foot and yelled outside. "Spotty! Freckles! You puppies get in here right now if you know what's good for you!"

Jeb walked over to Liza. He couldn't kiss her, so he had to be content with teasing her a little about Denny. "I wonder where he picked up that tone of command." He was glad when she laughed instead of getting angry.

"I can't imagine," she said, still smiling. "You wouldn't catch me talking that way."

"Of course not. Here, let me take your coat. Wouldn't want you to get too warm in here."

She acknowledged his comment with a raised eyebrow. "Very funny."

He tried not to touch her very much, tried to be brisk in his movements, but still he felt as if he'd been electrocuted as he helped her off with the coat, and his hand came in contact with the warm silkiness of her blouse. It took effort to pull himself from the lure of her perfume long enough to hang the coat in the hall closet.

"Stand back," Denny called from the doorway. "Here they come!"

Jeb almost expected two barking whirlwinds of black and white to hurtle through the door as he came to stand behind Liza once more. He watched Denny pretend to fix the imaginary puppies' meal and give them water.

Liza's voice was low so that Denny couldn't hear. "I had no idea," she said softly. "I knew that he wanted a dog, but I didn't know how much."

Jeb wanted to hold her, to cradle her against his chest while they stood there watching. But he knew that wouldn't be any good. Not yet. "I didn't realize, either. Listen, I'm going to put all my efforts into this dog search next week."

"I appreciate that."

"What I mean is, I'll be looking for dogs, and you'll be practicing for your show. I'm wondering how we can—"

"Maybe we can't," she interrupted, her tone gentle. "Our lives are busy, Jeb. You said it yourself the other day."

"Yeah, and it seems to me I also said we'd work it out. But damned if I know how at the moment."

"Let's not push it, okay?"

"Liza, if you only knew how much I..." He left the sentence unfinished, allowing her imagination to fill in the rest.

"Maybe I do," she murmured.

Jeb felt as if someone had poured warm maple syrup over him. "That's nice to hear. I sure wish we could do more than talk about it, though." Her warm fragrant skin so close to his was making him forget everything else, including the little boy petting his imaginary dogs.

"Jeb, even talking is liable to get us into trouble. Change the subject, will you?"

"At the moment I can't think of any other subjects."

"Then find something to do. How about the grill for the cookout? Don't you have to set that up?"

"The way I feel right now I could stand beside it and create spontaneous combustion."

"Jeb, I mean it."

"Are you saying that I bother you?"

"Yes, you do."

"I'm so glad." He couldn't restrain himself any longer. He had to have one little taste. Placing a brief kiss against the curve of her neck, he stepped away before either of them could react. "I'll set up the grill."

He heard her quick intake of breath and treasured the sound of it as he crouched next to Denny and scratched behind a pair of invisible floppy ears. "How're you doing, Freckles?"

Denny snorted. "Can't you tell them apart? That's Spotty. Freckles is over here."

"Well, they do look a lot alike."

"Not to me," Denny asserted. "Look, Jeb. They ate every bit of their food. They're good puppies, huh?"

"They're great puppies. What do you say we take them out in the yard with us while we set up the grill for our cookout?"

"Sure. They'd like that."

"Would you like to learn how to light the coals, Denny?"

"You bet!"

Jeb felt the tension increase in the room and braced himself for Liza's protest. He should have warned her that he'd planned to do this.

She stepped toward them, poised to defend her offspring from danger. "I'm sure Jeb can take care of that, Denny. Besides, I could use some help with the potato salad."

"Aw, Mommy, I want to go outside with Jeb."

Jeb stood up and faced her. Silently he acknowledged

the light of challenge in her brown eyes. "Let him go, Liza. He'll be fine."

"Jeb, I don't think that—"

He kept his expression perfectly calm. "Trust me on this one."

"But—"

"It's okay, believe me."

At last she shrugged. "You're the fireman."

"Thanks. Will you get our coats from the chair, sport?"

"Sure, Jeb."

While Denny was out of the room Jeb grabbed the time for a brief explanation. "Liza, this is a proven technique. Gets rid of the forbidden fruit aspect." He could tell she wasn't buying it.

"Jeb, I don't allow any lighters or matches in our apartment anymore. And now you're—"

Denny stepped between them. "Here's your coat, Jeb."

"Thanks." He cast one more glance of reassurance at Liza as he put on his jacket, but she looked away, so he took Denny and left. He'd talk with her about it later, when Denny wasn't around. The trouble was, when Denny wasn't around Jeb's mind was on something other than talking.

Inside the kitchen Liza opened the refrigerator door and got out the bowl of cooked eggs and potatoes. She didn't like this, not one bit. Jeb had asked her to trust him while he gave her son more proficiency with matches. Where Denny was concerned, she couldn't trust easily.

She emptied the eggs and potatoes into the sink and positioned herself so that she could watch them through the kitchen window while she worked. Denny's red jacket stood out like the flash of a cardinal against the autumn shades of brown in Jeb's backyard.

Her movements were automatic and mechanical as she

sliced eggs and potatoes into the bowl. All her conscious attention radiated outside, focusing on Denny holding the box of kitchen matches, and Jeb teaching him how to strike them.

Not that she expected Denny to get hurt. Jeb wouldn't let anything happen to him. But he was exposing Denny once again to the lure of fire. Would he go home and decide to have his own cookout, minus the safety of a grill and charcoal?

What she'd told Jeb was true. There wasn't a single match in her apartment, even after all this time had gone by since the night of the fire. Would Denny pocket a few today when Jeb wasn't looking? Then she chided herself for thinking such thoughts about her son. Denny was bright enough to realize how dangerous his experiment had been. But seeing him with a flaming match in his hand made her very uneasy.

Finally the coals were lit, and Jeb stood talking with his arm around Denny as the flame slowly settled into the charcoal and disappeared completely. Then Jeb squeezed Denny's shoulder and led him back toward the house.

"Come on, Spotty! Here, Freckles!" Denny called as Jeb opened the back door.

"Why don't you play with them in the living room while I help your mother get lunch ready?" Jeb suggested.

"Okay," Denny said easily and patted his leg. "Let's go in here, puppies. I'll teach you to roll over."

When he'd left the room Liza turned to Jeb. "I'm really worried about exposing Denny to matches and fire again," she said, keeping her voice low.

Jeb pitched his voice at the same level. "I know. I should have told you about this earlier. The psychologists think giving a kid like Denny experience with friendly fire—charcoal grills, fireplaces, camp fires—reduces their urge to experiment. Kids used to have more of that before we got so modern with fake logs and gas grills.''

"Oh." She stirred more mayonnaise in with the eggs and potatoes. She stirred until her wrist grew tired, but she didn't dare glance up. He was so close, and Denny seemed completely absorbed with his "puppies" in the other room. The silence lengthened.

"Come here," he said at last, taking the spoon from her hand and pulling her away from the counter.

"Jeb, no," she whispered, but her resistance was minimal. She craved his touch.

"Yes, please." He gathered her into his arms. "I told Denny the puppies needed lots of playtime."

"But they've just eaten!"

Jeb grinned and tipped her chin up. "You're as bad as he is. The puppies don't exist, Liza, but I'm glad Denny thinks they do. It gives us a little privacy."

"You plotted this," she accused.

"Necessity is the mother of invention."

"And children are the necessity for convention."

Jeb laughed softly. "He'll be okay for a few minutes."

"But..." Even as the last word of protest emerged from her lips, she was molding herself to him, glorying in the muscled strength of his body.

"Be quiet." Slowly he lowered his head and tasted her lips. "You've been into the potato salad," he murmured.

"I don't know any other way to get it right."

"Let me see if it's right." He outlined her lips with the tip of his tongue. "Umm. I think it's perfect."

"Is it?"

"Yes," he said with a sigh as he matched the contours of his mouth with hers.

Her response was instinctive. She tilted her head and parted her lips in a surrendering gesture that wrenched a groan from his throat. His tongue followed the pathway that she opened for him, and her body ached for the completion that the intimate kiss suggested. She wanted him without reservation, and her abandon was frightening and wonderful at the same time. Reluctantly she broke free of his kiss. "Jeb, we shouldn't," she murmured.

"Shh." His big hands, roughened from his work, were surprisingly gentle as he cupped her face. "Just once more."

Liza couldn't deny him. She closed her eyes and clung to him while his mouth moved hungrily against hers.

"Oh, Liza," he moaned softly, lifting his head and gazing into her eyes. "I love holding you."

"But we have to stop, Jeb. I must look thoroughly kissed and...Denny's never seen me kissing anyone before."

Jeb looked at her in amazement. "Never? Not even with his father?"

"Denny never knew his father."

"You were divorced before he was born?"

"We, um, were never married," she admitted.

"Oh." Jeb looked at her steadily as the information sank in.

"Do you disapprove?"

"That depends on why you didn't get married, I guess."

"Simple." She forced herself to tell the truth. "He didn't want to."

His grip on her tightened. "What a stupid jerk. Although I should be glad he was. Otherwise you wouldn't be free right now."

Liza shook her head. "I wouldn't still be married to him. I realized later that he did me a favor because I didn't really love him, not in any way that could last."

He looked pleased with that information. "It must have been rough, deciding to keep Denny and be on your own."

"The decision was easy. Convincing my parents was the rough part. They expected great things of me, maybe even concerts at Carnegie Hall, after all the music lessons and the baby grand. They sure made me feel guilty. But my little sister, Helen, stepped right into my shoes."

"She's a musician, too?"

"She's *the* musician of the family. Got a scholarship to Juilliard, which made my parents very happy. Believe me, I didn't make them happy by becoming a piano tuner."

He shrugged. "I figure you have to ignore that kind of thing and live your life. My folks don't approve of my job, either, my mom, especially. She's always on my case."

"Because of the danger?"

"Yeah, and the crazy schedule. They blame that for the fact that I haven't found a wife and settled down, which they want very much for me. You know, carry on the family name and all that. They say a woman would be out of her mind to marry somebody who has my job."

Liza leaned back against the curve of his arm and considered what he'd said. "I suppose being a fire fighter's woman is no bed of roses."

"No," he said quietly. "It's not."

"I've started hearing the sirens more now, Jeb."

His blue gaze was steady. "I won't kid you. Some women can't take it. I wasn't going to bring this problem up unless you did, but here it is. Would you rather not risk the relationship? You could get out now with minimal damage to everyone."

She would have thought he was in perfect control if

she hadn't noticed his convulsive swallow. Her answer meant a lot more to him than he wanted her to know. "Jeb, I haven't felt this way about a man in a long time…maybe ever. I'd be a fool to turn away from you because your job is more dangerous than that of other men I could meet. For all I know, that's partly what attracts me to you."

He grinned with relief. "The erotic perfume of danger, huh?"

"You must admit the women flocked to see Indiana Jones in action."

"Speaking of that, have I shown you all my awards? I am one exciting guy. I put Jones in the shade."

"Go check the grill," she said, giving him a playful push.

He brightened. "Hey, that's it. You can come outside and check the grill with me."

"No, I think not." She stood on tiptoe and kissed him quickly. "Have a little patience, Jeb."

He groaned and headed for the back door. "Lady," he said over his shoulder, "patience is not my long suit."

BY THE TIME LIZA ARRIVED at Rags and Riches that night, her mind was far more involved with a certain sandy-haired fireman than with Dulcie's problems at the club. During the break she sat down at the bar, and Dulcie placed the mineral water in front of her without saying anything.

As Liza sipped her drink and contemplated Jeb and their day together, she didn't register Dulcie's silent behavior for several minutes. When Liza finally realized that Dulcie hadn't engaged her in their usual break-time chatter, her boss had moved to the other end of the bar and was serving a customer. Liza had to wait for her to finish.

Dulcie measured the liquor into an ice-filled glass and added a spray of soda. Then she handed the drink to the customer, a regular, without smiling or making jokes the way she usually did. The man asked her something Liza couldn't hear and Dulcie shrugged and looked away. The man, obviously thwarted in his attempt to make conversation, picked up his glass and moved from the bar to a table in the corner.

Liza shook her head. If Dulcie started treating all the customers like that, she'd soon have no one walking through the doors of Rags and Riches. People came here for good cheer and a sense of welcome. They also came to hear the merry sound of banjo strings and piano keys, but without the warmth of Dulcie's usually vibrant personality, Liza doubted the music would hold the customers.

When Dulcie made no move to return to Liza's end of the bar she decided to call her over. Maybe some discussion of the new act would boost the older woman's spirits. "Hey, Dulcie," she said. "I'm sure getting lonesome drinking by myself down here."

Dulcie glanced up in surprise, as if she'd forgotten Liza was sitting at the bar. "I'm not very good company tonight."

"Bad company's better than no company, I always say."

Dulcie approached her with obvious reluctance. Her step was slow and her face looked old. Even the gardenia in her hair seemed to droop tonight.

"My goodness, Dulcie, am I breaking out with some contagious disease? You don't look at all glad to see me."

"It's not you, honey." The plump face crumpled. "It's...it's..." She turned away and fumbled for a tissue in her skirt pocket.

"Dulcie?" Liza wasn't quite sure what to do. Dulcie was about to cry, something Liza had never seen happen in the four years they'd known each other. Well, maybe once when her son had gotten married, but those had been tears of joy.

"Give me a minute," Dulcie mumbled, sniffing. "And don't look so sympathetic. I'm fine as long as nobody looks at me like that."

"Okay." Liza purposely stretched her lips in a wide smile. "You can look now," she muttered without changing her expression. Dulcie glanced sideways and saw Liza's clownlike grin. She started to laugh, but the laughter soon changed to sobs.

Liza jumped from her stool and pushed open the swinging door at the end of the bar. She took the crying woman in her arms and held her as best she could, considering that she couldn't quite reach around Dulcie's plump body. The gesture felt peculiar. Many times Dulcie had comforted her like this, but Liza had never expected the day to arrive when Dulcie would need comforting.

Glad as she was to help Dulcie, Liza felt a sickening loss of security as the normal order of things turned upside down. She glanced over at Bill, who was laughing and enjoying a beer with some of his buddies. He hadn't noticed Dulcie's breakdown, and neither had anyone else, apparently. Gently Liza guided Dulcie into the small, brightly lit kitchen behind the bar. The room was empty as usual. Rags and Riches didn't serve hot food, and the kitchen was used primarily for storage.

"It's going to be all right, Dulcie," she crooned, finding a battered chair and settling Dulcie into it. "The new act will bring in more customers." Dulcie's tissue was shredded, and Liza handed her a clean paper towel.

Dulcie blew her nose into it with a noise like an angry goose. "I know."

"Bill's friends are handing out flyers. We'll begin the act on Thursday. And Bill and I can certainly wait for our paychecks this month."

Dulcie's cheeks quivered as she took a deep breath. "I know that, too."

"You're not going to lose this place, Dulcie."

Dulcie's gray eyes filled with tears again. "God, I hope not, but I'm so scared."

Liza got down on her knees and held the woman's plump hands. "Don't be scared. We won't let them run us out."

"Leonard called today," Dulcie said in a small voice.

Liza nodded, remembering that Leonard was Dulcie's son. "Was he upset about the rent?"

"Not really. I guess that's what got me so scared. He said it was time for me to retire, anyway, and come live with them. He acted as if I'd lose the place for sure, and I might as well make plans for when I did."

"Oh, dear." Liza struggled for something to say. Dulcie idolized her son, and his calm acceptance of this catastrophe meant he didn't understand his mother at all. Well, Liza thought, so what was new? When did the generations understand each other? "I'm sure he was trying to be of help, Dulcie," she said. "After all, how many newly married sons would ask their mothers to live with them? He loves you very much."

"But he's ready to put me out to pasture, and I'm not even sixty years old yet! What does he expect me to do, sit around all day and hook rugs?"

"I'm sure he doesn't. Maybe he knows of some good jobs in his area."

"Jobs, my foot. He distinctly said the word 'retire.'"

There's not a dirtier word in the English language. Not for me, anyway.''

''Well, don't worry about it, because it isn't going to happen.''

''The new act—it's really ready to go?''

''By Thursday it will be.'' Liza pushed away thoughts of Jeb, of spending a few hours with him alone.

''Thank goodness.'' Dulcie sighed. ''Bill said so, but I worried that with Denny, and your tuning jobs, and this fireman—''

The waitress poked her head through the doorway. ''Dulcie? I need two gin fizzes. Want me to make them?''

''No, no. I'll do it. Be right there.''

''Okay.'' The waitress left.

''We'd better get back to work.'' Dulcie stood up.

''That's right.'' Liza got to her feet and brushed off her skirt. ''Can't keep thirsty customers waiting.''

''Liza...thanks, honey.''

''Are you kidding? After all the times I've cried on your shoulder? It's about time I returned the favor.''

''We will beat this thing, won't we?''

''You bet we will,'' Liza said, as she dismissed all hope of having time alone with Jeb in the next few days. She wondered how it was possible that she could already miss what she hadn't yet had.

CHAPTER EIGHT

ON SUNDAY LIZA PRACTICED most of the day with Bill, and Sharon came with him to act as a combination baby-sitter, cook and audience. She'd performed this function before, and the three adults worked well together, but Liza couldn't help resenting the fact that Bill had his romantic partner here with him and she did not.

Instead, Jeb was fighting fires that day. Much as she tried to ignore the sound of sirens, Liza heard every one that came within earshot. At five o'clock she insisted that they all take a break and listen to the evening news on television. For Denny's sake she made up a story about being interested in the weather, but Sharon and Bill knew that Liza needed to hear that no Melwood Park fire fight-ers had been injured on the job so far that day.

After Sharon and Bill left at eight and Denny was in bed, Liza watched the late news, too. The newscasts couldn't calm her fears about the sirens that screamed at midnight, however, or the ones that sounded in the pre-dawn darkness. His shift was over at eight in the morning, about the time she walked Denny to the bus stop.

When she returned to the empty apartment, she fought the urge to call him and make certain he had survived his shift. If she called and revealed how she'd worried through her entire twenty-four-hour duty, he would know that she wasn't worthy of a relationship with a fire fighter. He would tell her to find a nice, quiet teacher to care for, or maybe a stockbroker. She would be just like his parents, asking him to live more safely so that they would be spared this agonizing worry.

So she didn't call, but she thought about him all day as she tuned pianos and grabbed moments at home for extra practice on the new act. By evening she was hoping that he might call her, but he didn't. Denny's questions about the dogs went unanswered, and Liza crawled into bed soon after she tucked Denny in. Between practice and lack of sleep, she was exhausted, and she missed Jeb with a fierceness that amazed her.

By Thursday morning her emotions had changed from loneliness to anger. She could wring Jeb's neck. Was a simple phone call too much to ask? Sure, they'd agreed that they'd both be busy, but this was ridiculous. Yet she was determined not to call him and behave like some clinging vine. After all, wasn't he the one who'd seemed so desperate to get together?

She had no tuning appointments Thursday morning, and she'd slated the time to put the finishing touches on her portion of the new act while Denny was at school. Bill had told her last night at practice that he thought she was ready, but Liza had planned a few hours more to put the cap on her performance—to make it perfect. Maybe Jeb would surprise her and show up at Rags and Riches for the big opening night.

When the telephone rang she finished an especially difficult chord progression before answering it. Jeb's voice on the other end came as such a shock that she couldn't speak for several seconds.

He seemed as surprised as she was. "Liza, is that you? I thought I'd get your answering machine."

"No, it's…it's me. How are you?" *What a dumb, banal question,* she thought.

"I found a litter of puppies."

Puppies. Safe subject. "Jeb, that's fantastic! Denny will be so excited."

"Yeah, I thought so, too. How about if we pick them up on Sunday? I'm on duty Saturday, so that's out, but Sunday would be fine."

"Sure. Sunday's fine," she repeated, wondering how she would survive until Sunday without him. Saturday would be another long day and night of sirens that could mean Jeb's life was in danger. "Won't you be tired, though, after twenty-four hours on the job?" She'd be tired, even if he wasn't. Waiting and worrying was the hardest work of all, she'd discovered.

"I can sleep later. This is important."

She held the receiver with both hands, as if that would keep him on the line. "I really appreciate your efforts to find the puppies. It must have taken a lot of time."

"A fair amount. We'll have about a thirty-mile drive on Sunday. I'll pay for gas if we can take your car."

"Don't be silly. I'll pay the gas money."

"Well, we can settle that on Sunday, I guess."

She was afraid he was going to hang up, and she needed to hear his voice a little longer. "Is there any chance you'll drop by to catch the new show tonight?"

"I was considering it, but I wouldn't want to make you nervous."

Liza smiled at his comment, which sounded as if she were giving her first piano recital. He wasn't used to being around professional performers. "I'd love to have you there," she said.

"I wouldn't give you the jitters?"

"Nope. I'll probably have butterflies before we start playing. That's pretty normal. But once we begin I'll be fine."

"Okay, that settles it. I'll be there."

"Good." She relaxed a bit. At least she'd see him to-night, although there wouldn't be much time for conversation.

"I guess you're practicing now, since you're home."

"Yes, I am."

"I suppose you should get back to it."

"Yes, I suppose, but—I'm glad you called. I've been wondering…"

"Me, too. How you are, what you're doing. But this is an important week for you, and I was afraid to call and interrupt you. Besides, I figured hearing your voice would make me want to see you even worse."

Her heart began to pound. "And does it?"

"Liza, don't tease."

The urgency in his voice made her tremble. "I didn't mean to. I just…"

He didn't respond for a moment. When he spoke, his tone was soft. "Just what?"

Wanting him cut into her, sharp and demanding. But she couldn't ask. She closed her eyes and tried not to think of the warmth of his arms, the sweet pressure of his lips. "Never mind. I'm sure you're busy, too."

There was another pause before his reply came, low and gentle. "I'll be there in five minutes."

She opened her mouth to protest, but he'd already hung up. *Five minutes.* It took her three tries to get the phone back on the hook. What had she done? Jeb wouldn't drive to her apartment and break every speed limit on the way to have a cup of coffee and listen to her practice.

And what about her practice? Liza wondered if later she'd feel guilty about throwing away practice time. Right now she had no room for guilt with all the other emotions roiling around inside her.

Five minutes. She scurried through the living room grabbing Denny's toys, dropping as many as she picked up. As she threw an armful on his bed she remembered that she had on no makeup. Besides that, she should brush her teeth again and put on cologne.

As she raced into the bathroom and squeezed toothpaste onto her brush, she thought of how carefully she'd dressed for Saturday's cookout in one of her best blouses and a new pair of slacks. And what was she wearing now? Her jeans with the hole in one knee and an oversize man's flannel shirt. Great.

When her teeth were brushed, and she'd dabbed cologne behind her ears and on her wrists, Liza bounded into her bedroom and threw open her closet door. She was reaching for a blouse to replace the plaid shirt when the doorbell rang.

With a wail of frustration she closed the closet door. Her hair was still in a ponytail, and her lips hadn't so much as a hint of lipstick. Some sexy temptress she was. Maybe Jeb would have coffee and watch her practice, after all.

She opened the door and looked into blue eyes that smiled at her with unrestrained joy. A wave of pure happiness washed over her, and she knew that none of it mattered—the toys, her unadorned face, the oversize shirt. Nothing mattered but the expression on Jeb's face when she'd opened the door.

Wordlessly she stepped back as he walked into the room. Then she turned around and leaned against the door, closing it with both hands still on the knob. For a while they stood staring at each other, almost in disbelief that this moment had come.

Delicious privacy surrounded them in the sweet butterscotch light of morning. When Jeb took off his coat and tossed it onto the couch, sunlight flashed across his sandy hair, turning it momentarily gold. Liza couldn't take her gaze away.

He didn't spare a glance for the toys still on the couch or the open magazine on the coffee table. Without a word he drew her into his arms. "Thank you," he said, just before he kissed her.

His lips carried the flavor of peppermint drops, but soon all Liza could taste was the heady tang of desire. He buried his fingers in her hair and carefully removed the elastic fastener. Then his touch moved to her shoulders and down her back until he reached the loose hem of her shirt.

Without pausing he slipped both hands underneath and slid them up the unobstructed length of her bare back. His moan of delight when he discovered that her breasts were unfettered beneath the oversize shirt told her that perhaps her outfit was right, after all. She clung to him as he filled both hands with her softness and stroked her nipples to stiff attention.

Then he was lifting her in his arms, supporting her back and cradling her beneath her knees. He found her bedroom without her direction, and she reveled in his take-charge attitude. There was no halfway measure about Jeb. Once the decision had been made, he carried her off without asking if she was sure, or ready, or any other time-wasting questions.

But she had one question, and as he set her on her feet and began unbuttoning her flannel shirt, she closed her hands around both of his and asked it. "Jeb, before we take this any further, you should know, that I...I'm not exactly, uh, prepared. Are...are you?" In the silence that followed she felt the awkwardness of the question, but years ago not asking it had cost her dearly. No matter how much she ached for Jeb, and she did ache, they would not continue without birth control.

He took her by the shoulders and gazed at her tenderly. "Yes. It's okay. We'll be fine, Liza."

She relaxed and wrapped her arms around him. "I think maybe we will," she murmured.

"I love the way you look right now." He cupped her chin and tilted it up as his gaze roamed over her flushed skin. "I love it because this is how you'd wake up in the morning, with no makeup and your hair all mussed and your skin warm from sleep." His thumbs rubbed lazily against her cheeks. "I like knowing how you'd look to the man who slept beside you."

She sighed as he nibbled at the corners of her parted lips. "Jeb, you can't ever spend the night. I don't want Denny to—"

"I know." He began unfastening the rest of her buttons. "I'm just dreaming, that's all." He slipped the shirt from her shoulders. "And that's what dreams are made of," he whispered, gazing at the rounded swell of her breasts. "You're so beautiful, Liza."

She struggled for breath as he ran his calloused hands over her collarbone and down the slope of her breasts. He reached for the fastening on her jeans, and she quivered with an excitement that hadn't been part of her life for years, maybe never.

He glanced up with quick concern. "Are you cold?"

She shook her head.

"You're shaking." He pushed the jeans past her hips.

"Yes. I...I want you."

His blue eyes blazed with passion. Without a word he stepped to the bed and threw back the covers. Then he swept her up in his arms and settled her in the soft sheets. In an instant her jeans and socks were gone and he was undressing, too, tossing his clothes aside as he watched her lying there waiting for him.

His body was magnificent, as she'd imagined it would be, but he had an ugly purple scar on his chest and another along the muscle of his thigh.

He noticed her looking at the scars. "The price of being a fire fighter," he said simply.

Her throat closed at the thought of what he risked every day of his life. That beautiful body, that generous smile, the tender, caring man before her could be wiped out in the course of a day's work. "Jeb, I'm so afraid for you," she whispered.

Concern shadowed his face, and then he smiled at her. "Why? Are you dangerous in bed?"

"You know what I mean. How can you joke about it?"

Clad only in his briefs, he lowered himself beside her. "There's no other way," he said, stroking her hair back from her face. "If I think about dying, I won't be able to do my job. I won't be able to go into a fire."

Good, she wanted to say. *Think about it. Then maybe you'll keep yourself from harm.* But she didn't say it. Instead she pulled him into the shelter of her arms. She moaned at the welcome weight of his chest, the friction of his skin. He was so alive, more than any man she'd known. She wouldn't think about the danger, either, just the living, just the loving.

And the loving took her breath away. Jeb was completely present, completely *there* as he stroked and kissed her writhing body. He murmured her name over and over, leaving no doubt that he was loving her and not some ideal, some fantasy creature of his imagination.

Any fears that she'd had about making love to a man after five years of abstinence crumbled with the force of Jeb's ardor. When at last the moment came when she begged him to complete their union, she nearly went crazy with wanting while he made himself safe for her.

At last he was back, his blue gaze intent on her face. "Liza, my Liza," he murmured, stroking her intimately as he eased between her open thighs. As he pushed gently into her, he bit his lower lip and closed his eyes. "Oh, God," he whispered. "This is so good."

"Yes." Tears streamed from the corners of her eyes at the exquisite pleasure of having him inside her, filling the void of longing. She gripped his back and arched upward as he began to move.

His eyes were open once again, watching her reaction as he increased the pace. Tiny drops of moisture beaded his forehead, and his shoulders glistened, the muscles bulging as he held most of his weight away from her.

She returned his gaze for as long as she could, but he was pressing, urging, rocking against her until the intensity of it made her cry out. She looked away, embarrassed to reveal this primitive part of herself to him.

"No. Look at me," he insisted. "Be here with me. We'll do this together, Liza. Together."

Feeling more naked than ever before in her life, she turned her head and stared into the fiery depths of his eyes. His movements continued to wring sobbing cries from her throat, and she dug her fingernails into the bunched muscles of his shoulders.

"That's it, Liza. That's it." He moved faster. "No, look at me. Look at me!"

With one final thrust he achieved his goal and sent her into violent convulsions that were soon mated with his.

Eyes wide, still shuddering from her own climax, she watched with awe as his face twisted with the ecstasy of release. His eyes lost their focus for a moment, but as his trembling grew less he gazed down at her once more, and a current of electricity seemed to arc between them.

"There," he said softly.

She couldn't speak. There were no words adequate to tell him that he'd loved her as she'd never been loved before. If she never lay in his arms again, she would be miserable beyond belief, but at least she would have known what was possible with a man who gave all that he had and demanded no less from her.

"I didn't mean to make you cry." He kissed the tears from the corners of her eyes.

"Yes, you did," she murmured.

"You're right. I did. I meant to make you cry and moan and feel—really feel. Some people live their whole lives and never let go like you just did."

"And you."

"Yeah." He kissed her full on the mouth before easing to his side. "Don't go away. I'll be right back."

While he was in her bathroom Liza snuggled under the covers, and when he returned she enjoyed every moment of his walk back to the side of the bed. "Can you cuddle for a while?" she asked, folding back the covers on his side.

"I can cuddle all day. You're the one with a schedule. Is that all we have time for? Cuddling?"

"Afraid so."

"Then I'll take it." He slid beneath the sheets and drew her close. "Cuddling is nice, too," he said, stroking her hair as she rested her head against his chest.

"Uh-huh."

"Maybe I'll be able to control myself for a little while. But you really inspire me, Liza. When I first saw you, I began remembering what it could be like to pour all that passion into one tiny segment of time. I'd almost forgotten that there was drama like this that I didn't have to risk my neck to find.''

Liza didn't think Jeb was speaking in the abstract. Someone in his past had touched him deeply. ''Who was she, Jeb?''

He hesitated before answering. ''Just a girl.''

''I don't believe you. You wouldn't have fallen in love with 'just a girl.' She must have been special.''

''Well, she was,'' he admitted with a sigh. ''I really cared for her.''

''What happened?''

''The day I took the exam to become a fire fighter she accepted some other guy's proposal. I didn't think she was serious about walking out if I joined the department, but she was.''

''That must have hurt.''

''It hurt like hell. Funny thing was if I'd known she was so serious, I wouldn't have taken the exam.''

''You wouldn't? But I thought you loved the job.''

''I do, but I've been riding on ladder trucks for eight years, and it's in my blood now. At twenty-one I was still malleable, and with my parents arguing against it and the woman I loved ready to leave, I might have changed my mind, despite my dreams of glory. But it was too late by the time I understood how she really felt. Besides, my pride was hurt because she snapped up the other guy's offer so soon. They're divorced now.''

Sudden fear shot through Liza. ''Do you ever see her?''

''She came by the station once after the divorce, to let me know she was free.''

''And?'' Liza was clammy with uncharacteristic jealousy.

''And?'' He arched one eyebrow. ''Do you think I'd be here in this bed if there was an 'and' to the story?''

"I don't know. After all, I don't know you all that well."

"Yes, you do. Your intuition does, if you'd listen to it. I'm not going to hurt you, Liza Galloway. What you see is what you get, a guy who is strongly attracted to you and has no women hanging in the wings in case you don't work out."

Liza still wasn't satisfied. "Why didn't you rekindle the flame with her, Jeb?"

"Nosy little thing, aren't you?"

"Damn right."

"You have every right to be, after what we've just shared. So I'll tell you. The price was too high. She expected me to give up my job, still, after all these years."

"That's outrageous."

"She didn't think so. She'd found me a better job, in her mind, working with her father in his Chicago brokerage firm. All I had to do was take a few accounting courses, which the firm would subsidize."

Liza looked up at him and ran her finger along his bottom lip. "I think I understand that woman. She wanted to keep you safe."

"Do you?"

"Yes, of course. But I'm beginning to understand why I can't."

"Keep working on it."

She gazed into his eyes. "I will."

THAT NIGHT LIZA WONDERED if she'd been so wise to invite Jeb to the show. She sat at a back table twisting a cocktail napkin to shreds as she watched the crowd come in. Bill and Sharon sat to her right, and they both seemed completely relaxed.

Ever since Jeb had left her apartment at noon, Liza had

been able to concentrate on little else but the wonder of their lovemaking. Plumbing the depths of her sexual response had been a traumatic and exciting experience this morning, and she didn't feel like the same woman who had practiced a musical act with Bill the night before.

"Easy, Liza Gayle," Bill said, laying a hand over her nervous twisting of the napkin. "The show will be fine. You'll be terrific."

"And the crowd will be good," Sharon added. "The flyers must have brought in some people."

"I guess." Liza swallowed hard. "I wish I hadn't asked Jeb to be here tonight." She hadn't told Bill and Sharon about her morning, only that she'd invited Jeb to watch their opening show.

"You know, Liza," Bill pointed out, "the man could have shown up here whether you had invited him or not. It's a public place. We *want* people to come. That's the whole idea."

"Yes, but he would have stayed home if I'd asked him to."

"You're a professional," Bill said. "You don't need to play those games. Five seconds into the set, and you'll forget all about him."

Liza doubted that she'd forget all about Jeb, but she also knew that Bill was partly right. Once she started performing she'd be okay. The waiting always got to her.

"There's a good crowd," Bill said, repeating Sharon's assessment, "but not nearly the numbers I'd hoped for."

"It's Thursday, Bill," Liza said, taking her turn at soothing. "By tomorrow night we'll be able to judge if we've really— Oh, my God."

"What?" Bill looked at her with concern. "Liza, you're as white as a sheet."

"My parents just walked in the door."

"No kidding. Those ogres you never speak to?"

Liza nodded. "I can't imagine what they're doing here."

"Which ones are they?"

"The balding man in the gray topcoat and the woman in the fake fur."

"That's strange. I don't see any horns protruding from their foreheads, and their teeth don't look sharpened."

"Very funny. Oh, no, they're looking for me. They're coming over. Dammit!"

Sharon leaned across the table. "Maybe they want to make up," she whispered.

"And don't forget that they're paying customers," Bill said in an undertone.

Liza stood up as her parents approached. She hadn't seen them since Denny's birthday last summer, when they'd dropped a package by and left soon after. The familiar longing tugged at her until she reminded herself that if her parents had succeeded in their campaign, Denny would be another woman's child right now.

"Why, Mom and Dad, what a surprise," she said, forcing a smile.

"Isn't it?" her mother agreed. "You look wonderful, Liza."

"Thought we'd better see what you were up to," her father added with a wink, as if Liza were a continual source of amusement.

Liza gave her mother and father an obligatory hug, although she hated the hypocrisy of it. They'd fallen into those habits years ago, and even the bitter arguments in the past few years hadn't disturbed their traditional greetings.

Outsiders wouldn't guess the antagonism they felt toward each other, Liza decided. In this case, that was just as well. She motioned to Bill and Sharon, who by now were also standing. "Mom and Dad, I'd like you to meet my partner, Bill Buckhalter, otherwise known as Billy Bach, and his good friend Sharon Denby."

Sharon nodded and Bill shook hands with them. "Pleased to meet you, Mr. and Mrs. Galloway," he said with a broad smile.

Liza was relieved that he didn't add the usual "I've heard so much about you." He had heard a lot, and most of it was negative. "So," Liza said, "what brings you to Rags and Riches?"

"I saw one of your little flyers," her mother replied. "I decided to go downtown for the fall sale at Marshall Fields, and I saw the Xeroxed picture of you two taped to a lamppost."

Bill stuck his fist in the air. "All right! We got at least two from that paper barrage."

Liza realized her jaw was clenched, and she made a conscious effort to relax. "Little flyers" indeed. How typical of her mother to diminish her eldest daughter's efforts.

Her father's gaze roamed the interior of Rags and Riches and settled on Dulcie holding forth behind the bar. "Cozy place," he said, watching Dulcie interact with the customers in her jovial manner. "That woman bartender seems to be having fun."

"She owns the place," Liza said, remembering how little "fun" Dulcie had enjoyed last Saturday night as she sobbed in the kitchen.

"Really?" Her father glanced at Dulcie with more respect. "Well, good for her."

"I've been meaning to call you," Liza's mother said, "but I just never did. We thought showing up tonight would be a nice surprise. Who knows? Maybe we'll make a habit of it."

Liza hoped not. "That would be nice," she forced herself to say.

"How's Denny these days?" her father asked. "Probably grown another inch since we saw him last."

"I... Yes, I think he has grown." Liza couldn't imagine what they were up to. She and Denny were just an obligation to them, weren't they? Why this fuss all of a sudden?

Liza's mother touched her husband's arm. "Maybe we'd better be sitting down, Curtis, if we want to be sure of a good seat."

"Yes, that's a good idea," he agreed. "Well, nice meeting you, Bill and Sharon, and good luck to our performers here. What do you say in a situation like this? Break a leg?"

Bill stuck out his hand again. "That's it. Thanks, both of you. We're glad you came."

"Will you be staying until after the show?" Sharon asked politely.

Liza's mother laughed and looked away. "I don't know if we'll make it that late. We both have to work in the morning."

"Yeah, we old folks have to get our rest."

Liza felt the old stab of disappointment that came when her parents dangled their support and then withdrew part of it. But it was better if they didn't stay, she argued with herself. Then she'd be able to talk with Jeb after the show without having to deal with her parents, too. No doubt they wouldn't approve of her relationship with Jeb, either. "Then I'll talk to you both later, I guess," she said.

"Yes," her mother said. "We'll keep in touch. Good luck, now."

"Thank you." Liza sank to her seat as they walked away. All the words sounded so normal, as if her mother would phone her tomorrow and they'd chat about the show. She and her mother hadn't chatted about anything since Denny had been born.

Bill put his hand on her arm. "You okay?"

"I think so."

"I hate to say this, but they didn't seem so awful."

"They're not, Bill, unless you're the daughter who failed them." She realized with dismay that she was about to cry, which would ruin her makeup ten minutes before show time. She had to be alone for a few minutes and get control of herself.

"They came here tonight," Bill pointed out. "That's saying something."

"I think it's only saying that they're curious," Liza said, pushing her chair back. "Otherwise wouldn't they stay until the music is over and congratulate their little girl?"

"Maybe they're uncomfortable in this setting."

"Maybe they are, and dammit, they've made me uncomfortable, too. Did they ever consider that?" Liza swallowed the lump forming in her throat. "I'll be in the bathroom until show time. I need to powder my nose." She pushed through the maze of tables and ran right into Jeb.

"Hey, the stage is the other way, Miss Gayle, ma'am."

"Oh, Jeb," she faltered. "I didn't see you."

He looked closely at her face. "What's the matter? Is something wrong?"

"My...my parents are here tonight."

"And you're about to cry?"

"It's a long story. I've told you that my parents and I have some...differences."

"Why are they here?"

"I have no idea."

"Liza, I hate for you to be so upset. Is there anything I can do?"

She shook her head. "I need to be alone for a few minutes before the show, to pull myself together. I was heading for the bathroom."

"When I stopped you. Listen, I understand. Go ahead. This is a big night for you. But before you go, I'm damned curious. Which ones are your parents?"

"By the far wall, four tables from the front. He's going bald, though he combs a few hairs over the spot, and she's wearing a fake fur. You can look after I'm gone."

"Thanks. And I know you'll be terrific tonight." He smiled, and she responded with a halfhearted effort before turning away from him.

In the bathroom she gripped the edge of the sink and fought back tears of frustration. This show was so important—to Dulcie, to Bill, and to her if she wanted to buy that little house someday. But between Jeb and her parents tonight she felt like a live power wire full of uncontrolled and dangerous energy as it danced and sparked upon the street.

She should never have allowed Jeb to come over this morning, she thought. Maybe the extra practice hadn't been necessary, but she would have been better off cleaning the apartment or doing her nails. The time spent with Jeb, wonderful though it had been, had increased her stress level, and already it had been pushing maximum overcharge. A woman with any sense would end the relationship now, before her world exploded.

CHAPTER NINE

LIZA FELT CALMER BY THE TIME Sharon opened the bathroom door.

"Bill asked me to come and get you. It's time," she said, looking concerned. "Are you going to be all right?"

"Yeah, I think so."

"Listen, if you ever need to talk, without Bill around, let me know."

"Thanks. I'll remember that."

"Sometimes he's so wrapped up in his music that he doesn't try to understand what you might be going through, but I can see you're under some strain."

"I really appreciate that, Sharon." Liza wished she had time to talk with Sharon right now about Jeb, about Denny, about her parents. She was beginning to realize how isolated she'd been, how lacking in a confidante.

"It's none of my business, but you don't seem to have many close friends."

Liza glanced away. "Friendships take time."

"Yeah, but they're worth it. Especially when the going gets tough."

Liza smiled grimly. "You mean when the going gets tough, the tough have friends?"

"Something like that." Sharon hesitated. "Sometimes I can get free for lunch."

"I'd like that."

"When?"

"Um, I'll let you know, Sharon. And thanks." She squeezed Sharon's arm and checked in the mirror to make sure her mascara hadn't smudged. "We'd better go."

She and Bill took their positions before the spotlights were turned on. Bill thought it looked classier that way and Dulcie always worked the lights for them. They could begin playing a split second before the lights came up, and the effect took the place of a curtain lifting.

Because the stage was dark, Liza could easily see the audience seated around her. Once the lights were on her vision was more limited. She spotted Jeb immediately. He was sitting with the couple whose piano she'd tuned last week. She wondered how much he'd told them about Saturday, about this morning. She felt her cheeks flush and willed herself to stop that train of thought immediately.

Then she glanced over at her parents. Her father sipped his usual Scotch and soda, and her mother fingered the stem of her wineglass. They looked vaguely uncomfortable, but expectant, too.

Liza thought of how the audience of Rags and Riches usually responded to the show, with catcalls and stomping feet. If they liked this show, and she prayed they would, their reaction would be the same. Her parents once had hopes that she would receive the polite applause of a symphony audience. They couldn't possibly be happy with this rowdy display. Liza's stomach began to knot as she became convinced that they would disapprove.

"Let's do it," Bill whispered. "On the fourth beat. One, two, three, go!"

Ordinarily they opened with an old favorite sing-along such as "Baby Face," or "Take me Out to the Ballgame," but tonight they began with one of Bill's most challenging new instrumentals, an arrangement that called for all of Liza's skill and concentration. The rhythm was fast and complicated, and Liza's fingers raced from one end of the keyboard to the other. She didn't have time to think about Jeb or her parents; she just played.

When they were finished the audience went wild, and Liza grinned up at Bill on his perch. He glanced down at her, and the look of triumph on his face made her glow with pride. His talent was being rewarded at last, and she was helping him achieve that reward. She prayed that she wouldn't let him down.

"Thank you, kind people," Bill said into the mike. "Now we'll slow it down a bit, but not a whole lot. We want you revved up and rarin' to go."

The regular audience that had followed Liza Gayle and Billy Bach since they had opened four years ago hooted their approval, and the rest of crowd was carried along with them. Liza wondered how her parents were taking it. Her hand faltered a little on the introduction to the next tune, but she steadied as they began the rollicking melody punctuated with slightly bawdy lyrics.

"Okay," Bill whispered to her as enthusiastic applause greeted the end of the second number. "They're warmed up. Now we'll put them away with the love song."

At Bill's nod, Dulcie turned off half of the spotlights, leaving only the blue ones trained on the stage. Liza had always considered the song itself easy to play and sing. The hard part was evoking the right mood, the exact balance of tenderness and passion. Bill sang the melody, and Liza harmonized on the gentle love song.

Three bars into the song, Liza knew that she was in no shape to do the number. Its message of caring and enduring love struck too close to home tonight. She struggled with the words as images of Jeb, of Denny, of her parents, swirled through her head. Halfway through the song she was crying. Somehow she continued to play, but Bill had to finish the song without any vocal harmony.

At the end of the number she bowed her head as tears fell on the black and white keys and dribbled between the crevices. The cheering and clapping of the audience seemed to be coming from far away, and she wondered why they were so pleased with a number that was so messed up.

Dimly she heard Bill speaking into the microphone again. "Thank you so much. We'll take a quick break and be right back. We've got some of your favorite sing-alongs sill coming up, as well as more of this newfangled stuff."

Liza knew they weren't scheduled for a break yet, but she was grateful when the blue spots winked off and she was in semidarkness again. She felt Bill's arm around her shoulders, and she let him guide her from the stage and around the end of the bar. Soon they were standing in the kitchen, and Bill sat her down in the same worn chair where she had comforted Dulcie a few nights before.

"Hey, babe," he said, taking a cocktail napkin and wiping ineffectually at her cheeks. "Don't crack up on me, okay?"

"I'm sorry, Billy." Liza looked at his blurred face. "I've never really listened to that song before."

"Hey, I didn't know you were so close to the edge. Want a drink of something?"

"No. I…I think I'll be fine if we can sit here for a minute. Besides, that's the only song like that. I was okay with the fast ones."

"Yeah, but sweetie, you've got to go out there and sing it again tomorrow night, and the night after that."

"I will. It's just today. Everything seems to be happening at once."

"How's our girl?" Dulcie bustled into the kitchen and squatted down next to Liza. "What gives? Is this becoming our crying chair?"

Liza's smile trembled. "Looks that way, doesn't it?"

"Your makeup's smeared, honey."

"I'll fix it. I'll be fine, really."

"I know you will." Dulcie squeezed her hand. "That big fireman wanted to come back here, but I told him to wait a minute. Want to see him?"

Liza glanced up in dismay. "No, absolutely not! I have a show to do, and he's a good part of the reason I'm having trouble doing it."

"Yeah," Bill added, "and then her long-lost parents showed up tonight to put the icing on the cake."

"Well, if that ain't enough to give hives to a horsefly. No wonder you were breaking down out there."

Liza blew her nose on the cocktail napkin. "Do you think everyone could tell, Dulcie?"

"Not really. The fireman was watching you like a hawk, so it's not surprising that he knew you were upset, and I suppose your parents know you well enough to tell, but the song came off fine."

"Yeah." Bill laughed. "That's the irony of it. Except at the last when you dropped out, you did a better job on that number than you ever have, Liza. You get those tears under control and keep the emotion going, and we could have a hit on our hands."

Liza cleared her throat and stood up. "I'll promise to eliminate the tears, Bill, but I don't know if I can afford to keep the emotion in. It costs me."

"Emotion costs us all, honey," Dulcie said, patting her shoulder. "But without it we might as well be dead."

"If you say so, Dulcie. Right now I could do with a

little less in my life. Bill, if you'll ask Sharon to bring me
my purse I'll do what I can with this face.''

"You bet.''

The waitress stepped into the kitchen as Bill stepped
out. "Need you at the bar, Dulcie,'' she called and left
again. Dulcie patted Liza's shoulder one more time and
returned to her duties.

For a brief moment Liza was alone with her thoughts,
and they weren't pleasant ones. Jeb was turning into a
liability, yet she'd agreed to getting the puppies on Sunday. Unless she wanted to disappoint Denny completely,
she was locked into some sort of arrangement with Jeb.
At the moment he assumed they would continue the pattern they'd begun this morning, but Liza couldn't let herself be that vulnerable. She couldn't be breaking down on
stage. People didn't come to see that.

Jeb had opened up a whole area of her emotions that
she'd kept in check for years, and the results could play
havoc with her professional life. She'd have to call a halt
to what had begun so beautifully this morning. She
couldn't afford to be someone's lover right now. As she'd
said to Bill, it cost too much.

She got through the remainder of the performance without incident. During the final number, which was one of
the old favorite sing-alongs, the waitress brought Liza a
note. As applause echoed around her following the final
chorus, she read the short message in her mother's handwriting.

"Great job, Liza. We enjoyed it. Love, Mom and
Dad.''

She glanced quickly at the table where they'd been sitting, but they were gone. Was the note sincere? She'd
probably never know, she decided. Her gaze moved
around the room and settled on Jeb and the Talbots. All

three of them were clapping wildly, and the two men added occasional earsplitting whistles to the noise. She braced herself for the inevitable conversation with Jeb.

Bill was flying high. "I think they liked us okay," he said, his face bright as a searchlight as he took Liza's hand for another bow.

"I always said you were a genius, Billy-boy." Liza squeezed his hand.

"How about if you and Jeb join Sharon and me for a celebration?" he suggested as the applause died down and the crowd began to drift out of the club.

"I'd love to, but I can't leave the baby-sitter stranded. Besides, I'm ending this business with Jeb."

"Don't do anything rash. It was just one song."

"I know what I'm doing, Bill."

"Okay. It's your life." He picked up his banjo case and carefully stored his instrument inside it.

"That's the point I keep trying to make, but not everyone sees it that way."

"You know I do, Liza."

"Yes, and that's why we're still partners."

"Here he comes now, complete with bodyguards. I wouldn't mess with the one with the mustache if I were you. Wait until you get Jeb alone to lower the boom."

"Right." Liza smiled her thanks for his support. "See you tomorrow night. You were great."

"You, too." Bill hopped from the stage and waved to Jeb before heading back to Sharon's table.

Liza stepped down from the stage to meet Jeb as he walked forward, trailed closely by Steve and Mo.

"Wonderful show, Liza," he said, his blue gaze searching hers. "The crowd loved it, and so did I."

"We didn't realize we had such a celebrity tuning our piano," Mo added. "By the way, I hope we're forgiven for our little deception. We do plan to call you to tune the piano again in six months. That part was for real.''

Liza smiled automatically at Mo. ''No problem. Jeb and I needed to iron out a few things, so you provided us with an opportunity to talk. And I'll be glad to tune your piano again. It's a lovely old instrument.''

''Well, Jeb.'' Steve fingered his handlebar mustache. ''I know you still don't have everything 'ironed out' with this young lady, so the missus and I will take a hike. We'll be waiting in the car, making out, probably. Just rap on the window to get our attention.''

Jeb threw an arm over his buddy. ''Just don't embarrass yourself, Steve. Remember you're in a public parking garage, okay? Some things can wait until you get home.''

''I'll do my best, brother.''

''That's what I'm afraid of.''

Liza watched Steve and Mo leave, arms linked. She envied them their tidy little life, their uncomplicated love for each other. They were nice people, and under different circumstances they could become her friends. But their loyalties lay with Jeb, and they wouldn't like her much for rejecting him.

''What happened up there, Liza?'' Jeb touched her arm.

''I think we'd better talk about that.'' She glanced up at him. ''It seems that when I allow myself to lose control in one area of my life, I begin to lose it everywhere.''

''You were crying because of what happened this morning?''

''Not entirely, to be fair. My parents showing up unexpectedly also threw me for a loop. But I could have handled that if I hadn't already been on an emotional binge. The combination was too much, especially with Bill's song.''

"Which is beautiful, Liza. I nearly cried myself when you sang it."

She looked away, not wanting to see the tenderness in his eyes. "I *can't* cry. I'm supposed to be the professional around here, bringing out the feelings in other people. I'm sorry, Jeb, but you're a luxury, and you're far too expensive. We've got to…end what started today."

He met her statement with silence, and finally she turned, expecting to find an expression of pain or at least anger on his face. Instead he gave her a soft smile. "I had a feeling you'd say that. But it's no good."

"What?"

"Pushing me away is not the answer."

"I think it is, and that's all that counts."

"But you're wrong."

She clenched her fists. "That's one of the problems. You always think you're right. You always know what's good for me."

"Not always, but this time I do. You can't go backward, Liza—just forward. You can't undo what happened today, and if you were anything like me, you thought about it constantly afterward." He lowered his voice. "I can't believe you don't want to make love again. It was too good."

"What I want and what is wise are two different things, and I'm a thinking human being, not a passion-crazed animal."

His smile grew wider. "I'm betting that you're both."

"I feel like punching you in the mouth."

"Yeah, I know. I have that effect on you sometimes, mostly because you're resisting what's going on between us. Don't fight so hard, Liza. It'll be so much easier if you stop the fighting."

"Easier? For you, you mean."

"No, for you." He brushed her cheek with his knuckles. "Any free time tomorrow?"

"I can't believe this. You're not taking me seriously!"

"Oh, but I am."

"Then listen carefully. We are through."

"Okay." He shrugged. "I guess you have to say these things. Is Sunday still on for the puppies?"

"You're impossible."

"Well, is it?"

She folded her arms. "Yes. I can't disappoint Denny at this point."

"I'm glad of that, at least. I'll be by around eleven. Your place is on the way, so we'll leave from there."

"Okay. And Jeb, I really mean every word I said. We're finished, you and I."

"I know you mean it." He dipped his head and brushed her lips with his. "For now." Then he turned and left the club.

LIZA HAD HOPED FOR EVEN larger crowds at Rags and Riches the next two nights, but the expected rush of business didn't come. Although Bill wouldn't listen to her on the subject, she wondered if her emotional reaction during the love song the first night had anything to do with it. The regular customers would forgive her, but they wouldn't drag their friends in to see some woman cry. Bill insisted she was paranoid and that business would pick up eventually.

On Friday Liza came home from her tuning appointments and found a message from her mother on the answering machine. Her mother wondered if they could get together someday soon for lunch. Liza shook her head. Suddenly everybody wanted to make lunch dates.

She played the message over three times while she tried

to decide what her mother wanted. Judging from past experience, Liza guessed that her mother would take the chance to criticize her daughter's nightclub career. Liza didn't return the call.

In the early hours of Sunday morning the sirens screeched several times, once only blocks away, and each time Liza pulled the covers tight around her and curled into a ball of fear. The man who had loved her so tenderly in that same bed was out there riding through the cold darkness on the back of a ladder truck. Soon he might chop his way into a blazing room to engage a monster with flaming breath. Liza tried not to think of him, tried not to care about the possible danger he was in, but each time the siren shrieked she was wide-awake and shivering.

Denny was up before the first light of dawn, as if this were Christmas morning. He scurried into her bedroom and jumped up beside her. "Ready to get up, Mommy?" he chirped, giving her a little shake.

"Denny, Jeb won't be here for hours yet."

"What time?"

"About eleven."

Denny peered at the digital clock radio beside Liza's bed. "Now it's six-oh-seven. How much longer?"

"Almost five hours, Denny."

"Five hours? Oh, Mommy!" He flopped on the bed in despair.

Liza hauled out one of her old tricks. "Maybe it will make the time go faster if we make chocolate chip pancakes."

"Maybe."

Liza had never heard such a lukewarm response from Denny to a suggestion of chocolate chip pancakes. This puppy apparently was the most important thing that had ever happened to him. She hoped Jeb would arrive on time. No sirens had sounded for quite a while, and he must be okay, or he would have called. Of course, if he were hurt really bad, he wouldn't be able to call, and if he'd been... *Stop it!* she cried to herself. *Jeb is fine.*

"Denny," she said, rolling over and ruffling his hair, "I have a riddle for you. How are dalmatian puppies and chocolate chip pancakes alike?"

His brown eyes began to sparkle. "Spots."

"Right. What else?"

"Um, I don't know." He squinted his eyes in concentration. "They're both real good," he ventured.

"That's two things. Any more?"

"Well, they're warm. That's it—they're both warm!"

"Excellent, but I can think of two more."

"I can't. I'm all thinked out."

"One is that they both start with the letter *p*."

"Hey, yeah, they do." Denny popped his lips as he chanted, "Puppies and pancakes, puppies and pancakes, puppies and pancakes, puppies, and—"

"And the last one is," Liza said, holding her hand over his mouth, "that we don't have either one yet. But we can at least have the pancakes while we wait for the puppies. Okay?"

"Okay!" Denny bounded out of bed and ran to the kitchen while Liza fumbled for her bathrobe and slippers. Making and eating the pancakes might take them to seven, even seven-thirty if she dragged out the process, but what then? Maybe Jeb would be early.

As it turned out, Jeb was early, but Liza wasn't encouraged by the dismal expression on his face.

Denny, already dressed in his red jacket, leaped upon Jeb when he walked through the door. "Hey, Jeb, did you remember to bring the collars, huh? And the leashes? I think those puppies will need leashes. Come on, Jeb, let's go." He grabbed Jeb's hand and tugged in the direction of the door.

"Hold on there a minute, sport."

Liza felt sick to her stomach. Something had gone awry. The evidence that Denny wouldn't get his puppy today was written all over Jeb's face.

He crouched down and put his arms around Denny, who had suddenly become quite still. "I called the woman a little while ago to remind her that we were coming. She was all upset because she'd forgotten about us, and somebody took all the puppies an hour ago."

"All the puppies?" Denny's face went white.

"Yes. There were three left this morning, and a man came over to get one. He ended up taking all three."

"But they were our puppies," Denny protested, his chin quivering. "We'll make the man give two back."

"I'm afraid we can't do that, Denny. We hadn't reserved them, put down a deposit or anything. The lady completely forgot that we were coming over this morning, but even so she had no obligation to hold those puppies. It was unusual, someone taking three. She didn't expect it."

Liza ached as if she had the flu. Poor Denny. He'd talked of nothing else for almost five hours. After the pancakes, they drew pictures of dogs, and read stories about dogs. Finally Liza made up some songs about dogs on the piano. They had planned to sing them for Jeb later on.

Big tears began rolling down Denny's cheeks.

"I'm very sorry, sport," Jeb said, his voice husky. "We'll get some puppies, I promise. We'll get some newspapers today and start looking through the ads. Maybe we'll even—"

"I don't want to look at old newspapers!" Denny shouted, twisting away from Jeb. "I want my puppies!"

"You'll get them. It will take a little more time, that's all."

Denny's face was scrunched tight with misery. "You said we'd get the puppies today," he wailed, "and now we can't. You're stupid!"

Liza started toward him. "Denny, that's enough."

"And so are you!" he shouted, running for the door and flinging it open. "You're both stupid, stupid, stupid!" He dashed into the hall.

"Denny, come back here this minute!" Liza ran after the fleeing boy.

"Leave me alone!" Denny pounded down the stairs with Liza in pursuit. She caught him at the first landing and grabbed his arm. "Let me go," he pleaded, looking up at her with his eyes brimming. "Please, Mommy, leave me alone for once, okay?"

His words shocked her into releasing her grip on his arm. She'd been about to march him back to the apartment and force him to apologize to Jeb. But if she were in Denny's shoes, would she feel like apologizing? "All right," she said, "but stay near the apartment building. Don't go over to Eric's unless you come back and tell me."

Denny nodded as tears still trickled down his cheeks. Liza tried to think of something comforting to say, but she had no words to take away the bitter disappointment Denny felt. Maybe he was right to want to be alone for a little while. She stroked his hair once and walked back up the stairs.

In the apartment Jeb glanced past her as she came through the door. "Where's Denny?"

"He wants to be alone for a while. I let him go, but

I'll talk to him later about his bad manners. I apologize for the way he spoke to you."

"Don't worry about it. I feel responsible for all this, anyway."

She sighed and closed the door. "It's not really your fault."

"I'd probably feel better if you'd get mad at me."

"That wouldn't solve anything." She flopped down on the couch. "This is why I was so reluctant to get involved with puppies. So much can go wrong."

"I think this was a fluke. Next time—"

"Oh, Jeb, let's not risk this again, okay? Let's give it up as a lost cause."

He peered down at her. "Hey, are you crying?"

"No." She lowered her head.

"Yes, you are." He squatted down in front of her and took her hands in his. "I'll find other puppies for Denny. I promise."

"It's not just the puppies," she said, sniffing. "It's everything. I can't seem to cope anymore. I—" A sob shook her.

"Oh, Liza." He sat beside her and gathered her into his arms. "My poor Liza," he crooned, rocking her gently as she fought a battle to hold back the sobs and lost.

Once she let the tears flow freely she couldn't stop them, and her frustration and grief poured out in a cleansing rush. For the moment Jeb's arms created a sanctuary from pain, and she cried until the tears all drained away. Finally she lifted her cheek from his damp shirt, and he reached in his back pocket for a handkerchief.

"Thank you," she mumbled, wiping her eyes and blowing her nose.

"Better?"

"I guess. I...don't usually do that."

"Maybe you should try it more often."

"No, thanks." She sighed. "At least I got it out of my system before Denny came back."

"Listen—about Denny. When he comes back, why don't we—"

She looked him in the eye. "No, Jeb. I'll handle Denny when he comes home. I appreciate you putting up with my hysterics, but maybe you'd better let me take it from here. I'll...I'll be in touch."

Jeb took his handkerchief from her and gazed at her in silence. "If that's the way you want it."

"It is. Please understand."

"I'll try." He got up from the couch and walked to the door. "Good luck."

"Thanks." She watched him leave. If she were smart, that would be the last time she'd ever see Jeb Stratton.

By the time she'd washed her face and combed her hair, Denny still hadn't returned, and she decided he'd been gone long enough. She put on her coat and went to look for him.

She checked the small plot of grass in front of the apartment building and the alley in back. She wandered up and down the sidewalk, glancing between buildings and up into trees with low-hanging branches. No Denny.

After deciding that he must have gone to Eric's without permission, Liza returned to the apartment and called Eric's mother, but she hadn't seen Denny, and Eric was out with his father raking leaves. This time Liza covered the hallways and stairwells of the four-story apartment building before going back outside. Then, after another circuit around Denny's usual playing territory, she went back to the apartment to wait.

She would give him fifteen more minutes, and then she'd call the police. Unable to sit still, she paced the living room while the hands of the clock inched, minute by minute, toward the deadline she'd set. *Please come home,* she begged silently. *Please be all right.*

Three minutes before the scheduled call for help Denny opened the apartment door. Liza resisted the urge to snatch him up and shake him until his teeth rattled.

He walked past her toward his bedroom without saying a word.

"Where have you been, young man?"

"Outside." He didn't look at her.

"I went outside. I couldn't find you."

He didn't answer.

"Were you hiding from me?"

He looked at the floor and said nothing.

"You really scared me, Denny. I thought something terrible had happened to you. Don't hide like that again, okay?"

"Okay," he said to the floor.

"And Denny, you were rude to Jeb. And me. I won't have you talking that way to adults. Is that clear?"

"Yes." He kept his gaze averted. "Can I go to my room now?"

She sighed. "Yes."

He left and closed his bedroom door behind him.

Liza slumped to the couch feeling totally defeated. She wished that she had someone to talk with, but a runthrough of the people she knew yielded no prospects. She hadn't taken time to make any close friends in the building. Dulcie had her own problems, and although Bill and Sharon would be glad to listen, they'd packed a picnic and driven to one of the beaches on Lake Michigan.

Eric's mother was nice, but Liza hated the thought of revealing her problems to someone who seemed to have none. As for Jeb, she'd just told him that she could handle everything, and besides, he was part of the problem. Last of all, her parents certainly wouldn't want to hear about the latest mess she'd gotten into.

As she sat staring into space and wondering how to improve her increasingly crummy situation, the wail of a siren grew nearer. The sound came closer, and she heard people bustling out in the hall. Curious and a little relieved for the distraction, she opened her door and looked out. Mr. Peters was hurrying down the hall zipping his jacket as he went.

"What's going on, Mr. Peters?" Liza called to him.

He paused and glanced back at her. "Somebody said our trash dumpster is on fire."

CHAPTER TEN

LIZA GREW COLD AS SUSPICION of the person she loved most in the world gnawed through layers of denial. She glanced back at Denny's closed bedroom door and shuddered.

No. Her child, who loved chocolate chip pancakes and Mickey Mouse, who hugged her so fiercely and placed wet kisses on her cheeks, couldn't have done something so deliberately destructive. The papers in his room had been an experiment, an accident almost. Denny wasn't bad, just curious, hyperactive at times—and sensitive, so very sensitive.

But what if he had set that fire? She couldn't turn her back on the possibility, not if she loved him. And what if he'd left some evidence, what if someone had seen him do it? She'd swear that he'd been in the apartment if necessary. Nobody would treat her child as a criminal. She would take care of everything her own way.

A knock on the door halted her pacing. When she opened it to the stern presence of Mrs. Applebaum, she went on instant alert.

"Where is your son?" the gray-haired woman snapped.

Liza struggled to keep her tone mild. "What seems to be the problem, Mrs. Applebaum?"

"A fire engine is down in the alley putting out a fire in our trash dumpster, that's the problem."

"So?" Liza's heart pounded with fear. Had her landlady seen Denny do anything?

"I want to know where your little firebug son has been this afternoon. I want to know if he's been out in that alley."

She relaxed. The woman was fishing for clues. "Mrs. Applebaum, I will not have you making unfounded accusations against Denny. Unless you have evidence that he started that fire, I won't listen to any more of this."

"I'd say that fire he built in his bedroom is evidence enough. That kid's a menace. I told the firemen as much."

Liza glared at her. "How dare you slander Denny's name without proof!"

"Then prove he didn't start the fire!"

"That's not how it works in this country, Mrs. Applebaum," Liza said, proud of her composure. "People are innocent until proven guilty. Now leave my apartment before I press charges of harassment."

Mrs. Applebaum backed away, apparently intimidated by her manner. "Perhaps it won't be your apartment much longer, missy," she threatened as she edged down the hall.

"You throw us out of this building without just cause, and I'll sue you for discrimination." Liza slammed the door and twisted the lock. "And don't think I wouldn't," she muttered.

"Who was that, Mommy?"

Liza glanced around. "Our landlady."

"What's the matter?"

"There was a fire in the dumpster," she said, watching him carefully.

"Oh."

"Didn't you hear the sirens?" Her suspicion grew. Denny always noticed sirens, and these were right beside the building. Why hadn't he run out to see what happened?

"I guess so."

"Come with me, young man." She grabbed his hand and marched into his room. "Where are they?"

"What?" He tried to pull his hand away.

"The matches."

"I don't have any." His eyes were wide with apprehension.

"Don't lie to me, Denny."

"I'm not! I don't have any."

"Then I'll have to look myself. You stand right there and don't move." She took his bed apart and emptied his toy chest. She took everything out of his closet and combed through his dresser drawers before finally searching Denny himself. She found nothing.

Doubt became a welcome cool breeze through her fevered mind. After all, he was only five years old, and the dumpster was a huge rusty bin twice as tall as he was. Setting a fire in it logically could be the work of older kids. Still, she couldn't ignore his disinterest in the sirens.

"Did you make that dumpster catch on fire?"

His chin quivered. "No."

"Then why didn't you want to go out there when you heard sirens?"

"I just didn't. It might be Jeb."

The explanation made some sort of sense if she considered that he was angry with Jeb about the puppies. However, she couldn't be fool enough to believe him completely. She'd have to double her surveillance of his activities from now on.

"Listen," she said, crouching down as she took him by the shoulders and put her face close to his. "This fire business is nothing to kid around about. People get hurt and killed with fire. You do know that, don't you?''

Denny nodded. '''Cept when the firemen come.''

''No, that's not true. Sometimes even the firemen can't save people. Denny, you've got to promise me that you will never, ever mess around with fire. If I discover that you have you will be a very sorry boy.''

Denny put his arms around her neck and hugged her. ''I love you, Mommy.''

''I love you, too,'' she said as tears came to her eyes. She remembered a phrase from a song, ''you and me against the world.'' Ever since she had first learned that she was pregnant with Denny, that was the way their life had been. She'd had to fight to keep him, and now she fought to protect him from people like Mrs. Applebaum. She was all Denny had and she wouldn't let him down. But maybe, just to be on the safe side, she should look into some counseling for him.

JEB SAT IN THE CAB OF HIS red pickup reading the latest horror novel by Stephen King and eating a bologna sandwich. Every time a car drove up he glanced from the pages of the book to the street in front of Liza's apartment. It was a wild guess that she'd come home for lunch, but he'd catch up on his reading if he was wrong. Maybe he'd leave a note on her door if she hadn't arrived by one-thirty.

At 12:10 he was rewarded with the sight of her blue Mustang parallel parking in front of the apartment building. He tore off a piece of the tinfoil he'd wrapped his sandwich in and used it as a bookmark. He knew that she'd seen him. A red truck was hard to miss.

She stood by her car and waited as he crossed the street. Her hair was loose and blowing in the breeze, her trench coat unbuttoned. He sucked in his breath. He had to work this out. He just had to.

"You might have waited out here all day, you know," she said without smiling. "I don't always come home for lunch."

"I had a book to read."

"And a sandwich to eat." Her brown eyes twinkled for a moment. "You have mustard in the corner of your mouth."

He wiped hastily at the spot. "You don't look very surprised to see me."

"I'm not. I understand word spreads quickly in a fire-house."

"That's not why I'm here. Well, not exactly why." He drew near enough to catch her scent and notice the un-certain flutter of her eyelashes. She feared him, dammit, because of his job. He didn't want that.

"Denny doesn't know anything about the dumpster fire," she said.

Jeb nodded.

"You don't believe that, do you?"

"Let's face it—if you were five years old and pulled a prank that got out of control, would you confess, espe-cially if no one knew for certain you did it?"

"Jeb, that dumpster is huge. Denny's a little boy. Be-sides, he knows the danger of fire."

"No, he doesn't, not really. But I agree that nothing's proven right now, and I'm not here to pin the blame on Denny. I'm here to help."

Liza frowned. "I told you I would handle it."

"Please listen. The puppy situation has been botched from the first, and don't think I don't feel guilty about it. If Denny started that fire—"

"He didn't."

"All right, but the disappointment yesterday wasn't particularly good for him."

"No kidding."

"I've decided what to do about it."

"So have I." She tucked her hair behind her ear. "We'll forget the whole idea. I've seen a big stuffed dog in the toy store, and I'll buy him that instead."

"That's not going to replace a live animal, and you know it."

"Maybe not, but a stuffed dog is within my control. I don't have to depend upon you to make sure Denny gets it."

"Liza." He gripped her upper arm in an instinctive attempt to hold on to her. "Don't shut me out of your life, or Denny's. Not now. Please."

She tensed under his fingers and emotion sizzled for a moment in her eyes. "Give me one good reason why not. You haven't made my life a bed of roses, you know."

"I know. Let me try again. For Denny's sake, if for no other reason."

"I am thinking of Denny, and the look on his face yesterday when you told him the puppies were all gone."

"That won't happen again."

"You can't guarantee that, unless you're willing to take mongrels instead. I don't know why you had to set your mind, and his, on dalmatians."

"It was a whim at first. I've always wanted one, so I thought, why not? Later I realized that the association for Denny would be positive. If he had a firehouse dog, he couldn't very well set fires, could he?"

"He doesn't have a firehouse dog. If he has anything right now, it's a broken heart. I won't have him set up for that kind of disappointment again."

"He won't be. I'm buying the puppies from the pet shop."

Liza appeared surprised. "Those pedigreed dogs? I couldn't accept that from you, Jeb."

"You're not doing the accepting: Denny is. I can swing it. I've got a savings account."

"Which you aren't using to buy dogs, Jeb. I won't have you making that kind of sacrifice."

"It's no sacrifice. I finally realized that if I could have prevented what happened yesterday I would have gladly paid twice that much." In the silence that followed he looked into her eyes and wanted to shout with joy. Her expression had changed. She agreed with him.

"Let me buy one of the puppies."

"Absolutely not. This was my plan all the way, not yours."

"But—"

"No." He took hold of her other arm. "No, Liza." He fought the urge to kiss her right there, in front of anyone who cared to watch.

She stood looking up at him, and he could see the battle raging in her, as well.

"God, I miss holding you," he whispered.

"Jeb, I can't deal with a relationship now. Everything seems to be closing in on me, with the club, and Denny, and now the puppies. Even my parents had to show up last week, and my mother's after me for something, Lord knows what." Her lower lip trembled as she gazed into his eyes. "I'm on emotional overload."

He held her for a few precious moments longer and then released his grip. "That wasn't my intention."

"I know, but that's the way it has turned out. I'm not saying never, but can you give me some time?"

Time. He supposed that from her perspective it

stretched out in limitless amounts. She hadn't watched her best friend die. She hadn't faced the possibility of death each morning when she arrived at work. Although Jeb refused to dwell on the risks of his job, they brought an immediacy to everything he did.

He couldn't force her into an understanding of that, however, or he might scare her. He'd already lost one woman who had realized all too well that tomorrow might never come for them. Connie had been a coward, and he didn't think Liza was a coward, but now wasn't the moment to test it.

He smiled at her. "Sure. Take some time."

"Thank you."

"Are you free on Saturday to get the puppies?"

"Yes, that's fine."

"Ten in the morning? You and Denny can have lunch at my place again."

"I don't know...."

"Come on, Liza, it's only lunch."

"Everybody seems to be fixated on lunch these days."

He grinned. "I beg to differ with you."

"Jeb, don't start."

"Okay. Lunch?"

"Only if you'll let me provide everything for the meal."

"You don't have to... Well, okay. Yeah, that would be nice." He realized that fixing the lunch would provide her with a sense of participation that she needed. He took too much control of things, always had.

"I'll be at your place by ten on Saturday, then," Liza said, turning to leave.

"It's a good thing we're getting these puppies."

She glanced back with a ghost of a smile. "I guess it is."

"They'll give me something to cuddle while I wait," he said, grinning.

"Jeb, for heaven's sake."

"Can't help it. Firemen were born to flirt."

"I'm beginning to understand that. But don't overdo it just yet, okay?"

"Aye, aye, Captain." His jaunty grin faded as she turned and walked away. Well, he hadn't lost her, but he hadn't won her, either. Now she'd asked him for the most precious gift that he had to give, the one that involved more sacrifice than she'd ever know. She'd asked for time.

WITH THE PUPPIES BACK ON the agenda, Liza decided to temporarily postpone the idea of a counselor for Denny. She'd explained carefully to him that the dogs were being held at the pet store especially for Jeb and that no one else could have them. At first Denny had tried to protect himself by not believing her. Then gradually as she explained the power of a deposit, he understood that on Saturday he couldn't be disappointed barring a disaster in the pet store. Denny spent most of the week worrying about that possibility.

On Saturday morning he dragged Liza out of bed at dawn once more, but they carefully avoided their routine of last Sunday for fear they'd jinx the outcome of the day. They had cornflakes instead of chocolate chip pancakes and played with Denny's trucks instead of making up stories and songs about puppies.

Finally the moment arrived to pile into the car and drive to Jeb's house. Despite the chilly fall day, Liza's hands were damp on the steering wheel. She'd made a promise to herself that she wouldn't be drawn under Jeb's spell today—no touching, no kissing when Denny wasn't around.

Why had she allowed him to make love to her? She felt like someone dying of thirst who'd been granted one swallow of cool water. The memory of that sip was driving her crazy for a second, and a third. Yet she feared that in trying to satisfy her craving, she could easily drown.

When they rang Jeb's doorbell he answered with his coat on. "Let's go," he said, ushering them back out to the porch.

His nearness brought the now familiar churning sensation to Liza's stomach. She felt like a mountain climber on a ledge that had collapsed on either side of her. Returning to the days before she'd made love with Jeb was impossible, but going ahead was out of the question.

They drove to the pet store with Denny belted into the back seat and Jeb in the passenger seat by her side. Denny kept up a steady stream of anxious questions. Did Jeb have the collars and leashes? Were the puppies still there? Could he hold one on the way home? Could he choose which one was his?

Jeb answered in a gentle tone meant to soothe the excited boy, Liza was sure. Unfortunately that tone had the opposite effect on her. She remembered it far too well from a morning last week, when Jeb had been loving her.

"What's in the cooler, Denny?" Jeb asked when the little boy paused to catch his breath.

"Doggy biscuits!" Denny announced. "Wanna see?" He opened the chest beside him and pulled out two cellophane-wrapped objects shaped like bones.

Jeb laughed and turned to Liza. "Is that what we're having for lunch?"

"I just stuck them in there because it was easier."

"Hey, Mom, can I have one of the carrot sticks?"

"Sure," Liza said, thinking it might stop the endless rain of questions for a while.

"Doggy biscuits and carrot sticks," Jeb said. "What else?"

"Ham sandwiches and some potato chips. Oh, and there's a container of baked beans we can heat up."

"Umm. Sounds great. I hope it wasn't too much trouble?"

"Not really. Denny got me up at five, so making lunch gave me something to do."

"Five, huh? And what time did you go to bed?"

"The usual for Friday nights, about one-thirty."

"That's not good. Three and a half hours."

"It's probably more than you got." She didn't tell him that she hadn't slept a full three and a half hours. The sirens woke her up, as they did every night he was on duty.

"I'm used to it. Besides, last night was pretty quiet."

"What's your definition of quiet?"

"A kitchen fire, nobody hurt, and somebody locked in a back bedroom with a gun, threatening suicide. We got to him in time."

"Who got to him?"

"I did."

Liza shivered at the thought of Jeb facing a loaded gun. "Wouldn't that be a job for the police?"

"Yeah, and we called them after we got there, but we were afraid he might do something while we waited for them to arrive. So I went in."

She didn't like hearing about the danger, but not knowing was worse. "I just never thought of you in some situation like that, with guns."

"People call the fire department for lots of things that aren't really a fire."

Liza detected the note of pride when he said that. She glanced at his chiseled profile. "You really like the job, don't you?"

"I like helping people."

She was touched by the lack of pretense in his statement. His motives were straightforward. Even in dealing with her and Denny, he'd been clear about his purposes. One was guiding Denny away from the danger of fire, and the other was becoming her lover. He'd never pretended that his sole interest was in Denny while he quietly tried to maneuver her into bed. She appreciated his honesty.

"Well, here we are," she said, pulling into a parking space in front of the row of stores.

"Hurry, hurry," Denny begged as he waited for Jeb to get out of the seat and tip it forward. "Let me out."

"Don't run," Liza called as Denny scrambled through the opening and dashed to the sidewalk. "The puppies aren't going anywhere."

"But I have to *see* them!" Denny shouted back as he pushed open the glass door with both hands.

Jeb smiled at her. "This is the right thing to do."

"I guess so. Ready?"

He winked. "Always, gorgeous."

She rolled her eyes. "I forgot that I don't dare say a word to you."

"Relax, Liza. Have some fun for a change."

She glanced up at him. "Okay. I'll try."

The pet store was filled with the sound of barking, whining puppies as each dog in the two tiers of cages tried to get attention from the little boy on his knees in front of them. But he seemed oblivious to other wet noses, other bright eyes and wagging tails. He pressed his hand up against the wire where the two white puppies dabbed with black were trying their best to lick his stubby fingers.

Liza and Jeb walked over to the noisy cages and gazed down at Denny. He didn't even hear them come up behind him.

"Nice puppies, good puppies," he crooned. "Want to lick my fingers? I bet you don't like it in that little cage. I bet you want to come out."

"Can I sell you folks a puppy?"

Jeb and Liza turned as a young man who looked as if he might be working his way through college approached them.

Jeb put out his hand. "I'm Jeb Stratton."

"Oh, Mr. Stratton! The boss said you'd put a deposit on the dalmatians," the young man said. "I sure hope that little boy is with you. He wants one of those dogs in the worst way."

"He's with me," Jeb said.

"Great. Let me get one of them out for you." He crouched beside Denny. "Which one would you like to hold?"

Denny didn't hesitate. "That one," he said, pointing to the puppy with a black patch over one eye. "He's mine."

"She," the clerk corrected gently. "That one's a female."

"You mean it's a girl?" Denny looked confused.

"Yes. The other puppy is a male, a boy."

"Oh."

Jeb squatted down to join Denny and the clerk. "If you want the boy, that's fine with me. I like girls."

What an understatement, Liza thought.

"I like girls, too," Denny said. "But I thought my dog would be a boy."

"Your dog can be a boy. That other puppy is a fine-looking animal," Jeb said. "But we can decide that later, can't we, sport? Why don't we take them both home and think about it?''

Denny shook his head. "Nope, 'cause I'm gonna hold my dog all the way home. And I want the one with the spot over its eye, because that's Spotty. That's my dog, even if he is a girl.''

The clerk grinned. "Looks like we have a decision. Would you like to hold your dog now, Denny, just to make certain you two get along?''

"I *know* we'll get along, but I sure would like to hold him, I mean, her.''

The clerk unlatched the cage and picked up the female puppy. "Come on, Spotty, let me introduce you to your new owner. This is Denny, and he's going to hold you very carefully under your rear end, so you don't fall.'' The clerk put the wiggling puppy slowly into Denny's outstretched arms. "Hold her firmly, but not too tight. You don't want to squeeze the breath out of her.''

"No, I don't!'' Denny made little chuckling sounds of delight as the puppy squirmed against him and tried to lick his face. "He likes me,'' he said, and giggled. "I mean, she likes me.''

Tears gathered in Liza's eyes. She'd never seen Denny so happy. She glanced at Jeb and found that he was looking at her instead of at Denny and the puppy. Silently they gazed at each other, each enjoying the little miracle of joy they'd created.

"Sir, would you like to hold your dog?'' The clerk had the other puppy out of the cage.

"Why, um, sure.'' Jeb took the chunky little body with both hands and brought the puppy to his chest.

Liza watched his face soften as he stroked the black and white fur and murmured to the puppy, who was sniffing his shirt and trying to chew on a button. The sight of this brawny hulk of a man cradling a puppy warmed Liza's heart with a glow that she hadn't felt in years.

I'm falling in love with him, Liza thought in amazement. *The game is over.* She'd foolishly imagined that she could dictate the level of her involvement with this fireman, dig a trench of indifference around their blaze of passion and get on with her life. But every contact with him struck a new spark, and now the flames were burning out of control. How long would it be before he noticed?

CHAPTER ELEVEN

THE PUPPIES DOMINATED the rest of the day, and for that Liza was grateful. She wasn't quite sure what to do with her newly discovered feelings for Jeb, and the hubbub of the puppies covered up her own confusion. Physical attraction was one thing; love was quite another. Love tied you to someone, made them part of your life forever, even if the relationship ended. Love could hurt as nothing else could hurt. She'd learned that much.

Jeb drank a beer with lunch, and another during the afternoon as they sat in lawn chairs and provided an audience while Denny pretended to put on a circus show with his "trained" puppies. As the show continued, Jeb slumped lower in his chair with a sleepy smile on his face and his eyes half-closed.

Liza realized that his exhaustion plus the beer had dulled his perceptions. Normally he would have noticed that she gazed at him more than once with obvious longing. Had he questioned her about those searching looks, she might have blurted out the truth, but he wasn't even aware of her concentration on him.

Finally about three o'clock she decided that Jeb needed rest more than he needed to watch Denny play with the puppies. She shook the arm of his chair. "Hey, sleepyhead, you're fading fast. Why don't we go home?"

He sat up straighter. "No. Don't go. I'm fine."

"You look like you've been run over by a Mack truck."

"Thanks. You're lovely today, too."

"Jeb, you need sleep."

"No, I don't," he said, his blue eyes alert now. He lowered his voice. "But I wouldn't mind going to bed."

She ducked her head to hide the flush that rose to her cheeks. "Never too tired to make bawdy comments, are you?"

He gazed at her. "Never."

"Well, you may not be willing to admit it, you big macho fireman, but you're dead on your feet." She stood. "Denny and I are going home so you can sleep."

"But I hate sleeping alone."

"You won't have to. Those puppies would love to hop into your bed."

"That's just great," he said without enthusiasm. "I'm really excited."

"You wanted them."

"Does that mean I can have whatever I want?"

Liza studied the rumpled, sleepy, lovable man in the lawn chair. *Yes,* she thought, *you probably can.*

"Hey, Liza, you didn't say no."

"I'll get Denny," she said, averting her gaze. "He won't be happy to leave, but he'll have to learn that he can't live over here."

"He can if he'll bring his mommy."

"Jeb, you're…impossible."

"How about tomorrow?"

She thought it was a proposition and stammered her response. "I—I can't—"

He chuckled. "I mean how about bringing Denny over again tomorrow to see his puppy?"

"Oh." She was blushing again, and Jeb was watching

her closely, too closely. "Well, you see, I promised Bill we'd practice all day. The new show isn't attracting the customers as quickly as we'd like, and there are a few little variations he wants to try."

"So you're busy."

"I'm afraid so, yes."

"Okay. Then can I have Denny for the day?"

"Uh, I guess so. But Jeb, this is your time off. You must have other things—"

"Not tomorrow. I left the day open because I knew Denny wouldn't be at school and could play with the dogs. I was hoping you'd come along, but I guess the act is more important."

"That's not fair. You make it sound as if I don't care about this." She swept her arm toward Denny and the tumbling dogs. "But if Bill and I don't get that act to work for us, Rags and Riches will be history. That will hit Dulcie hardest, but Bill and I will suffer, too."

He ran his hand over his face and shook his head. "Yeah, I know."

"Do you really?"

"I think so. It's just that I—" He glanced up and looked directly into her eyes. "I love being with you."

The words came before she could stop them. "I love being with you, too."

He was on his feet instantly. "Liza—"

"Forget I said that." She turned away.

"Fat chance. Come clean, Liza. What's going on in that pretty head of yours? Is it yes or no for us?"

His warm breath was close to her ear as he stood behind her. She decided that she'd be all right if he didn't touch her. "You're rushing me, Jeb."

"Damn right I am." He took her by the shoulders and brought her around to face him. "Every minute of every day is like gold. Can't you see that? God, we're wasting time!''

She began to tremble. ''Are we?''

''You bet, and there's one sure way to prove it to you.''

''You wouldn't…''

''Not with Denny here. I'll have to talk some sense into you instead.'' His blue gaze was fierce. ''More than a week has gone by and I've barely touched you. You must have had a few hours at home alone, without Denny. We could have filled those hours with beautiful lovemaking, but now the week is over. Those chances are gone. Do you understand?''

''I need time,'' she insisted.

''Bull. You need me, Liza.'' He gripped her hard. ''You need me.''

''I'm scared.''

''I know you're scared. But there's something else in your eyes. You're tempted, too.''

''I…yes, I am,'' she admitted softly.

''Then make time for us. We can be good for each other. I know we can.''

With his lips so near, his gentle hands caressing her shoulders, she wanted to believe him. Would this love she'd found nurture her, or would it tear her apart? She searched his face for reassurance.

''I won't hurt you,'' he murmured. ''I've told you that.''

''Even if I said yes, I don't know when we might—''

A flame of victory leaped in his blue eyes. ''Get a baby-sitter for tomorrow night.''

''I can't. Denny has a baby-sitter three nights a week. I don't want to add a fourth.''

''All right. I'm on duty Monday, so how about Tuesday? Have you got a break in the day?''

"Yes...."

"Come over then."

"I don't know, Jeb."

"How much time is it? An hour? Two?"

"Two hours. Between two and four in the afternoon."

"I'll take it. Say yes, Liza. Please."

"You work until eight that morning. You won't have much chance to sleep if I come barging in here at two."

"Please barge in." He took a ragged breath. "Sleep is of small consequence."

"I worry about you, Jeb."

"And I worry about you. See how well that works out?"

"Maybe." Her smile trembled. "Maybe it does."

"Damn right. You'll be here on Tuesday?"

"I shouldn't, but I... Yes."

"Oh, Liza." His face was filled with relief. "At last."

LIZA DRAGGED DENNY AWAY from Jeb's house that afternoon with difficulty. The only reason he agreed to leave at all was because of Jeb's solemn promise that he'd bring Denny back early on Sunday for another day with the puppies.

Jeb kept his word the next morning, and Liza watched sadly from the window as they drove away in Jeb's red truck. For the first time she resented Dulcie's problems and Bill's ambition. All that time devoted to the new act hadn't produced results. Liza wondered if she'd be better off as a cocktail waitress in somebody else's nightclub. At least she wouldn't have to practice to do that.

Yet when Bill arrived full of enthusiasm for a new number they would polish that day, Liza squelched her negative thoughts. Sharon hadn't come with him because they hadn't needed someone to look after Denny, so the team of Liza Gayle and Billy Bach immersed themselves in their music. By the end of the day Liza felt better about their chances of success.

"We just have to reverse the trend—get Rags and Riches to catch on," Bill said as he packed up his banjo. "This new song and the changes in the others might do the trick. I'm trying to talk Dulcie into advertising in the *Tribune*, but she's afraid to spend more money."

"I know. Every time she hears from that son of hers she's on the gloom and doom trip. That's not helping business, either. The regular customers expect a jolly woman behind the bar. If she doesn't perk up soon she'll be a liability to us."

"One or two really good nights of cash register receipts, and she'll be smiling again."

"Me, too, Bill. We might get paid."

"That would be nice. Say, when's the fireman bringing Denny home?"

"I'm not sure. We didn't set a time, but he knows Denny has to be in bed by eight-thirty."

"The puppies are working out pretty well then?"

Liza made a face. "Finally. Took a heap of cash, though. Jeb's cash. I still don't feel right about that."

"I'd accept the situation. It's for Denny's benefit."

"True. Jeb's going to have his hands full, though. Denny will want to be over there every spare minute, and during the week I don't have time to take him. Jeb will have to handle the transporting."

"I doubt if he minds. He seems like a nice guy."

"You think so?"

"Yeah, I think so. How about you, Liza Gayle? What do you think of him?"

She ran her knuckle over the black keys on the piano. "He's okay, I guess."

"I saw that little smile. You're not fooling me. I'd say you two were getting along pretty well."

"For now," Liza said, holding up crossed fingers. "As long as he doesn't try to take over my life, we'll be fine. But I've been on my own too long to say 'yes sir' and 'no sir' to a man."

"I can't picture you ever doing that."

"Of course I did, Bill. I was the most obedient person you'd ever meet until the day my parents told me to give up my baby. Since then I've been making all my own decisions, and Jeb Stratton isn't going to change that."

"If he's smart he won't try. Well, I'd like to stay and say hello to Denny, and to Jeb, for that matter. But Sharon expects me to take her to dinner. Considering our finances I've given her a choice of McDonald's or Kentucky Fried Chicken."

"Yeah, that sounds like the choices I give Denny. Fortunately he's a kid and loves them both."

"Some day," Bill promised as he put on his coat, "you and I will treat our loved ones to dinner at the Pump Room."

"I'm looking forward to it. Now go on home to your ladylove and tell her hello for me. I've been thinking she and I ought to get together sometime."

"I think so, too. See you Tuesday night for practice, Liza."

"Right." As she closed the door behind Bill she wondered if she'd be able to keep her mind on music Tuesday night after spending the afternoon in Jeb's arms. The thought of their rendezvous gave her goose bumps.

Jeb and Denny arrived a little before eight, both looking tired but smiling like circus clowns. Liza hustled Denny out of his clothes and into the bathtub before returning to where Jeb waited in the living room.

"He's fed and everything," Jeb said proudly. "I wanted to prove to you that I could take care of him and not bring him home filled to the brim with orange drink."

Liza touched his arm. "I know you can." Jeb hadn't taken off his jacket. Unless she invited him to stay, he might leave now that Denny was home safe and sound. "Would you like a cup of coffee?"

"Yes."

She started for the kitchen and paused. "Cookies? They're store-bought."

"Yes." He tossed his jacket onto the couch.

"I have the feeling you'd say yes to anything."

"You've got that right, lady, if you're offering. You're wearing my favorite outfit again."

She glanced down at her practice clothes—an oversize man's shirt and jeans. "My glamour look."

He crossed the room and lowered his voice. "Have you got anything on under that shirt?"

"I'm not about to tell you."

"Then maybe I'll have to find out." He reached for her, but she moved away.

"Jeb! Not now," she whispered.

"Just let me hold you."

She shook her head. "I want to be very careful around Denny," she said in a soft voice.

"I wonder if he'd mind that I like to hug his mommy?"

"We're not going to find out, not at this point."

"At what point, then?"

"Don't push, Jeb."

He groaned and lifted his hands upward in a helpless gesture. "How can I help it when you prance around like that?"

"Like what? Any normal man would think this was a

dopey outfit. Can I help it if you're turned on by faded jeans and old shirts?''

"Maybe it's not the clothes.''

"I'm going to make the coffee. I'd advise you to sit on the couch and read something.''

"Couldn't I help you? I'm great at brewing up—''

"Trouble,'' Liza finished. "No. You stay here.'' With one more warning glance she turned and left the room. Alone in the kitchen she wondered if inviting Jeb for coffee was such a bright idea. Their playful banter could instantly become words of passion, and they both knew it. She would not, however, give in to her feelings for him with Denny in the next room.

She put on the coffee and got out the package of Fig Newtons. She'd have to make sure Denny was in bed before she brought out the cookies or he'd demand some. Voices drifted in from the living room, and she peeked in to see what Jeb and Denny were up to.

Fresh and pink from his bath and dressed in his Mickey Mouse pajamas, Denny leaned against Jeb, who was reading him a Dr. Seuss book. She thought again about what Jeb had said. Would Denny mind if he knew how she and Jeb felt about each other?

She decided the question was premature. She wasn't planning to give Denny any indication of the situation until she was certain where it was headed. Right now Denny accepted her relationship with Jeb in the same way he treated her association with Bill. Her son didn't need to know any more right now. Leaving the cookies and coffee in the kitchen, she walked into the living room and sat down on the other side of Denny.

Jeb glanced over Denny's head and smiled at her. "Cozy, huh?''

"Very.''

"Come on, Jeb, read the rest," Denny said.

"Okay, but then it's bedtime."

"Aw, Jeb, couldn't we read one more?"

"Nope. The old clock on the wall says it's twenty hundred hours and twenty minutes, and you have to be in the sack, lights out, at twenty hundred hours and thirty minutes."

"Did you hear that, Mommy? That's fire station talk. That's how they tell time there."

"Very impressive."

Jeb cleared his throat. "*Some* people thought so."

"So do I, Jeb. So do I," she assured him.

"I can tell. Well, sport, let's finish this cliff-hanger and get you in bed."

"What's a cliff-hanger?"

"An exciting story, like this one."

"Oh. Cliff-hanger. I like that." Denny settled against Jeb while they finished the book. Then he asked if Jeb could put him to bed.

"Okay," Liza said, although she felt a pang of jealousy. Was Denny switching his loyalties that easily? Then another thought struck her. Was she afraid that Denny would be upset if he knew about her relationship with Jeb, or was she secretly worried that her little boy would become Jeb's little boy?

The idea that she might be unwilling to share Denny's love wasn't a very comforting one. Still thinking about the possibility, she wandered into the kitchen to load up the tray with coffee and cookies. As she was returning with their snack, Jeb came out of Denny's bedroom.

"He wants you to kiss him good-night, too."

So Denny hadn't quite discarded her, Liza thought ruefully. "Okay. I'll be right back. Help yourself to the cookies."

"When you finish kissing Denny, I'd like to get in line."

She frowned at him. "Stop that."

"Nope."

Shaking her head, she walked into the dim light of Denny's room. He held out his arms, and she leaned over to kiss his cheek.

"Mommy, will you read me a cliff-hanger tomorrow night, like Jeb?"

"Sure, honey, but that was just one of your regular books."

"I know, but he made it seem different."

"Jeb makes lots of things seem different," Liza said more to herself than to Denny.

"Yeah, and real exciting."

"That, too. Good night, sweetheart."

"Good night, Mommy."

She closed the door gently and returned to where Jeb lounged on the couch eating a Fig Newton. He patted the cushion next to him, but she sat down a good two feet away.

"Closer."

"I think not." She picked up her coffee cup.

"You're no fun," he protested.

"Not tonight, I'm not. What did you and Denny do all day?"

"My parents came over to see the puppies. We had lunch." He picked up the other cup and took a gulp of coffee.

"That sounds nice." Liza noticed the way his shirt collar pulled away from the back of his neck when he leaned forward to drink. She remembered how the nape of his neck felt, the creased, sunburned part and the sensitive places behind his ears.

"They got a kick out of Denny," Jeb continued, taking another sip of his coffee.

She liked to watch the curve of his lower lip as it pressed against the rim of the cup. She was remembering how he had... No, she mustn't think of that now. "I hope Denny wasn't too wild."

"Not really. Just cute, you know. My folks are used to my sisters' kids, so they understand little ones pretty well." He studied her through the steam rising from the surface of his coffee. "Denny liked them, too."

"Good." She gazed into his blue eyes and thought of what they would share the next time they met.

"I thought so. On the way home, I asked him about his grandparents, if he had fun with them."

Her warm cocoon of sensuality began to unravel. "He doesn't have much chance, I'm afraid."

"I guess I knew that, but it seems kind of sad, especially because his father's parents are out of the picture, too. I know my sisters' kids think my mom and dad are about the niftiest thing going."

Liza's spine stiffened and she put down her coffee cup with elaborate care before she answered. "My mother and father didn't want me to keep Denny, remember?"

"Well, yeah, but that was before he was born, before they knew him. They were thinking of you then. They must care about him, Liza, if they bring him presents twice a year."

"They do that out of a sense of obligation, Jeb. They're very socially correct people."

He flinched. "Ouch. That's hard, Liza." He put his cup next to hers and leaned forward. "I can't believe you're still angry."

"Jeb, I've tried to establish a relationship with them." She was dismayed to discover that no matter how much she resisted the urge, she was about to cry. "But every time I deal with my parents they act as if they have a right to run my life. I won't let them be in charge. I won't."

He laid his hand on her arm. "Whoa. I wasn't suggesting that, by any means."

"Then what were you suggesting?"

"Bringing more people into Denny's circle, people who love him. You're carrying the whole load. That's not so good for you, or for him."

She blinked back her tears. "Careful, Jeb. You're treading on dangerous ground, advising me what to do with my son."

He sighed and sank back into his corner of the couch. "I know. If I had any brains I wouldn't have brought up the subject."

There was a long silence. "Jeb, about Tuesday. Maybe it would be better if we didn't—"

He sat forward immediately. "No. Don't say that. Forget I mentioned anything about Denny's grandparents. Just don't cancel Tuesday. I'm living for that day."

"But what's the point, if we're always fighting?"

He squeezed her hand. "We're not always fighting. Not by a long shot. But we are learning about each other. No two people agree on everything, and I haven't been through what you have with Denny and your parents. I probably spoke out of turn."

Liza's shoulders sagged. "You also touched a really sensitive spot."

"That's not the sort of sensitive spot I had in mind," he said, his tone gently teasing. "In fact, I thought maybe here," he continued, stroking the inside of her wrist, "or here." He drew an imaginary line from the hollow of her throat to the point where her shirt buttoned.

"No, Jeb." She pulled away as his touch electrified her, sending messages of need to every part of her body. "Don't do that now."

"It's tough not to. I want you, Liza."

"Maybe...maybe you should go."

"Maybe I should. My natural instinct is to spend every possible minute with you, but if we can't—"

"We can't."

"Okay." He stood and looked down at her. "Tuesday?" he asked softly.

She closed her eyes. She was a fool, but she ached for what he offered. She nodded. "Tuesday."

CHAPTER TWELVE

ON TUESDAY THE FIRST COLD fingers of winter stroked the air and turned a steady rain into sleet. Liza bundled Denny up for school and shielded him with an umbrella while they walked to his bus stop. The weather was miserable, but other than protecting Denny, she barely noticed the bitter chill. Anticipation of the afternoon filled her with steaming heat.

She used the scant half hour she'd scheduled for lunch to rush home and take her second shower of the day. The hot water clouded the small bathroom, giving it an otherworldly appearance that suited Liza's mood perfectly. There was no time to dawdle; she washed quickly and reached for a towel.

Despite the need to hurry, however, her brisk motions became more languorous as she imagined stepping from the relaxing warmth into Jeb's arms. She regretted that he wasn't waiting in the next room, and for the first time in years the thought of living with a man brought pleasure instead of apprehension.

Yes, she was falling in love with Jeb, she admitted, and he seemed to feel the same way about her. Smiling, she drew a heart on the fogged mirror over the sink and put Jeb's initials and hers inside. If he were there, she could call him in to see it.

But he wasn't there, and she had a tuning appointment at one o'clock. Arriving late would only shorten her time

with Jeb. She wrapped herself in the towel and dashed
into her bedroom.

Liza moved quickly without sacrificing any of the steps
she'd planned. She smoothed lotion everywhere she could
reach before touching cologne on all the spots Jeb liked
to kiss. Then she put on the new underwear she'd bought
the day before, silken tap pants and a camisole, both in
purest white. Feeling them against her skin made her
shiver with delight.

She went light on makeup, remembering Jeb's statement about liking her without any. Perhaps that was why
she could imagine living with him, Liza thought. From
the beginning there had been no pretense between them,
and Jeb seemed to prefer it that way.

The weather dictated the rest of her outfit. A black and
white patterned sweater, black wool slacks and black
socks under her fur-lined boots would keep out most of
the cold. After giving her hair several strokes with the
brush, Liza went out to the kitchen to pick up the trench
coat that she'd left drying on the back of a chair.

That morning she'd zipped the lining into it as she had
every winter for the past six years. Each time the ritual
reminded her of her last shopping trip with her mother,
before the pregnancy, before the battles over what would
become of the baby. Her mother had bought the coat as
Liza's reward for a good semester. Liza hadn't wanted the
style with the lining, but her mother had insisted that she
needed the versatility. Dammit, her mother had been right.

As Liza drove to her one o'clock appointment, she reviewed once again the almost-fight with Jeb on Sunday
night. The equation always came out the same when she
thought of the situation with her parents. Sure, Denny
should see more of them as Jeb had said, but Liza
wouldn't trade that for her independence. Jeb was threat

enough to her self-sufficiency, but she was willing to take the risk with him because of the incredible joy he offered. Thinking of that joy, she wondered how she could possibly tune Mrs. Triblet's piano while her fingers were shaking with excitement.

Somehow she managed, and Mrs. Triblet didn't appear to notice anything amiss. Liza waited impatiently while the woman wrote out a check and chattered about her daughter's progress with piano lessons. When Mrs. Triblet paused long enough to offer Liza a cup of tea, she politely declined and murmured something about another appointment before racing through the sleet to her car.

By the time she pulled up in front of Jeb's house her heart was thudding rapidly and her mouth was dry. She couldn't remember ever *planning* to make love before. With Kyle everything had seemed to occur spontaneously, by her agreement but not her devising. In contrast, the events of the next hour and a half were happening by her choice.

She felt like Mata Hari as she turned up her coat collar, opened her umbrella and hurried up the walk. Halfway to Jeb's door a gust of wind blew the umbrella inside out, and she raced for the shelter of the porch. Just her luck, she'd arrive looking like a drowned rat instead of a sultry siren.

The front door opened as her foot touched the bottom step, and the umbrella was tossed aside as Jeb swept her into the house.

"Damn weather," he muttered, unbuttoning her trench coat. "Got you all wet, and now you might catch cold, and—"

His mother hen behavior made her smile. "You sound quite put out."

"I am. Have you seen the roads?"

"No, I keep my eyes closed when I drive in weather this bad."

"That's not funny. I hate for anyone to be out on days like this." He slipped the trench coat from her shoulders and draped it over a chair.

"Talk about crazy—you ran out there in just your socks."

He glanced down. "Yeah, well, when I saw your umbrella go I reacted without thinking." He leaned down and pulled the socks from his feet. "That's the beginning of my strip-tease act."

She laughed and realized that her nervousness was gone. She was completely at ease in his company. "Where are the puppies?"

"Zonked out in their bed in the kitchen. During a break in the rain I ran the pants off them in the backyard so they'd sleep this afternoon."

"Clever man. I won't even take a peek in case I might somehow wake them up." She sat on a chair and took off her boots.

"You wouldn't want to wake them up. They're not wonderful when they have to be cooped up on a day like this." He watched as she stood up and walked toward him. "God, I'm glad you're here. It's a wonder you didn't have an accident driving on those slippery roads."

She placed both hands on his shoulders "Jeb, for heaven's sake. I'm fine. I've lived in this area all my life, and I'm careful under these driving conditions. And getting wet won't hurt me. It just makes me look bedraggled."

"You look wonderful." He wrapped her in a bear hug and buried his face in her damp hair. "I have the most vivid imagination, and I don't enjoy imagining you in any danger."

She snuggled against him and abandoned herself to the luxury of holding him tight. "That's pretty silly," she murmured, "when you're the one who's in danger all the time, not me."

"I know." His voice was muffled against her hair. "I never used to worry like this, but..."

She realized that the tension in him hadn't abated. He *had* been worried about her, unreasonably so. She lifted her head and looked up. "What, Jeb? What is it?"

He hesitated. "Forget it."

"No. Something's bothering you."

"I've become too much of a worrier, that's all. You see..." He paused and brushed a damp strand of hair from her cheek. "My best friend was killed three months ago."

"In a fire?"

"Yes."

Terrible images assaulted her but she fought to stay calm. He didn't need her fears piled on top of his agony. "Were you there?"

He nodded.

She had no words for something so monstrous, so she laid her head against his chest and held him. As she listened to his strong heartbeat, she quivered in dread of his own danger, but she couldn't speak of it. It was real enough without saying it aloud and making it loom even larger.

He rested his cheek on top of her head. "I'd never lost anybody I loved before that. Maybe I didn't believe it could happen. Now at the drop of a hat I worry about everyone—my parents, my sisters, Steve, you...."

She gripped him tighter. Unless she'd misunderstood him, he'd just included her in a list of people he loved. "I guess that's a natural reaction," she said, her voice unsteady.

He rocked her in his arms. "Please don't let anything happen to you, Liza. Promise me you'll be careful."

"I promise, Mr. Fireman."

"I want to be able to hold you like this forever. I don't want some stupid accident to deny us this."

Forever. She basked in the warmth of the word. "Neither do I."

He tilted her chin up, and his expression was open and soft. "Come on," he said gently. "Come and see what a cozy place I've made for us." He guided her toward the bedroom, where the curtains were drawn against the stormy day, and a bedside lamp cast a welcoming glow over turned-back sheets. A single red rose lay across the nearest snowy pillowcase.

His preparations touched her. "How sweet," she said, releasing his hand to walk over and pick up the rose.

"I cut off the thorns."

She sat on the edge of the bed and breathed in the springlike scent of the rose. "Of course you would."

He crossed the room and sat beside her. "I've never understood why something so beautiful has thorns."

"The world's not perfect, I guess."

"This part of it is," he said, taking the rose from her fingers and placing it on the nightstand. He cupped her face in his hands. "Except that you have to leave too soon."

"Don't think about that," she whispered, leaning back across the bed and drawing him down on top of her. "Not now."

"You smell fantastic."

She smiled against his clean-shaven cheek. "On purpose. I used my lunch hour to freshen up."

He grew still. "For me?"

"Yes, for you."

His gaze swept over her face. "I'm very flattered."

"I wanted this afternoon to be special."

"I never had doubts about that." He slipped her sweater up over her breasts and drew it gently over her head. "God, I love to look at you." He ran his finger along the lace trim of her undergarment. "Very pretty," he said, his voice thick. "What's it called?"

"A camisole. I...dressed up a little for you."

"Dressing up underneath. I like that." He moved his hand over the swell of her breast, and her nipple puckered, pushing against the smooth material. "Nice," he murmured, rubbing his finger across the spot.

Liza moaned. "Yes."

He smiled down at her. "See how much we agree?"

"Mmm." She reached for his top button.

"Wait." He caught her hand. "I'm not quite finished." He unfastened her slacks and pushed them over her hips. His blue eyes lit with approval as he studied the tap pants. "Sexy." He caressed her thigh. "With the leg openings loose like this, I can move my hand from here all the way up to—"

Her heart pounded as he reached beneath the thin material. "No fair," she said, gasping. "You're still dressed."

"So I am." Ignoring her protest, he finished removing her slacks and both socks.

She found it difficult to speak as he continued to touch her in all the ways she'd dreamed of for so many days and nights. "Jeb, please...take off your clothes."

"I thought you might do that."

"I tried, and you—"

"Try again."

Eagerly she reached for the buttons on his shirt, nearly pulling one off in her desire to run her hands over his bare torso. When the shirt was open, she pushed him back on the bed and placed lingering kisses over his chest and across the long scar, as if she could kiss away this reminder of his vulnerability. Her camisole provided a whisper of friction between them as she nibbled her way up the column of his neck.

"You're something," he breathed, just before she covered his mouth with hers.

Made bolder by his encouragement, she became the aggressor, dipping her tongue into his open mouth as she unbuttoned his jeans and caressed the cotton fabric straining across his aroused manhood. She slipped her fingers beneath the elastic waistband and down. The groan that rose from his throat vibrated against her lips.

"Do you like that?" she murmured between kisses.

"Do I...mmm...Liza...Liza..."

She grew drunk with power as she listened to his labored breathing and looked into eyes filled with the need she was building within him.

He sucked in his breath and grasped her wrist. "No more." His voice rasped with desire. "If you won't get rid of the rest of these clothes, I'm going to." He sat up and took off his shirt in one swift movement. Then he pulled away the jeans and shorts with a sigh of relief and turned to her. "Now you."

His eyes were bright as she crossed her arms and grasped the hem of the camisole. She pulled it up and flung it away in one motion.

"Oh, Liza." He pressed her back against the sheets and drew off the tap pants. "Liza, my wonderful woman."

She arched her back as he took her nipple into his mouth. She held his head, burying her fingers in his sandy hair and closing her eyes in ecstasy. The ache within her grew, and as if in answer he moved his hand down across her taut belly, through the damp bed of curls to assuage that ache with a circular pressure from his palm.

He wound the tension tighter and tighter, until it was her turn to hold his wrist while she gasped for breath. "I want to wait for you," she choked out. "I want us to be together."

He lifted his head and gazed into her eyes. "So do I, my love. But first, I have to get something." He turned away and reached into the nightstand drawer.

Her passion erased all timidity. "I want to...put it on."

He turned back to her, surprise changing to desire in his blue eyes. "All right."

She opened the package with trembling hands. Carefully she sheathed him in the pliant material, and she could feel him trembling, too. She met his gaze.

"That was beautiful," he said in a husky voice.

"So will this be." She moved over him and took him slowly inside the moist recesses of her body. She watched his lips part and his pupils dilate with pleasure as she rotated her hips.

"I love...the way your breasts move when you do that," he said softly.

"Do you?" She moved in the opposite direction, taunting him as long as she could before her own response robbed her of control. "Is that all you love?"

"No." He grasped her hips and began to guide her movements for even greater pleasure. "I love the feeling of being inside you like this."

Gradually she began a slow up-and-down rhythm. "And this?"

"Yes, my God, yes."

She was so in tune with him that she barely heard the whimper and scratching from outside the door. Then she heard it again. "Jeb, the puppies."

"Forget the puppies."

"You may be..." She struggled to stay rational as he increased the pace. "You may be sorry."

"No, I won't. Just don't...stop."

She gazed into his eyes and forgot everything else but the intense need she saw there, a need reflected in her eyes and echoed by the movements of their bodies. Understanding flowed between them as they undulated closer and closer to their moment of truth.

The flash of release sparked in his eyes at the same moment that convulsions racked her body. She slumped against him, and he held her tight as the quivering slowly subsided. He crooned words of praise in her ear and stroked her hair until at last she felt strong enough to lift her head and smile at him.

He combed her hair back with his fingers and studied her face for a long while. "You have so much to give."

"So have you."

"I like this arrangement, giving to each other."

She laughed softly. "You may not be so happy about it if you go outside this door and find puddles on the floor. I still hear the puppies."

"I don't care what I find. This was worth it."

"Yes, it was." She thought about telling him how she felt, of her newly discovered love, but the puppies began howling and whining even louder. "But those dogs will get you evicted if you don't take care of them."

"I wonder who thought of buying those mutts in the first place," he grumbled.

"Someone with a big heart."

"Yeah, and a teeny tiny brain."

Reluctantly they left their retreat, and Liza took her third shower of the day, while Jeb checked on the puppies.

He walked into the bathroom in his jeans with his shirt unbuttoned just as she turned off the water.

"No problems," he announced. "They were lonesome. It's stopped raining so I put them out for a while." He handed her a towel as if he'd been doing it for years.

"I bet they miss Denny."

"Yeah, I was wondering if I could bring him over here for a short time tonight while you practice with Bill."

"I guess so, if it's not too late." She drew the towel across her damp back and noticed that he was staring at her. "Anything wrong?"

"No. Everything's fine. Here, let me help."

"Help?"

"Let me dry you."

"I..."

"Humor me." He took the towel from her unresisting hands and rubbed it gently over her breasts.

She clutched the towel rack as she began to quiver. "Jeb, I have to leave in twenty minutes. You do realize that."

"Unfortunately." He sat on the closed toilet seat and held the towel with both hands while moving it down her rib cage. Then he sank to his knees to dry her legs. He worked from the bottom up, until finally there was only one place left to dry.

"I can finish this," she begged. She'd tried to remain detached, but her whole body was flushed pink from his ministrations with the towel. If he touched her there, where she was already moist and throbbing, she'd never get to her next appointment.

He tossed the towel behind him and grasped her hips. "I want to give you something to remember until next time."

"Jeb..." She started to resist, but his grip was strong

and her resolve weak. "Jeb," she whispered again as his tongue and lips worked their magic. She placed both hands on his shoulders to keep from falling as the dizzy spinning began. Quickly, sooner than she could have imagined, he brought her to the edge and then beyond the edge. She clutched his shoulders and cried out as her body shuddered its response to his loving.

Carefully he guided her to her knees until they were face-to-face. "I don't want you to forget what happens when we're together like this, without distractions, when it's just you and me."

She took a quivering breath. "You make an eloquent statement."

"We won't be able to see each other tomorrow. I have the day off, but I'm spending it with a couple of boys."

"Boys in your program?"

"Yes."

She nodded. "And Thursday you work. Saturday's out, so how about Friday?"

"Name the time."

"My first appointment isn't until eleven. You could come over after Denny leaves for school at eight."

"I'll be there."

She thought again about telling him that she loved him, but now didn't seem like the right moment, just before she had to leave. But on Friday she'd say something for sure. He should know how she felt, how his wonderful lovemaking affected her. On Friday they'd have more time.

"OKAY, BUDDY, OUT WITH IT. Admit you're in never-never land, romanceville." Steve sat across the firehouse kitchen table from Jeb and sipped on his fifth cup of coffee of the night while Jeb munched on a diminishing pile of Oreos.

Jeb grinned. "Get a life, walrus-face. Then you wouldn't have to pry into mine." He and Steve were alone in the room while the rest of Ladder Company Three and Engine Company Nine dozed upstairs on their cots. Jeb and Steve preferred to stay awake on their shifts rather than trying to sleep. Like Jeb, Steve hated to wake up to the sound of an alarm coming in. They'd spent many nights like this one, keeping each other company as the hands of the wall clock edged past midnight and started a new day.

"I beg your pardon," Steve said, feigning great indignation, "but wasn't I the guy who hatched that brilliant plan, the one that rescued you from the brink of disaster? Without Mo's piano, you and Liza would be history, lover-boy."

"I would've found a way," Jeb maintained staunchly.

"You?" Steve slapped his forehead with the heel of his hand. "*Mamma mia!* You can't find your way to a five-alarm fire unless I point out the smoke. Without me around you'd be a sorry excuse for a fire fighter."

"Steve, my friend, you are so full of—"

"Ah, ah." Steve waggled his finger across the table. "Watch that language. You are now a role model for little boys. We can't have Fireman Jeb talking nasty, now can we?"

Jeb laughed. It was good to joke and tease again. Kevin's death had stifled much of the banter in the firehouse, especially when Jeb was around.

Steve got up for another cup of coffee. "How'd yesterday go with those two boys, anyway?"

"Great. I took them to the top of the Hancock Building, where they'd never gone before. We even discussed the danger of fire in multistory buildings. I can't believe those two will mess around with setting fires anymore."

"It takes a lot of your free time, being a big brother to these kids."

"So what else am I going to do? Liza's busier than a one-armed paperhanger, and I don't have a house of my own to take care of, or a family. I've got the time, and the people at juvenile have the kids, apparently. They've got another one like Pete and Mike—a boy suspected of starting fires although there's no hard evidence yet. I want to get to that type before they do something they can be jailed for."

"I've been thinking I should help. You know, at least until Mo's pregnant."

"I'd love to have you, Steve."

"Some of the other guys have been saying the same thing. Most of them don't have the time you've got, but they see what's happening, and they'd like to spend a couple of hours a week. You're proving something to them, buddy. They didn't think your idea would work at first."

"So who's interested?"

"Eddie, and Bob, and I think Aaron said something about it, too. They, um, don't want to horn in, though, if you want to run this show solo."

"Are you kidding? Do I look like an egomaniac to you?"

"No, you look like a sex maniac."

Jeb gazed at the ceiling. "Here we go again. Can I help it if I'm a legend in my own time?"

"I'll mention that to Liza next time I see her. I wonder if she has the proper respect for your prowess?"

"You do that and I'll clue Mo in on your bachelor party. I seem to recall a sweet little redhead who..."

"Blackmailer," Steve grumbled. "I should know what to expect from you by now."

"That you should, my boy. Especially after—"

Jeb's statement was cut short by the harsh jangle of the alarm. Both men listened for instructions from the loud-speaker in the kitchen.

"*Fourteen-twenty East Maple,*" the man on watch blared. "*Engine Company Nine goes, Ladder Company Three goes, Chief goes.*"

Jeb followed Steve out to the apparatus floor where the others were sliding down the pole and hurrying toward their gear. Within seconds Jeb had pulled on his boots and slipped his arms into the sleeves of his turnout. The big front door opened, and Jeb hopped on the ladder truck as Steve drove it into the night air.

When the icy wind hit him, Jeb wished he'd had time to buckle his coat closed. Much more of the chill damp air and he'd be ripe for his annual winter cold. Steve was already working on his, and Bob had been coughing all during dinner. The kitchen counter was cluttered with over-the-counter cold remedies and would be until spring, when the fire fighters wouldn't have to rush from a heated firehouse into the deep freeze of a Midwestern winter.

Two blocks away from the site Jeb smelled the acrid smoke and knew they had a working fire. This time of night, he hoped to hell the building wasn't occupied. People were so easily killed in their sleep.

The building was a warehouse, only two stories. Smoke billowed from a high window on the second floor, but the fire hadn't broken through the roof yet. Jeb knew that Bob would have to open it up from the top. He'd taken Kevin's place as the roof man on most jobs, and Jeb had been careful not to forge a close friendship with him. He felt like a coward for avoiding Bob, but he couldn't help it.

A small crowd had gathered to watch the show. The people stepped aside, creating a path to allow the ladder truck through. As Jeb stepped off the truck and started to buckle his turnout, Chief Gregorio was already shouting orders.

"Nobody's seen the night watchman come out," he yelled in Jeb's direction. "You and Aaron take masks and see what you can find."

Jeb finished buckling and took his mask from the truck. Aaron followed suit and grabbed a halligan tool to force the front door. Life came first, and then the fire. Before the engine company could turn the hoses on the blaze, Jeb and Aaron had to find the night watchman.

They got through the flimsy lock on the front door without much trouble and dropped to their knees. The smoke was thick and hung low over a maze of crates and huge rolls of what looked like newsprint. Jeb remembered the sign on the front of the building—Great Lakes Paper Company. The fire had apparently started upstairs in the back. If it ever reached this area, the place would be an inferno.

Jeb motioned Aaron to one side of the building, and he took the other. They crawled beneath the layer of smoke and searched for signs of the watchman. He might not be here, Jeb thought. He could have stepped out for a pack of cigarettes. He might have set the fire himself and left the scene. But they had to look, had to be certain. If either of them found him, they'd signal the chief and each other on the radios they carried.

They followed their prearranged pattern for searching a large area out of sight of each other. They'd work until they only had enough air to get back out. Then someone else would go in with a fresh air supply.

Jeb had covered his side of the first floor when the bell

rang indicating that he was low on air. He hoped Aaron had found the guy, because he hadn't and the fire was roaring over his head. If the watchman was unlucky enough to be on the second floor, he wouldn't have much of a chance.

As Jeb crawled toward the front of the building, he noticed a door that blended in so well with the wall that he'd missed it with the first sweep of his flashlight. The wall took a right angle just past the door, and there was enough space for a small room, maybe a utility room of some sort.

Jeb stayed on his knees and felt upward for the knob. The door was locked. Jeb knew he should leave it. What would a night watchman be doing behind a locked door? But he had to be sure the room was empty. He crouched a short distance from the door and hurled himself against it.

The lock snapped but the door only opened a few feet, releasing a wedge of light into the smoky warehouse. Sweating from the heat and exertion, Jeb pushed hard and felt the door give a little. Something or someone was behind it. The effort to get through the door was using up his air too fast. At this rate he'd be out before he could make it to the front entrance. But he had to know what was holding the door.

He squeezed through the opening and nearly fell over the night watchman. The man slumped against the wall was huge, at least three hundred pounds. The empties from a six-pack of beer were scattered around him. Apparently he came in here to drink on the job and locked the door so that he wouldn't accidentally be discovered in the act. The door had kept out most of the smoke, although enough had seeped in to render the man unconscious. Jeb took off one glove and checked the man's pulse. He was alive.

Jeb knew the air in his mask was virtually gone. Hauling the man out of the warehouse would finish it in a few seconds. Without pausing to think about it, he unhooked the mask. Instantly he began to cough as smoke filled his lungs. Keeping as low as possible, he began dragging the man around the door and out into the warehouse.

Once there he dropped to his stomach, wrapped the man's arm around his neck, and began inching forward. He felt as if he'd hooked Moby Dick. Their progress was slow, so damned slow, but Jeb couldn't leave him. As he squirmed forward he swallowed back the urge to vomit from the combination of the smoke and the man's alcohol-laden breath. Soon they would reach the entrance. Soon he could breathe the cold, fresh air. Soon.

His eyes burned like hot embers as he strained for sight of the front door. The beam of the flashlight seemed to grow dimmer. Were his batteries going dead? Then everything became hazy and began to revolve. He shook his head, but the room wouldn't stop spinning. *The smoke,* he thought. *The smoke is getting thicker.... Got to get out.* He fought the blackness, but it lured him with the peace of oblivion. With a sigh he rested his head on the concrete floor and closed his eyes.

CHAPTER THIRTEEN

JEB AWOKE FLAT ON HIS BACK. His first sensation was that the ground underneath him was moving. He tried to speak, but an oxygen mask covered his nose and his mouth, and he was strapped down. The jackhammer pain inside his head made thinking difficult, but eventually he grasped the reality of the ambulance that was carrying him to the hospital.

Slowly it all came back—the struggle to reach the door, the giant man he'd tried to save. Was the guy dead? Someone, Jeb hoped more than one person, must have come in after him when he hadn't shown up outside with Aaron. He swallowed and decided a football covered with barbed wire was lodged in his throat. He closed his eyes again. He felt like hell, but he was alive.

As his mind began to clear he remembered that today was Friday. After he got off work this morning he was supposed to drive over to Liza's apartment. A rendezvous of lovers. Silently he reviewed his entire vocabulary of swearwords as he realized that he hadn't a prayer of making love to her today. With as much smoke as he'd taken in, he'd be lucky if they didn't keep him incarcerated until tomorrow or the next day. Why did this have to happen now, just when he and Liza were developing some real feeling between them? He thought about the morning's lost promise and groaned.

Immediately a face appeared above him. The ambulance wasn't from the fire department, apparently, because he didn't know the man who asked if he was in pain. Slowly Jeb shook his head. The medical technician didn't have a single thing on board that would take care of Jeb's problem.

LIZA HAD FORMED THE HABIT of watching the morning news on television whenever Jeb had been on duty the night before. She didn't have time to sit in the living room and watch, but she kept the volume loud enough so that she could hear the news from anywhere in the apartment.

She was stirring a pan of Cream of Wheat for Denny's breakfast when the announcer mentioned a Melwood Park warehouse fire early that morning that had sent two people to the hospital, the night watchman and a fire fighter. Liza dropped the spoon and raced into the living room, but the report was over, and an attractive brunette was explaining that the Midwest was in for more cold, rainy weather.

She glanced at her watch. Seven-thirty. The firemen on Jeb's shift would still be there. If Jeb was okay, he would be there, too, and know that she'd called like some nervous Nellie the minute she heard that someone was hurt.

To hell with it, she thought. *Let him know that I'm worried about him.* After turning off the burner under the cereal she reached for the phone and dialed the number of the firehouse. When someone answered she asked for Jeb, figuring there was no point in pussyfooting around. Then she paced the floor of the living room while she waited for the reassuring sound of his voice on the line, telling her that he'd be at her apartment in an hour or so.

Instead someone else came to the telephone. "This is Steve Talbot. May I help you?"

"This is Liza Galloway, Steve. I just wanted to speak briefly with Jeb, but if he's busy..." She tried to sound casual. Jeb was probably changing clothes and couldn't come to the phone.

"He, um, took in a little too much smoke last night, Liza. He's in Melwood Park General."

Her blood seemed to freeze in her veins. "It was him," she whispered almost to herself.

"Liza, he's not too bad. The doctors want to observe him for a while, that's all. It happens."

"I...I suppose." The first shock had worn off, and now her heart was thudding with alarm. "Can I see him?"

"I'm sure he'd love it. Room 232."

"You've been there, then. Is he—"

"Ornery as ever. Not a happy camper. Maybe seeing you will help, though."

"I'll go this morning. What happened, Steve?"

"You know Jeb. That crazy guy is determined to be a hero. Tried to drag a three-hundred-and-twenty-pound man out of a warehouse last night. He might have done it, too, except his air supply gave out, and he ditched his mask. When he didn't show up outside the building Bob and I went in after him."

"Thank you." After she said it she felt silly.

"You're welcome," Steve replied gently, "but it's my job."

"Somehow I feel as if this is more than a job to all of you."

There was a pause on the other end of the line. "Jeb told me you were something special. You're right, Liza. This isn't just a job for us. Not for the good ones, anyway."

"You're certainly one of those, Steve."

"So is Jeb. I'm glad he's found you. Give him hell for me."

"Okay. Goodbye, Steve." She hung up the telephone

and realized Denny was standing next to her, his expression worried. "Time for your cereal, or we'll be late for the bus," she said, herding him into the kitchen.

He stiffened his back and resisted her efforts to guide him into a chair. "Who were you talking to?"

"A friend." She gave up her attempts to get him seated at the table and turned the heat back on under the rapidly congealing cereal. Denny didn't like it thick. She reached for the box of raisins and dumped a few into the pan.

"I heard you ask something about Jeb," Denny accused. "And you acted funny on the telephone. Besides, you never call anybody in the morning before I go to school."

Liza knew she'd have to tell him something. The weekend was coming up, and he anticipated Jeb taking him over to see the puppies. She decided to use Steve's words. "While Jeb was fighting a fire last night he breathed in a little too much smoke. The doctors want to keep him in the hospital for a few days to make sure he rests."

"Jeb's in the hospital?" Denny's eyes rounded in fear.

"Yes, but he'll be fine soon. Then we'll have a big welcome home party for him, okay?"

He looked doubtful. "With cake?"

"Sure, why not?"

"I'd like that. So would Spotty and Freckles. Those dogs love cake. Especially chocolate."

"Then it's settled."

"When, Mommy? When can we have a party?"

"I'm not sure. We'll have to find out exactly when Jeb can leave the hospital."

"What if I'm in school?"

Liza made a quick decision. "If it's on a school day, I'll let you stay home."

"Oh, boy!" He looked at her slyly. "Wish I could stay home today, too."

"Not today, Denny. Eat your cereal now. I put raisins in it for you." She wished he wouldn't ask to stay home so often. Denny wasn't doing particularly well in either kindergarten or the play school where he was enrolled for the afternoons. The teachers insisted that he was bright but unmotivated. Unfortunately the description sounded too much like Liza had felt in college. She knew the dangers of parental pressure, so she hadn't pushed Denny to improve his schoolwork.

Denny sat down at the table with a martyred sigh and began sprinkling sugar on the cereal. "Look, Mommy, it's snowing on my Cream of Wheat."

"Just don't turn it into a blizzard, or your teeth will rot and fall out of your head."

"I *want* my teeth to fall out. Eric had a tooth fall out, and he got a whole quarter from the tooth fairy." Denny splashed milk into his bowl. "Now there's a flood, and all the raisins are drowning, and the Cream of Wheat is turning into quicksand." He grasped his spoon in his fist and stirred the mixture vigorously. "Those raisins are done for now. They're calling *help, help, save me!*"

"Denny, please stop playing with that cereal and eat it." Her parenting was halfhearted this morning, she realized. Her mind was filled with a picture of Jeb lying in a hospital bed, and she was impatient to go to him and find out for herself that he wasn't seriously hurt.

Denny slurped away at his breakfast while Liza drank a cup of coffee and munched on some toast, more out of something to do than from hunger. She thought about how Jeb had risked his life to pull the huge man out of the fire. She'd been so certain that they would be together this morning, that she'd be able to tell him that she loved him. Instead he was almost snatched from her forever.

No wonder Jeb lived for the moment. What a fool she'd been to demand time to think things over. If he hadn't pushed her on Saturday, Tuesday afternoon might never have happened. Now she was greedy for every second she could spend with Jeb, even if it meant sitting with him in a stark hospital room. She wondered if she should take him something, and if so, what. None of the shops would be open at this hour, anyway.

"What about Spotty and Freckles?" Denny asked with his mouth full of cereal.

"Don't talk with your mouth full, sweetheart."

Denny swallowed. "Well, what about them?"

"Why, I don't know. Jeb will make some arrangements, I suppose, until he can come home."

"But I have to see Spotty tomorrow. She's expecting me to come, Mommy."

"Well, yes, I know, honey, but..."

"We could go over there, anyway. Jeb wouldn't care."

At that moment Liza knew what she could bring Jeb, an offer to feed and exercise the puppies while he was in the hospital. It was the least she could do after all he'd been through to buy them and care for them. "I can't promise anything, Denny, but I'll ask Jeb if he'd like us to check on the puppies for him."

"Yeah! That would be cool! It would almost be like they're really ours." Denny scraped the last of his cereal from the bowl. "I wish we had a house, so we could have Spotty all the time."

"That would be nice, Denny." She tried not to think how faraway that dream seemed, or how insignificant in the face of Jeb's injury last night. "Right now we have to get you to the bus. Go brush your teeth." One thing at a time, she counseled herself. Jeb's condition was her first priority right now. She didn't have time to worry about the house and yard Denny wanted, or the lack of customers at Rags and Riches. Not until she'd satisfied herself that Jeb was all right.

Once Denny was safely on the yellow school bus, she hurried to her car parked at the curb in front of the apartment house. After quickly scraping the layer of ice from the windshield she drove to Melwood Park General Hospital. Knowing the room number helped. She could go right up without inquiring and perhaps being turned away because it was too early for visiting hours. At the moment she didn't give a damn about visiting hours.

The door was partly ajar and she rapped gently.

"Come in." The voice was hoarse, but it sounded like Jeb's.

She walked through the doorway, and her eyes filled with tears of relief. He was pale, but otherwise he looked fine. He'd even shaved this morning.

He gazed at her in disbelief. "How did you know?" He stopped to cough. "I tried to call a few minutes ago, but you weren't home."

"I heard it on the news, and I phoned the station and talked to Steve." She crossed to the bed and sat down in the upholstered chair drawn up beside it. "I'm here to keep our date."

He grinned and motioned to the bed. "That's great. Climb in," he said in a raspy voice.

"You sound terrible. Don't talk." She shrugged out of her coat and left it on the back of the chair.

"Go over and lock that door, and I won't say another word."

"Jeb, I was teasing."

"I'm not." He reached for her hand and tugged.

"Come closer, pretty lady. Sit on the bed and give me a kiss."

"What will the hospital staff think?"

"Ask me if I care." He started to sit up and fell back with a groan. "I feel as if I've been up all night drinking with Steve, except I don't remember having much fun."

Instinct overcame Liza's reluctance, and she sat on the bed so she could stroke Jeb's forehead. "I heard you were very brave, risking your life to save that night watchman."

"Mmm." He lay still with his eyes closed. "I just did it so that you'd sit by me and rub my head."

Her heart ached at his nonchalance. He wasn't about to admit he'd done anything heroic or out of the ordinary. "In that case I wish you'd have asked me before you went running around in burning buildings. There are easier ways to get my attention."

"Like what?"

"I think," she said, kissing his forehead, "that you already know what they are."

"Yeah?" He looked up at her.

"Yeah. Now close your eyes and relax and stop talking." She continued to massage his forehead and temples.

"You enjoyed Tuesday afternoon?"

She smiled to herself. "More than I can say."

"How much more?"

"Jeb, we're in the middle of a busy hospital. People are walking up and down the hall outside, and a nurse or a doctor could pop in here at any moment. I'm not getting specific with you, okay?"

"Damn. I love getting specific."

"When you're better. When you're out of here."

"Promise?"

"Promise."

"Great." He sat up and grimaced from the pain in his hand. "If you'll hand me my clothes out of the closet, we'll leave now."

"I most certainly will not." She pushed gently on his shoulders. "Lie down."

"Not unless you will, too."

She laughed at his petulant expression. "You look about Denny's age."

"I feel about Denny's age." He coughed violently. "This place takes away your dignity, putting you in these funny nighties that open in the back and telling you what to do and when to do it."

"Then if I were you I'd be careful not to land back in here again." She poured him a fresh glass of water from the pitcher beside his bed and handed it to him.

"Yeah." He drank the water, squinting as it slid past his raw throat. Then he eased back onto the pillow. "Well, if I'd known that big old watchman would get me in this fix, I would've—"

"Done the same thing," Liza said softly. "You could no more turn your back on someone in trouble than fly, Jeb Stratton."

Jeb shielded his mouth with one hand and pretended to whisper to someone next to him. "The plan worked. She admires the hell out of me."

"Will you knock it off? You did a wonderful thing, and you won't take credit for it. I do admire the hell out of you, and don't make it into a joke. There's another man in this hospital who's alive today because of you, and I'm sure he doesn't consider it a joke."

He looked at her steadily for several seconds. "It's a trick of the trade, Liza. If we take any of this too seriously we might crack."

She stared back at him. Then she took a deep breath.

"How much more do I have to learn about being a fire fighter's woman?"

He squeezed her hand and smiled. "You're doing just fine. No evidence of panic this morning."

"And not because I didn't feel like it. When Steve said you were in the hospital…"

"I know. I've had plenty of experience dealing with my mother for the past eight years."

"Has she been here yet?"

"No, but she'll arrive soon, I expect."

"Maybe I should leave, then."

"Why? I'm sure she'd like to meet you."

Liza's stomach churned. Parents meant control. Parents meant judgments made, and usually they were negative ones. "How much does she know about me?"

"That you're a friend. She probably suspects that you're a very good friend, considering I had Denny all day Sunday and one of the puppies is for him."

"Does she know that Denny's father and I were never married?"

"No. That's for you to tell or not tell, to anyone you choose." Jeb took both her hands in his. "Look, I know you haven't gotten a whole lot of support on your decision to keep Denny and raise him without a father." He stopped and coughed.

"Jeb, you shouldn't be talking."

"This is important. I want you to know that I think you did the right thing."

"Thank you."

"Not to say you haven't had problems, and may still have more, but you did the right thing for you and for Denny. I can't guarantee that my mother or anyone else will see it that way, but I do."

"That means a lot to me, Jeb."

"Will you stay and meet my mother?"

She smiled to soften her refusal. "I'd still rather not—not yet." She saw that he was disappointed. "I'm sorry."

"It's okay. I understand."

"Before I go, though, I'd like to make my proposition."

His blue eyes glinted. "Hey, now we're getting somewhere."

"About the puppies."

"Well, hell. Puppies, huh?"

"If you'd like, Denny and I will take charge of them. I can go by after I leave here, and again for a little while tonight during the dinner hour. Saturday and Sunday we can spend more time, and perhaps by Monday you'll be home."

"Count on it. I'm leaving at the first opportunity. But I hate to make you responsible for the puppies."

"I want to do it. So does Denny, obviously."

"Well...it would relieve my landlord of the job. He feeds them when I'm on duty, but this is above and beyond."

"Then it's settled."

"Won't that be too much work for you? That's why I have them in the first place, to spare you this stage. I warn you, they don't always hit the newspaper."

"I'll manage."

"You're sure?"

"Yep. All I need is your house key."

"I knew it." He coughed and took another drink of water. "This is really a plot to get my key, so that you can sneak into my house and ravage my body whenever you want."

"How did you guess?"

"It wasn't a guess. It was wishful thinking. God, Liza, I wish we were someplace besides this hospital room."

"Me, too."

He sighed and opened a drawer in the stand beside the bed. "Here, you might as well take the whole key ring. I won't need it until they spring me from this joint. The house key is this square, silver one." He handed her the ring and held up the house key. "This still seems like a lot to ask, considering you have the show tonight and tomorrow night."

"Please, Jeb, don't worry about it. Just rest."

"How did the show go last night? Many customers?"

"No, but that's a whole other story."

"It's a good show."

"So Bill keeps telling Dulcie, but she's started talking about closing the club."

"That would be a shame."

Liza stood up and reached for her coat. "Your voice is getting worse, and I'm leaving."

"One kiss, Liza."

She glanced toward the half-open door.

"I'll get better twice as fast," he coaxed.

"You're ridiculous," she said, but she sat down again and leaned toward him.

"No, I'm desperate. I haven't tasted those lips for almost three days. I need my fix." He grasped her shoulders. "Come here."

She yielded to his gentle pressure and brought her face close to his.

"Have you been thinking about everything that happened on Tuesday, remembering it all?" he whispered.

Their surroundings faded away as Liza gazed into his eyes. "I haven't thought of much else," she admitted.

"Neither have I. I just wanted to make sure you were

thinking of it now. Don't kiss some poor invalid, Liza. Kiss the man who loved you three days ago.''

Slowly Liza settled her mouth over his parted lips. The contact took her breath away with its sweetness. With a soft moan she cupped his face with both hands and dipped her tongue into the inviting depths that she knew so well. He slipped his hand through her hair to the nape of her neck and caressed her tingling skin as he met her forays with thrusts of his own tongue.

Breathing hard, she forced herself to pull away. ''Much more of that, and I will climb into that bed with you.''

''Glad to hear it.''

''But I've really got to leave. I'll come back tomorrow, if you like.''

''I like.''

''I'll probably have to bring Denny,'' she warned.

''That's okay.''

''Which means no kissing.'' She hovered over his lips once more.

''Then one more for tomorrow,'' he murmured, urging her back to the haven of his warm lips.

Her willpower was nonexistent. She kissed him eagerly, nourishing her soul with their shared passion. He groaned and cupped her breast as she leaned over him. If someone hadn't rattled by with a cart of breakfast trays out in the hall, Liza might have totally forgotten where she was.

The noise jolted her back to reality. ''Jeb, this has to end. We're getting beyond kissing here.''

''Yeah.'' He grinned lazily. ''Ain't it great?''

''As long as we're somewhere private, yes.'' She stood up and put on her coat. ''But this doesn't qualify. I'll see you tomorrow.''

''Tomorrow, lover.''

She turned around and came face to face with a woman

in her early fifties who was standing in the doorway. Liza
had no idea how long she'd been there, but she knew
exactly who she was.

Jeb's gravelly voice broke the silence. "Hi, Mom. This
is Liza, as if you didn't know."

"Hello, Liza." The woman took off her leather gloves
and held out her hand.

"Nice to meet you, Mrs. Stratton." Expecting disapproval, she looked into the woman's face and saw only
curiosity. Liza remembered how her parents had regarded
potential boyfriends with misgiving. Judgments, usually
negative, were quickly made. Liza was disconcerted by
the woman's open interest. "If you'll excuse me," she
added, "I was just leaving."

"Don't rush off, Liza," Jeb said hoarsely.

His mother turned her attention to her son and walked
quickly to the bed. "You sound terrible, just like last time.
Steve told me you took off your mask. Why do you do
things like that? You could have died!"

This behavior was more familiar to Liza, and she
waited for Jeb's angry defense of himself and his chosen
profession. Instead he chuckled, which soon became a violent cough.

"Look at you," his mother scolded, handing him a
glass of water as Liza had done. "You might as well be
a chain-smoker for the condition your lungs are in right
now."

Jeb drank the water and smiled at his mother. "I've
always wondered how people did that. I've never been
able to light a chain myself."

"That's right, make your jokes, like you always do.
I'm telling you, if you don't get out of this line of work,
your father and I will—"

"Love me, anyway," Jeb finished, his tone good-natured. "Come on, Mom. You've delivered the lecture. Liza's had a chance to hear it, so let's move on to other subjects."

His mother sighed and sat in the chair Liza had recently vacated. "Are you really okay, like the doctors said?"

"Yep. A few days rest and I'll be good as new."

His mother glanced at Liza and shrugged, as if to say, *What are we going to do with him?* Liza was amazed at the interchange between mother and son. Jeb was passionately devoted to his job, and his mother was just as passionately opposed to his doing it, yet there had been no fight.

"Before I forget," Jeb's mother said, sliding her arms out of the sleeves of her coat and laying it over the back of the chair. "Steve asked me to give you a message. Before he left the firehouse this morning those two kids you've been working with came by on their way to school. They acted real nervous and made him promise to bring them over here this afternoon to see you."

"Is that right?" Jeb narrowed his eyes. "Very interesting."

"You must have made quite an impression on those boys, if they want to visit you when you're laid up."

"I'm not sure that's it. Thirteen-year-old boys aren't usually very big on hospital visits. There's something more to this."

Liza became curious. "Like what?"

"They may have some information about this fire if kids were involved. God, I hope they do. The warehouse isn't that far from the Madison Hotel, now that I think about it." His blue eyes lit with excitement. "Maybe I'm finally making progress."

The subject of young fire starters made Liza uneasy. Jeb hadn't told his mother about the circumstances of

Denny's birth, but had he mentioned how he'd met this woman he was kissing so passionately a few moments ago? What would the mother of a fire fighter think of a little boy who had played with a cigarette lighter that almost caused a serious fire—a little boy who was suspected of setting a second one?

Liza cleared her throat. "I really must be going," she said. "I'll see you tomorrow, Jeb."

"Get here early, okay?"

"I'll try. Nice to have met you, Mrs. Stratton."

"Call me June. I have a feeling we'll be seeing a lot more of each other. And give that little Denny a hug for me. When this fellow gets back on his feet, you'll have to come over and meet my daughters and their families. Denny would enjoy playing with those kids, I think."

"I— Why, thank you. That sounds nice. Well, goodbye for now." Liza hurried out of the hospital room before Mrs. Stratton—no, June—firmed up the invitation for a specific day.

Liza's safe little world was expanding faster than she liked. She wasn't ready to take Denny and thrust him into the middle of Jeb's family. Denny wasn't used to those sort of gatherings, and neither was she. There were always the questions, asked or implied, about her situation. Was she divorced, or widowed? And in this case, there would be another obvious question. How had she met Jeb?

As she walked rapidly down the bright hospital hallway, Liza imagined how the Stratton clan would respond if she told them the truth. *My son is illegitimate, and I met Jeb when he came to investigate the fire Denny set in his bedroom.* Would they welcome little Denny and his mother quite so readily then? Liza thought not.

CHAPTER FOURTEEN

JEB WAITED IMPATIENTLY for Steve to arrive that afternoon with the two boys. If they cared about him enough to see how he was, that would be fine, but if they had information for him, that would be even better. The chief had dropped by to see him about noon and had provided more details about the warehouse fire. It had been set, all right. The arson crew even found a gas can with some prints on it, but the prints didn't match any on file with the police department.

The torching of the warehouse was an amateur job, the chief had said, and the prints could easily be those of a kid. The chief had expressed his frustration but admitted they couldn't fingerprint every kid in town, not even the suspicious ones like the two Jeb was working with.

Jeb had kept quiet about Mike and Pete's scheduled visit this afternoon because he hadn't wanted the chief to put any pressure on the kids. This was his project, and he would handle it his way. Besides, he'd bet his next paycheck that the prints on the gas can didn't belong to either Mike or Pete. But they might match those of somebody the boys knew.

At three o'clock Jeb pushed the button that brought his bed to a sitting position, and from then on he watched the minutes tick by. What if the boys had changed their minds about coming? How much did they really trust him not to reveal their identity to the ones who'd set the fire? Pete was small for his age, and Mike wasn't any hulk, either. They might be afraid that Jeb couldn't keep their secret, and they'd pay the price in blood.

After glancing at the door a hundred times when he heard some noise in the hall, Jeb was finally rewarded with the sight of Steve, his smile jaunty beneath his waxed mustache.

"Got a couple of kids here who want to make sure you're still alive and kicking," Steve said, shepherding Pete and Mike into the room. "I told them you were too mean to get hurt bad, but they don't know you like I do."

Jeb grinned, hoping to put the boys at ease. "I bet they just wanted to see me in this nightie that ties in the back so they could have a good laugh."

Mike, a dark-haired kid with a Tom Cruise haircut, peered at Jeb. "Boy, your voice sounds like you have laryngitis or something."

"It'll go away in a few days," Jeb said. "Smoke can make your throat a little raw."

"Yeah," Pete agreed. He was of Scandinavian descent, with pale blue eyes and hair that was almost white. "We found that out the day we found half a pack of Marlboros."

"Pete..." Mike gave his friend a warning look.

"It's okay. Jeb's cool. He won't report us or anything."

"Yeah, but..." Mike angled his head slightly in Steve's direction.

Jeb rushed to Steve's defense. "I'd trust that man with my life," he said to the boys, "as well as my secrets. You don't have to worry about Steve."

"Yeah, well, if it's all the same to you," Mike said, glancing cautiously at Steve, "we'd like to talk to you in private."

"I'm outa here," Steve said immediately, without rancor. "When you guys are ready to go home, I'll be right down the hall in that waiting room we passed."

Jeb started to object to his friend's departure and then thought better of it. The boys did have some information, he realized with growing anticipation, and defending Steve's right to be here after he brought them over wasn't the big issue.

After Steve left, Mike walked quietly to the door and closed it. "I don't want anybody hearing us," he announced.

"That's for sure," Pete said. "Nobody knows we're here except you and that Steve guy. And we'll both be in our houses, safe and sound, before our mothers get home from work."

"And we aren't saying anything," Mike added, "until you give us your word you won't—what's that stuff they say on *Moonlighting*?" He turned to Pete.

"'Reveal your sources,'" Pete said. "You have to promise not to reveal your sources."

If the subject hadn't been so serious Jeb would have chuckled, but whether the boys knew the proper terminology or not, this whole business was no laughing matter. "I promise," he said, looking them straight in the eye one at a time. "If anybody asks, we never had this conversation."

Mike glanced at Pete. "What do you think?"

"You know what I think. Jeb almost got himself killed in that fire. Some other guy almost died, too." He clenched both fists. "Those jerks don't even care, either."

Jeb had always known that Pete responded to him more than Mike did. Mike had retained a certain amount of his original chip-on-the-shoulder attitude. Pete had probably talked him into coming here. Jeb crossed his fingers and prayed that Pete's influence would sway Mike, because if it didn't, Pete wouldn't take the heat all by himself.

"Okay," Mike said with a sigh. "Let's tell him."

Jeb sank back against the pillow in relief. Finally.

"We know who set that warehouse fire," Pete said immediately. "Jack Nesbit and—"

"Tony Dulane," Mike interrupted, anxious now to get his share of the story told. "They stole a can of gas from Tony's uncle's garage."

Jeb's heart beat faster. "How do you know?"

"They've been talking about it for weeks," Pete said. "All about how the night watchman gets drunk all the time, and the lock on the back is easy to pick."

"They were right about the night watchman," Jeb said. The memory of the man's breath mixed with the smoke was so fresh he felt nausea rising in him again. He took a drink of water. He wanted to ask why Mike and Pete hadn't told him about the plan to burn the warehouse, but he decided against it.

Pete was watching him, though, and apparently figured out what was going through his mind. "I guess we should have told you, but we didn't think they'd really do it, especially after what happened at the Madison."

"Pete, dammit!" Mike grabbed his friend by the arm. "What'd you go and say that for?"

Jeb tried to keep his voice steady. "You two know anything about the Madison fire?"

"No way, man!" Mike said immediately and looked threateningly at Pete.

Pete gazed down at the floor in misery.

Jeb decided to go for broke. "Listen, guys, you're best friends. You know what it's like to have a best friend. I lost mine in that fire."

Both of them glanced up, and this time the emotion on

their faces was the same shocked sympathy. Then they looked at each other.

"I say we tell him," Pete said. "His best friend. Jeez."

Mike's shoulders sagged. "Maybe then I'd stop having nightmares about it."

Jeb discovered he was trembling. He wanted to know who started the Madison fire, but he didn't want these two to be part of it. Still, he had to ask. "Were you there?"

"No, hell, no," Mike said. "Those guys have always been out of our league. But we heard about it, before and after."

"The same two guys?" Jeb asked carefully.

"Yeah," Pete confirmed, looking at him with both fear and pride that he possessed this information. "The same two."

"Thank you," Jeb said quietly. "Thank you both very much."

Mike stuffed his hands in the pockets of his worn jacket. "I hate to think of what could happen to us if Tony and Jack ever find out we told you this."

Jeb could tell that self-preservation was asserting itself in Mike's mind. "We're going to be very careful about this, Mike. You've got to trust me. I won't use your names, and for this last fire we have an ace in the hole. They left a gas can with fingerprints on it."

"Then you could have found out who they were without us?"

"No, because they don't have a record. Their prints aren't on file anywhere. You've led us in the right direction, but we can handle it from here, and you won't be implicated."

"How about the Madison fire?" Pete asked. "Did you find anything there?"

"Not much. They must have been more careful. But if

we can tie them to the warehouse fire and keep working
away at the other, they'll probably admit it. Or at least
one of them will.''

The boys nodded.

"It's getting late," Pete said, glancing at the wall clock.
"We'd better get home, or we'll have to make up some
story for our mothers."

"Yeah," Mike agreed. "See you later, Jeb." He smiled
faintly. "And the nightie is pretty cute."

"Thanks. Would you send Steve in for just a minute
before you go? I won't keep him long, I promise."

"Okay," Pete said, "if you keep it short and sweet."
He seemed pleased to be able to dictate his terms.

"Right," Jeb said, and wondered what other demands
these two might make on him now that they'd put him
forever in their debt. But he didn't care. He'd buy them
hot fudge sundaes for a month straight if that was what
they wanted.

In a moment Steve came through the door. "I'm not
even going to ask what went on in here," he said.

"Thanks, Steve. I did promise them everything would
be confidential. Look, I know you're probably exhausted,
but..."

"I got a few hours of sleep today. What can I do for
you?"

"Not me really, but Liza. Her club isn't drawing the
crowd it needs. I thought if we got a bunch of the fire
fighters from here and the surrounding towns to go tonight
and take their spouses and friends, it might help."

Steve smiled. "We?"

"Okay, you. I'd call, but my voice isn't holding up too
well."

"I'll take care of everything, buddy. But what will one
night do?"

"It'll give them all some hope down there, for one thing. Besides, the show is good, all my prejudice aside, and maybe some of the people who go tonight will spread the word."

"Especially if I tell them to, right?"

"I think it might work, Steve. The place just needs a little boost and it'll be fine."

"You've been doing lots of deep thinking lying there in that bed, haven't you?"

Jeb chuckled. "Not much else to do."

"You could admire the nurses."

"No interest. None of them are as pretty as Liza."

Steve shook his head in disbelief. "I'd better have a talk with your doctors, old buddy. You are really sick!"

"Get out of here, walrus-face, and take those two boys home before their mommas miss them."

"I'm on my way."

"You're a good friend, Steve."

"Takes one to know one." He gave a mock salute and left the room.

"MOMMY, DON'T WALK SO FAST!" Denny tugged on her hand to make her slow down.

"Sorry." She slowed her pace, but her shoes still clipped rapidly over the high gloss of the hospital corridor tile. The hall was lined with aluminum carts filled with breakfast trays. She hoped Jeb still had his tray in his room. She'd love to smack him in the face with half a grapefruit, just the way Jimmy Cagney had done to Jean Harlow in *The Public Enemy*.

"You're acting all mad, Mommy. Are you mad at me?"

"No, honey."

"Who, then?"

"Never mind. Okay, here's the waiting room, and the television has cartoons on. Sit right here in this chair, and I'll be back before you know it."

"But I want to see Jeb."

"In a minute. I have to talk to him about something first."

"What something?"

"Never mind," she said again. "Please just watch the cartoons, okay? Then in a little bit you can see Jeb, and after that we'll go over to his house and play with the puppies some more."

"Can we stay there all day?"

"Not quite all day, but for a long time."

"Okay!" Denny bounced into the chair she'd pointed out for him. "Hurry up, Mommy."

"Don't worry. This won't take long," she said grimly and continued down the hall to Jeb's room. When she walked in she noticed his color was better than yesterday, his eyes brighter. That was good. She didn't like the idea of chewing out a sick man.

He smiled when she appeared and then glanced past her. "Where's Denny?" His voice had only a trace of hoarseness.

"In the waiting room. You and I have some private business to discuss."

His smile faded. "If you'd said that in a different tone of voice I'd be all excited. What's wrong?"

"I'd like to know," she began, speaking with deceptive calm, "who elected you God?"

"What do you mean?"

"Sending all those fire fighters to Rags and Riches like that! I almost didn't find out what you'd done, but I overheard two men at a table talking about their job and wondered if it was a coincidence that they were fire fighters.

So I started table-hopping and discovered that nearly half the people there were connected with fire stations in the Chicago area. And I'd wipe that smug smile off my face if I were you. I'm not happy about this.''

"Was the place full?"

"It was packed! Or should I say *padded*?"

"What's wrong with that? I thought you wanted bigger crowds?"

"I wanted *real* crowds, not people who came out of a sense of obligation. The worst part is that Dulcie and Bill don't know about this yet. They were so ecstatic that I didn't have the heart to tell them the whole thing had been rigged. I suppose they'll find out tonight, when the club is half-filled as always. Jeb, how could you do this?"

"How could I? Easy. I saw how discouraged you were about the lack of business at the club, and I decided to help.''

"There's that four-letter word again. God save me from your brand of help. We've just about recovered from the situation with the puppies, and now you come up with this!''

"Have you considered that you might be wrong, that the club might be crowded again tonight?'' he said calmly.

"Why? Have you called up all the police precincts, too?''

He chuckled. He shouldn't have, because he could tell it made her more furious, but she was so indignant and protective of her independence that he had to laugh a little. Balancing that chip on her shoulder must take an enormous amount of energy. He wondered how long she'd continue to do it.

"Well?'' Her brown eyes flashed with righteousness.

"No, I haven't called up anyone else. But here's my

theory about Rags and Riches. What you had there, when you opened with the new act, was an ingrown group of people who liked you already. They'd brought in whatever friends would be interested, and you weren't likely to get any new blood from that bunch.''

"Yes, but the flyers—''

"Are a nice, cheap way to advertise that sometimes works and sometimes doesn't. In your case I think people needed a sample of your music, and that doesn't fit on the flyer. I have access to a large group of people—fire fighters—who will do just about anything for someone within their ranks. But any large group might have worked—the Kiwanis, Avon ladies, church members—and there's your new blood.''

Liza shook her head. "I don't know. All those fire fighters could go home, say 'that takes care of that' and never set foot in the club again.''

"Not if you and Bill are good enough. A percentage will come back, and they'll bring other people, not necessarily fire fighters, to show off their new discovery. It can spread like ripples in a pond, if your show is really good.''

Liza took a deep breath. "You're telling me that this is a kind of test, then?''

"Not in my mind. You see, I have no doubt that you're good enough.'' He watched her struggle to accept his faith in her. If she ever truly believed she was worthy of it, her defensiveness would crumble, and the chip would slide right off her shoulder. That wouldn't happen today, however. He could tell that from the conflicting emotions on her face. Eventually she took refuge in a self-protective phrase.

"We'll see,'' she said with almost no inflection in her

voice. "I'd better rescue Denny from the waiting room now."

She returned a few moments later with a restless Denny in tow. Once Jeb convinced the boy that the hospital gown and hospital bed didn't mean that his big fireman friend was really sick, Denny was satisfied with the visit and ready to be off to his puppies.

After they left, Jeb spent most of his day trying to convince the hospital staff to let him out that evening. Tonight would be important for Liza, and he wanted to be there. No one would listen to his pleas. The best his doctor would promise was possible release the next day if he checked out okay when the doctor made his morning rounds.

Jeb was left with a feeling of total helplessness, a feeling that did not make him a happy man. He considered calling Steve and asking him to round up another contingent of fire fighters for tonight's performance. He knew, however, the danger of that move and decided against it. He believed what he'd told Liza, that the show was good enough, but still, the public could sometimes be fickle. If he'd misjudged the situation, and the crowds didn't arrive tonight, he could very well lose her. The thought made him break out in a cold sweat.

He didn't sleep much that night, although he tried to relax and give his body whatever it needed to pass the doctor's exam the next morning. He'd ask Liza to take him home, and no matter what had happened at Rags and Riches, he'd make everything all right again. They'd be together—he, Liza, Denny and the puppies. She'd have to see how good it all was, even if he'd been wrong about how the show would catch on.

Mercifully, the doctor said he could be released as long as he promised not to begin working for another five or six days. Jeb's hand trembled as he dialed Liza's number. If the previous night had been a disaster, she might be angry enough not to pick him up at all. He could always call his parents or Steve, but that wasn't the point. He needed to see Liza today.

She answered the telephone with her usual cool and polite manner. No help there.

"It's me," he said. "They've decided to kick me out of the joint this morning, and I wondered if you might be free to pick me up." He'd decided not to ask about the club. She would tell him, sooner or later, and if he asked it might seem that he'd had doubts, after all.

"Today? Why, uh, sure. Sure thing. Just give me an hour or so, okay?"

"Look, you don't have to dress up or anything. Just come as you are. Denny, too. Will it really take you an hour?"

"At least. I have things to do."

"Oh. Well, yeah, I didn't mean to sound so demanding. I'm just anxious to leave here, I guess. Take your time."

"I'll be there as soon as I can."

He hung up, still not having any clue as to where he stood. She must not be terribly happy with him, though, or she'd postpone whatever chores she had lined up for the day until later. If their positions had been reversed, he wouldn't have taken a whole hour to pick her up.

It turned out to be an hour and fifteen minutes before she arrived, and by that time he had imagined everything from her complete disdain of him to horrible car accidents that had claimed both her and Denny. Once they were ensconced in her Mustang, she allowed Denny to monop-olize the conversation by describing the antics of the pup-pies yesterday.

He realized that she might be unwilling to discuss the

business of the club in front of Denny, so he waited impatiently for the ride to end. Once they got to his place, Denny would be absorbed with the dogs and he and Liza could steal a few moments alone. If she wanted any moments alone, that was.

As the three of them paraded up the walk to his front door, Jeb thought Denny would come apart with excitement. Jeb was surprised; the thrill of the puppies should have worn off a little bit by now, yet Denny behaved as if he were about to see them for the first time.

When Liza opened the front door he understood. He also understood the hour and fifteen minutes. She was a wizard to have created this effect in so short a time.

"Surprise!" yelled Denny, and dragged him by the hand into the room decorated with streamers and balloons. Across one wall was a large sign, written by Liza and embellished by Denny.

Jeb read the sign aloud. "Welcome home to our favorite fireman."

"We have cake, and ice cream, and *everything*," Denny announced. "We had to put Spotty and Freckles outside, though, because they were popping the balloons and playing with the streamers. Want some cake now?"

"Sure. I sure would." Jeb kept glancing from the sign to Liza. "Very nice."

"I promised Denny we'd have a party for you," she said, maintaining her calm exterior as she closed the door. "This was the best we could do on short notice."

"It's wonderful." He hoped to God this wasn't all for Denny's benefit, but he couldn't tell anything from her manner as she carefully took off her coat and hung it in the closet. Finally he could stand it no longer. "Okay, Liza, I have to know. What happened last night at the club?"

CHAPTER FIFTEEN

A SLOW GRIN SPREAD ACROSS Liza's face. She had been savoring her announcement for almost twelve hours. She would have given him the welcome home party in any case, but this made everything so much nicer.

He guessed immediately and his smile answered hers. "The place was full."

"Jammed."

"Standing room only?"

"Hanging from the rafters."

He whooped and grabbed her up in his arms. "I knew it! I just knew it!"

"You did not, you big oaf!" She laughed as he swung her around. "You were scared to death to ask me about the crowd in case your harebrained scheme hadn't worked."

"I wasn't scared. I was waiting for you to tell me."

"Baloney."

"Baloney!" Denny shouted, jumping up and down and clapping his hands. "Baloney, baloney!"

Jeb and Liza looked at each other as they both remembered the little boy was still in the room, and they were in each other's arms.

Jeb set Liza gently on the floor and cleared his throat. "Great news, Liza. Great news."

"Yes." She smoothed the front of her blouse where it had been twisted by their wild romp. "I thought so."

"Well!" Jeb rubbed his hands together and glanced at Denny. "Did I hear something about cake around here?"

"Yeah. It's a cake from the store because Mommy and I didn't have time to bake a real one. Come on." He grabbed Jeb's hand and led him toward the kitchen.

"Gee, it looks like a real one to me," Jeb said, gazing at the chocolate frosted cake. An inscription in white ran across the middle of the cake. It said Happy Birthday, Elmer. Jeb glanced at Liza. "Made the cake purchase in a hurry, huh?"

"I had to take what they had in the way of chocolate cakes at this hour on a Sunday morning. Elmer's cake wasn't picked up yesterday on schedule, so I canceled my order for tomorrow and took Elmer's." She grinned at him. "That's what you get for escaping early."

He gazed at her. "And that smile was one of the reasons I tried so hard."

She met his gaze for a brief moment, but it was enough to send a surge of desire through her that made her weak.

"Hey, you guys, are we gonna cut this cake?"

Liza glanced down at Denny's upturned face. She'd forgotten him again. "Right now, Denny." She put him to work setting the table with napkins and forks, while she served the cake and Jeb put on some coffee. She concentrated on her job instead of Jeb's presence in the kitchen; it was safer that way.

"I don't think I've ever had cake and ice cream in the morning before," Jeb said as they sat down.

"It'll ruin Denny's lunch, but I figured this was a special day."

"It won't ruin my lunch," Denny maintained as he shoveled in another hunk of cake dripping with vanilla ice cream.

"And it *is* a special day," Jeb added. "Rags and Riches

will take off like a rocket after last night. Wait and see. I bet Bill's excited.''

"He and Sharon are already talking about this as a career breakthrough for us. They've promised me that within a year I won't have to tune pianos anymore.''

"Maybe they're right. Maybe you two will become the toast of Chicago.''

"My mommy's not toast!''

Liza glanced at Denny and shook her head. He was lapsing into a silly mood. Then she returned her attention to Jeb. ''Whether I become rich over this or not, at least Dulcie will be able to keep the club if business continues this well. One more weekend of large crowds, and she's promised to call her son and tell him she's definitely not retiring.'' Liza smiled. ''She looked so triumphant when she told me that.''

"I'm sure she feels triumphant.''

"I haven't told her about the fire fighters yet. I haven't told Bill, either. Maybe someday I will, but not yet.''

"What do you mean, Mommy, about the fire fighters?''

"Nothing, Denny. Anyway, I'm very grateful to you, Jeb, and to all of your friends. I'm lucky that you have so many, I guess.''

"I'm glad it helped. Dulcie and Bill are flying high today, I'm sure.''

"I like to fly, Mommy!'' Denny jumped from his chair and ran around the room with his arms out. ''I'm flying high, too. Zoom, zoom! Look at me!''

"I am looking, Denny. Stop running in the house. You're liable to—'' Liza leaped to her feet as one of Jeb's lamps crashed to the floor. ''Denny, look what you've done!''

"It's not broken,'' Jeb said retrieving the lamp from the floor.

"Small wonder." Liza took Denny by the shoulders. "That was careless of you, Denny. Apologize to Jeb."

Denny bit his lip. "Sorry, Jeb."

"That's okay, sport."

"I think it's time you went outside and played with the puppies," Liza said. "Get your jacket."

"Will you come outside with me? Spotty and Freckles want to see you, too."

"Not right now, Denny. In a little while, maybe."

"Then I'll wait till you're ready."

"No, I want you to go out now, before something else gets knocked over."

Denny's shoulders drooped, and he stomped toward the door. "All right!"

"We'll be out in a bit," Jeb called after him as the little boy went outside and closed the door noisily behind him.

"I'm sorry, Jeb. The change in routine must have Denny a little too worked up."

"Don't worry about it." He wrapped her gently in his arms. "He likes to be the center of attention, like most kids his age."

"That's getting difficult for me to arrange." She gazed up at him. "I sometimes forget about Denny when you're around."

"I don't mind."

Liza sighed and relaxed in his arms. "But he does."

"That's because when the two of you are together he's used to having you pretty much to himself."

"I suppose so."

"Which leads into exactly what I wanted to talk about. Mom's invited us over for a family gathering next Saturday. They usually have them on Sundays, but I'm going back to work next Sunday, so they've scheduled around me. I think it would be a perfect way for Denny to start learning to share you and have fun at the same time with the other kids.''

Liza tensed at the suggestion. ''I...I don't think so, Jeb. Denny doesn't socialize all that well, or so his teachers tell me. He's great in a one-on-one, but...''

''So it'll be good practice for him.''

''It's not just Denny, Jeb. I'm not quite ready for your whole family, either. They might ask questions about Denny's father, or how you and I met.''

''They probably won't, but if someone became nosy you could change the subject. You have to handle those things sometime, Liza. You can't hide in your own little charmed circle forever. It's not good for you or Denny.''

''Jeb, don't ask this of me. Not yet. I—''

A crash just outside the back door ended the discussion and sent them both hurrying toward the noise.

''Denny!'' Liza stepped over the box of motor oil cans in front of the door and bent over her son. Blood oozed from a split in his forehead, and he started to cry.

''I'll get a washcloth,'' Jeb said.

''Denny, what happened?'' Liza sat on the cement stoop by the back door and cradled Denny in her lap. ''How did you fall?''

''Spotty...'' he said between sobs. ''Spotty pulled on my shoelace.''

Liza frowned. ''Spotty pulled you over?'' She glanced to a corner of the yard where the puppies cowered in confusion over all the noise.

''I was...on the...box. My head hurts, Mommy.''

''I'm sure it does, sweetheart.''

Jeb squatted next to her with a damp washcloth. ''Let's clean you up, sport, and see what the damage is.''

''I'll do it.'' Liza took the washcloth and dabbed at

Denny's forehead. The gash she revealed made her stomach clench. "Jeb, I think we'd better take him to a doctor."

Denny cried louder. "I don't want to go to the doctor."

"It's a good idea, sport," Jeb said. "We have to make sure that cut heals up just right. I'll drive your car, Liza, so you can hold him."

"Fine."

On the way to the emergency room Liza pieced together what had happened. The top half of Jeb's back door had small panes of glass in it, and Denny had dragged the box of oil cans over to the door so that he could see in. He'd been lonely outside by himself and had wanted to check on the grown-ups who had banished him from their company. While he was peering in, Spotty had upset his balance, and he'd hit the doorknob on his way down.

If she and Jeb had gone outside with Denny when he asked them to, this wouldn't have happened. The message was clear—she couldn't allow her feelings for Jeb to distract her from her job as a mother. She prayed that Denny's injury wasn't serious. At least this incident should end once and for all Jeb's insistence on Saturday's get-together by demonstrating what could happen when she didn't pay close attention to her son.

ON MONDAY LIZA CANCELED her tuning appointments and kept Denny home from school. The cut on his head had required only three stitches, and there were no signs of a concussion, but she wanted to make certain he was okay before sending him out into the world again.

Besides, he'd asked her to stay home, and her guilt over the accident wouldn't allow her to say no. She'd been so wrapped up in talk about her career and the heady feeling of being near Jeb again that she'd slighted Denny. Thank

goodness she and Jeb hadn't been involved in a passionate
embrace while Denny was perched on his box outside the
door.

She didn't call Jeb on Monday, either, although she
thought of him almost constantly. Sunday morning she'd
imagined that her world was almost perfect. The show
seemed destined for success, and Jeb was coming home
from the hospital. While she and Denny worked on the
welcome home party together, her son had bubbled with
happiness. But after what had happened at Jeb's back
door, Liza had to face the fact of Denny's jealousy.

Jeb's solution was to surround Denny with more people, specifically his family members. Liza wasn't about to
expose Denny to a bunch of strangers. Jeb thought her
son would be welcomed with open arms, but Liza could
easily imagine him feeling alone and abandoned among
all those people. He didn't mix well at school; Eric was
about his only friend. Why should the Stratton clan be
any different?

On Tuesday Denny returned to school. Once Liza was
alone in the apartment, all she could think about was Jeb.
An erotic dream the night before had left her aching to
hold him again. No matter how much she disagreed with
him about Denny, she couldn't forget how wonderfully
Jeb had made love to her. If they could keep the matter
of Denny out of their relationship, they had so much joy
to share. She wanted Jeb to know that despite the uncomfortable ending to Sunday's party, she still cared for him.

An hour—one free hour in her schedule that afternoon
tempted her with the possibility of spending it with Jeb.
An hour wasn't much time, she reasoned as she drove to
her first tuning appointment of the day. Jeb might have
plans, anyway. Yet she knew that his doctor had ordered
him to rest at home through the week. Even the frenzied

trip to the emergency room on Sunday hadn't been good for him. He'd coughed several times on the way home.

Maybe a visit from her wouldn't be good for him, either. She remembered how he'd prepared for her the last time, with fresh sheets and a rose in the pillow. She didn't want him to go through all that trouble when he was supposed to rest. Then slowly an idea came to her. She wouldn't call him in advance; she'd just appear. If he was alone, and they made love, she'd be the one in charge. Jeb wouldn't have to do a thing but lie back and enjoy....

At three o'clock that afternoon she rang his doorbell. The red truck was parked at the curb, so she knew that he was home, but when he didn't answer the door right away she worried that he was asleep. As she was debating whether to ring the bell again or leave, he opened the door.

"Liza!"

"I hope I didn't wake you." She gazed into blue eyes that looked anything but sleepy. Still, his hair was tousled and his feet were bare. Two black and white spotted faces peered from behind him and tried to wiggle past his legs.

"You didn't wake me. I wouldn't care if you had, but I wasn't asleep. Come in before these puppies knock me over. I was talking to the chief on the telephone, but I'll get rid of him in a hurry. Can you stay?"

"I have an hour, maybe a little less."

"Then the chief and I will finish our discussion later. Much later." He closed the door behind her and walked quickly to where the telephone sat on an end table beside the couch. The receiver was lying off the hook. He picked it up and covered the mouthpiece with one hand. "Take off your coat," he said to Liza. "Make yourself at home. I won't be long here, I guarantee."

Liza nodded and unbuttoned her warm trench coat. The

puppies were running around her feet, wagging their tails and trying to lick her shoes. But they didn't jump on her. Jeb had already trained them not to. She stooped down to pet them.

"Excuse the interruption, Chief," Jeb said, "but I'm going to have to get back to you in a little while, say an hour or so." He paused and listened. "Yeah, if they've confessed to the warehouse fire I think it's only a matter of time before they admit to the Madison one, too. At least they're locked up in juvenile hall where we don't have to worry about them setting anything right now. I'll think about the line of questioning to use and get back to you."

Liza stopped petting the dogs. So kids had apparently set the warehouse fire that might have claimed Jeb's life. She shivered and stood up.

"Yeah, it's a shame. Even at sixteen they're still pretty young, but that doesn't make Kevin any less dead. Well, so long. I'll call when I've had some time to think about this." He hung up the phone and turned to her. The dogs were still frisking around her feet, hoping for more attention. "Let me put these guys outside," he said. When he went to the back door and called them, both Spotty and Freckles dashed obediently into the chilly autumn air.

"You've done very well with their training, Jeb."

He smiled, evidently pleased. "I want you to have a polite dog when the time comes." He walked back to Liza, but didn't touch her. He was waiting for her signal, she realized.

"I appreciate that." She was still thinking about his telephone call. "Do you think you've found the ones who started the fire that killed your friend?"

Jeb nodded. "Yeah, and they're hardened little criminals already, despite their age. If someone had gotten to them a few years ago... Anyway, that's the point I'm trying to make with the chief. He's listening, but he's got budget problems, like everyone else. Still, I'd like to see some people get paid for what I'm doing. Depending totally on volunteers is tough. Everyone's not a carefree bachelor like me, with lots of free time.''

"I don't quite agree with the carefree part of your description,'' she said, walking over and placing her open palms against his chest. Awareness of her touch flared in his blue eyes. "You care about a lot of things,'' she added softly.

He covered her hands with his, as if to match her motions and not take anything for granted. "I care about one person in particular. I've been thinking about you ever since you left Sunday. How's Denny?''

"I kept him home yesterday.''

"I thought you might. I wanted to call, but I wasn't sure how things stood between us.'' He paused. "I didn't want to 'interfere,' as you phrased it.''

Liza placed her fingers against his lips. "Let's not talk about that now. I've learned a lesson from Sunday. When Denny's around, I have to concentrate on him. But he's not here today.'' She unfastened the top button of his shirt. "So I'm free to concentrate on you.''

He started to say something but apparently decided against it. His smile was slow and sensual. "I hope we have the same definition of the word *concentrate*.''

"If you'll follow me, perhaps we can find out.'' With a lingering caress of his cheek, she moved away and beckoned him as she turned and walked down the hall toward his bedroom.

"Lady, I'd follow you anywhere.''

She crossed the room to the bed and threw back the covers.

"I like this already," he said, coming up behind her and cupping her breasts.

She turned in his arms. "You're leading instead of following, and that's not allowed today. You're still recovering from the fire. The doctor told you to take it easy."

"And I told him I'd take it any way I could get it."

"I'll bet you did," she said with a grin. "Men always have to say that. But today you are going to do as he says, and take it *easy*." She unfastened the second button of his shirt.

"I thought you were in a hurry."

She looked him in the eye. "You let me worry about that." She finished with the buttons and slipped his shirt over his broad shoulders. "You let me worry about everything for the next hour. Can you do that?"

"You seem to doubt it."

"I do, my take-charge fireman." She unzipped his jeans and unhooked the metal button at the waistband. "Can you leave someone else in control?" His faded jeans crumpled to the floor, and she stroked the hardness thrusting against the white cotton of his briefs. "Can you?"

He took a shuddering breath. "Only a fool would say no."

She kissed his muscled chest. "Then lie down. You can watch me undress."

"Watch? I can't help?"

"No, not this time. Lie down, right there."

He complied with her demand, but he kept his blue gaze intently on her as she kicked off her shoes.

That morning when she'd decided to pay him a surprise visit, she'd chosen her skirt and blouse outfit for how easily they came off and her underwear for its sensual value. Slowly she raised her stocking foot and rested it

on the bedside table only inches from his head. Then she
pulled the loose folds of her skirt back and unhooked the
first fastener of the black garter belt holding her sheer
nylons in place.

She glanced at Jeb. "I guessed that you might be an
old-fashioned kind of guy, with old-fashioned fantasies,"
she murmured, unhooking the second fastener and rolling
the stocking gently down her thigh.

"Good guess." He moistened his lips with his tongue
as she peeled the stocking away and put her other foot on
the table. "How about if I do that?" he suggested.

"Not this time. Someday, perhaps." She guided the
second stocking over her smooth leg. His breathing had a
harsh, impatient sound as she removed the length of nylon
and turned to face him. She held his gaze while slowly
unzipping her skirt. Then she allowed it to slither down
and reveal a black garter belt with black bikini panties
underneath.

"God, but you're sexy."

"Am I?" She rounded her eyes in mock innocence and
unbuttoned her blouse. "And here I thought the only thing
that turned you on was the tomboy look of old flannel
shirts."

He caught his breath when she flung away the blouse.
Her black lace bra was made for effect, not comfort, but
the impact on Jeb was worth it. The underwires pushed
her breasts up until they seemed ready to spill over the
shallow cups into the hands of a waiting lover. The look
in his eyes made her flush with pleasure and desire.

His voice grew thick. "You like it, don't you, tempting
me like this?"

"Yes."

"Come here. Please. Let me touch you." He reached
for her, and she moved into his arms. With a groan he

buried his face against the swell of her breasts and pulled her pelvis tight against his. "Tomboy or temptress, you're one hell of a woman."

She nearly forgot her mission as he kissed her heated skin and fumbled with the catch of the bra. The binding material fell away, exposing her breasts to the stimulating caress of his lips and tongue. When he started to remove the garter belt and panties, she realized he'd taken command of the situation and she had to retrieve it.

"Wait," she murmured, rolling him onto his back and pinning his arms to his sides. "This is my show."

"Liza, I want you."

"And you shall have me. On my terms. Lie still."

His skin was salty beneath her lips; his muscles quivered at the pressure of her kisses. She rested her cheek over his heart and listened to its increasing tempo as she raked her fingernails lightly over his chest and across his taut nipples. "Remember what your doctor said," she teased. "Take it easy."

"My doctor's never had anyone like you in bed with him."

She brought her caresses lower, down the valley between his ribs to his flat belly. He gasped as she drew away the briefs and confirmed her intentions with a deliberate touch of her lips. "Two can play this game," she whispered. "I want to give you something to remember me by."

He groaned when she boldly took possession of him. He writhed beneath her, seemingly helpless before the onslaught of physical craving she built in him. She thought her plan would be complete until his fingers dug into her shoulder, and he pulled her up to him as if she were a rag doll.

His voice rasped in his throat. "We'll finish this together." Still holding her with one hand, he reached in the bedside table drawer. "Help me."

She'd tried to put her own needs aside, but his insistence destroyed her willpower. Together they sheathed him, and he tugged away her garter belt and panties. But when he attempted to roll her onto her back, she resisted and slid her knee across his stomach.

"This way," she said, bracing her hands on either side of his head. "This way," she repeated more gently as she took him deep inside her.

He gripped her thighs. "Love me, woman. Please love me hard."

"No. Easy. I'll love you easy." For a few moments she kept her resolution, but his harsh whispers urged her on, and her movements became more frenzied. Like a wave at sea, their passion gained momentum until it crashed in frothy magnificence against the shore, drenching them both in liquid desire.

Afterward she managed to keep her mind floating free, concentrating on nothing but his heartbeat against her cheek. The steady rhythm slowly formed the background for a chant that she gradually distinguished as the only words worth saying anymore. Her lips formed them silently at first, but at last she spoke them aloud.

"I love you."

His arms tightened around her. "What did you say?"

"I love you."

He rolled them over together, still joined. His blue gaze was tender as he studied her face. "And I love you back," he said. "But I think you know that. I think you've known for a while, even if I didn't say it."

"Why didn't you?"

"Didn't want to be pushy. You kept talking about needing time."

"I guess I did need time, but I'm beginning to realize what a precious commodity that is, especially if you love a fireman."

He kissed her gently. "Is that why you're here today?"

"I guess so. Perhaps I'm learning to seize the moment instead of debating endlessly until the moment is gone."

"I'm very glad about that."

"The trouble is, a moment is all we have today. If I don't get into your shower right now and get dressed," she paused for emphasis, "without interruptions—"

"I'll be good. I promise. What can I do to help?"

"Stay out of the bathroom until I've got all my clothes back on."

"Then I have to let you walk out of the house unmolested, when I know that you're wearing that bra and garter belt coyly underneath everything else? You ask a lot, lady."

"Can you do it?"

"Yes. Somehow." He lifted himself reluctantly away from her. "Go on now, while I'm feeling strong. I won't look until you're in the bathroom with the door closed. If I watch you gather all those little sexy scraps that are scattered around this room I may not be able to restrain myself." He lay back and closed his eyes.

She left the bed quickly and picked up her clothes. She was almost out the door when he spoke to her.

"I do love you, Liza. Very much."

She glanced over her bare shoulder and saw that his eyes were open again. She liked the fact that he couldn't keep them closed, that he had to watch her leave the room. "I love you, too. Stay there and rest."

Ten minutes later when she emerged from the bathroom fully dressed she discovered that Jeb hadn't followed her orders. He'd put his clothes on and remade the bed. When she walked into the living room to get the lipstick out of her purse, he was on the floor playing with the puppies.

He glanced up at her. "When can I see you again?"

"Not this week, unfortunately. My schedule's packed tight until Saturday."

"Then let's all go to my folks on Saturday, at least, okay?"

She stared at him in silence as apprehension swept over her. She'd told him that she loved him only minutes ago, and here was this request, the one she'd refused on Sunday. Did he suppose everything had changed, now that she had revealed her love? Worse than that, was he already using his knowledge of her feelings to run her life?

CHAPTER SIXTEEN

LIZA COULDN'T SHAKE THE BELIEF that his suggestion was deliberately timed. She considered her reply carefully. "I think for the time being we should keep the various portions of our lives separate. We can have our private times together, but dragging me and Denny into your family makes everything too complicated right now."

He stopped wrestling with the dogs. "You really aren't willing to go." It wasn't a question.

"Not this soon, no."

"How soon, then?"

"I don't know. Don't push me into this. Please don't. I really have to leave or I'll be late."

He stood up. "Wait a minute. I want to know what the big deal is about Saturday. You've already met my mother, and she isn't some ogre. Neither are the rest of my family members."

"I didn't say they were." She felt cold, so cold.

"Less than half an hour ago we said we loved each other."

There it was, she thought.

"If you love me," he persisted, "why shouldn't my family get to know you, and you them? Or aren't you sure of your feelings for me?"

"Of course I'm sure." She gripped the back of the

chair beside her for support. "That doesn't mean we have to bring other people into it and spoil everything. What's wrong with finding moments like this to be together? Isn't that enough?"

He looked at her in uncomprehending amazement. "No. No, it isn't enough. My God, that's the same attitude you have about Denny, isn't it?"

Panic welled in her. "I don't know what you're talking about, and I don't have time to find out."

"Time? You use it as a weapon, don't you, to keep everything in neat little boxes. To keep *me* in a neat little slot."

"No more than you do, always threatening me that you'll be killed, and we have to make the most of everything now!"

His voice grew quiet. "Now is all we have, Liza. The next moment doesn't exist. Can't you see that?"

She struggled to keep some vestige of composure. "We can't settle anything today. As it is I'm going to be late." She put on her coat and started toward the door.

"Liza, I warn you, don't walk out on this discussion."

She turned. "Why not? Will you stop loving me?"

He shook his head. "No, but it's because I love you that I want you to stay and hear me out. Forget the appointment."

"I need the money. Denny and I will never get that house if I—"

"Do you think a house will solve Denny's problems?"

"Of course it will. He'll have a yard of his own, and we'll have Spotty all the time." At the sound of her name the puppy gamboled over to Liza and wagged her tail expectantly.

"Spotty's only a dog. This whole thing has to do with people."

"Then why in hell did you make such a big deal about getting these puppies?"

"It was a start, okay? I was grasping at anything to get Denny's mind off of fire. It was easier to get a puppy than change his whole life, for God's sake."

"But his whole life needs changing?" A terrible numbness was creeping over her, as if her whole body had been injected with Novocain.

"Yes, dammit! He's set two fires already—"

"You don't know that!"

"Yes, I do, and so do you. And unless the two of you break this closed little circle you live in he's liable to set more."

"I can't imagine what you're talking about. I'm an entertainer, for crying out loud. And Denny goes to school. Two schools, in fact. What's closed about that?" The numbness was complete now, and she'd begun to shake. Jeb had his arguments well marshaled. He must have been preparing them for a long time.

"You've already admitted Denny doesn't have many friends at school."

"He has Eric."

"Yeah, I've heard Eric's name once in a while, but not as often as most boys mention their best friends."

"It'll be different when we get the house." She threw her defenses out like pieces of furniture thrust in the path of an intruder, but he kept coming.

"Will it? And what about you? Sure, you entertain at a nightclub, but do you socialize with the people there?"

"Not the customers, but there's Dulcie, and Bill and

Sharon." The shaking grew worse, and she locked her knees and elbows in an attempt to stay upright.

"Dulcie. Have you ever gone to her house? Maybe taken Denny to spend the day, or invited Dulcie to your apartment?"

"No, but we talk at the club."

"Very controlled. You haven't opened your life up to her, Liza. And all your time with Bill is spent practicing or performing, I'll bet."

"Well, there's Sharon. She and I are planning to go out to lunch soon. Any day now." She had to get out of there. He was attacking her whole way of life.

"Doesn't sound like a close female friendship to me."

"All right, so I don't have any close friends. So I don't have a whole gang of people ready to rally at a moment's notice, like you do. I haven't had time to sit around drinking beer with the guys, or whatever ritual you use for making friends. I've been too busy raising Denny." She could barely hold on to her purse. Where were the tears? Tears would have been a relief, but instead all she could do was shake. "It's a rather large job, taking care of him."

"That's why you shouldn't be doing it alone, Liza! Open your eyes. Denny needs more caring adults in his life. He needs grandparents."

"I've warned you to stay away from that subject."

"I can't do it anymore. Have you thought about what your self-imposed exile from your parents is costing Denny?"

"They wanted me to give him away!"

He reached out for her. "Liza, please—"

"No!" Finally she tapped a wellspring of self-preservation and found the strength to wrench away from his grasp. "You think you know everything, but no one can tell me how to live my life. No one!" She jerked open the door and ran, praying that her rubber legs wouldn't collapse. Her progress was dreamlike, as if in slow motion. Reaching the end of the sidewalk seemed to take forever.

"Liza, wait."

She heard him running barefoot down the sidewalk after her. Then came the sound of the puppies barking happily at the gift of unexpected freedom. As she reached the car she heard Jeb's loud curse as he was forced to chase the dogs instead of her.

Liza opened the car door and glanced back in time to see Jeb carrying two squirming bundles back into the house. Quickly she slid behind the wheel and started the car. The Mustang's tires squealed on the pavement as she pulled away from the curb.

Her last image of him was in her rearview mirror as he stood on the sidewalk, becoming smaller and smaller while he stared helplessly after her. Then she turned the corner and erased him from the mirror, just as she would erase him from her heart. It was over.

BY THAT EVENING LIZA had calmed her hysterics enough to attempt a practice session with Bill. He kept glancing at her trembling hands but didn't say anything. Good old Bill. He didn't push her, or insist she change her life. He didn't think Denny was an arsonist, either.

Denny had been beautifully behaved ever since she'd picked him up from school. His stitches had made him a celebrity with his classmates, and he talked eagerly about his day without noticing his mother's troubled silences. When Bill had arrived he'd put up no argument about playing quietly in his room.

Jeb called about seven-thirty. Before she answered the phone she knew who it would be, and she braced herself. As she picked up the receiver she turned away from Bill and leaned against the wall, but she was still unprepared for the onslaught of conflicting emotions that swelled in her when she heard his voice.

"I don't want to talk to you," she choked out, hating herself for sounding upset, for revealing to Jeb and Bill the state she was in. "We're finished."

"I was afraid you'd say that." He sounded very tired. "Listen, whatever your feelings are right now, don't punish Denny along with me. We need to make arrangements for him to see Spotty."

She was silent for a moment. Damn and double damn. She never should have agreed to the puppy business. Why hadn't she followed her own best judgment in the first place? But Jeb hadn't made that very easy. He'd bowled right past her objections, and now he had custody of Denny's cherished dog, at least until she could buy a house with a yard. "What did you have in mind?" she asked finally.

"If you'll approve it with his school, I'll pick him up tomorrow afternoon and bring him back to your place before bedtime. I can do the same thing on Friday night."

She thought quickly. Bill would be here tomorrow night, so she could avoid being alone with Jeb then. On Friday night she'd be at the club when he brought Denny home. "Okay, I guess we can do it that way."

"Unfortunately I'll be busy on Saturday."

She clenched the receiver. Of course he'd be busy on Saturday. That was the day of the big family gathering, the event that had changed everything between them. She should probably be thankful that the issue had come up so soon, before the power of his personality had overwhelmed all her independence.

"I work Sunday," he continued, "so that cuts out the weekend for me. Of course, you could bring Denny over here anyway."

"I think not." She couldn't imagine spending several hours in rooms where his unspoken presence would be everywhere.

"That means Denny won't see the puppies all weekend, and he's used to spending time with them."

"Denny and I will manage. We've been doing it for five years. Is that all, then?"

"No, that's not all. I realize you don't believe this, but I love you very much."

The shaking started again. "You're right. I don't believe you." She slammed the receiver down and kept her back to Bill until she'd pulled herself together. Finally she walked to the piano bench and sat down. "Let's get to work," she said. "That last section is still a little rough."

"We don't have to finish this tonight. You look really bummed out."

"I want to finish this. I want to make lots of money, and buy that house for Denny, and—oh, God." She wrapped both arms around herself and rocked back and forth on the piano bench.

Bill was beside her immediately. "Hey, hey, now." He put his arm around her quivering shoulders and hugged her. "Want to talk about it?"

Liza shook her head.

"You just want a house."

Liza nodded.

"Then maybe you'd like to consider Dulcie's latest suggestion."

She kept rocking back and forth. It helped to keep moving. "What suggestion?"

"Add another night of entertainment at the club."

"Oh, I don't think so, Bill. You see—"

"Don't be too quick to say no. Another night means more money in the paycheck and more exposure. You'd get that house faster."

"Yes, but another night? What about Denny?"

"Denny's a trouper. He could take it, especially if you explained that it would get him his yard and dog sooner. Besides, if we build this show into something big, you may be able to give up piano tuning. Then you could spend more time with Denny during the day."

"That could be pretty far in the future, Bill."

"Maybe not, maybe not. Hey, what do you say we try it for a few weeks? If you think it's too hard on Denny, or the business isn't coming in the way we'd like, we can always cut back to three nights again."

Liza balanced the extra night of baby-sitting for Denny against the grueling process of dealing with Jeb week after week concerning the puppy. Once she and Denny were in the house, that would be over. Maybe adding a night was worth doing, at least until she had the down payment saved. She was fairly close to having enough, anyway.

She looked at Bill. "What night?"

"Sunday's the logical one. We could start a little earlier, because we'll close earlier. That might attract some senior citizens who don't like to stay out late."

Liza hesitated. Starting earlier meant leaving Denny for a longer part of his awake time. "I have to check with the baby-sitter. When would we start?"

"If you can get your sitter, I say let's do it this Sunday and see what happens. Sort of a trial run."

Liza shrugged. "Okay, why not? If you'd like, I'll call Sue-Ann right now and see if she's free on Sunday."

"Great." Bill smiled at her. "This will work out. You'll see."

In a few minutes Liza returned to the piano bench. "Sue-Ann wasn't available, but her cousin is. She vouched for this girl, and it'll only be for one night. Sue-Ann said she wouldn't mind adding Sunday night and getting the extra money. She just happens to have something scheduled for this week."

"Hey, that's terrific. I tell you, Liza Gayle and Billy Bach are going right to the top."

Liza gazed at him, so young and excited about their musical future. She took a deep breath and tried to match his enthusiasm. "You bet, Billy-boy. You bet."

BECAUSE JEB HAD PICKED Denny up after school on Friday, Liza didn't see her son until Saturday morning, when she was able to gather from his complaints that his celebrity status had worn off at school. He was restless and demanded to know why his mother couldn't take him over to Jeb's house to see his puppy. Determined to distract him, she suggested a visit to the Museum of Natural History.

Sight-seeing with Denny all day and performing that

night drained her of energy. She began to regret agreeing to the Sunday night gig. Sunday had always been a day to relax with Denny or catch up on housework. Knowing she had to work that night threw everything out of sync.

To top it off, Denny expected another full-day's outing, since she wouldn't take him to Jeb's. She compromised by treating him to a McDonald's hamburger for lunch and wondered in the process if she would save money by working extra hours, after all, considering that she seemed to be spending more to keep Denny happy.

And he still wasn't very happy, anyway, she concluded as he sprawled on her bed while she dressed for the club. His questions were asked in a belligerent tone, as if he knew the answers wouldn't be satisfactory.

"Who is this Denise girl?" he asked, rolling back and forth on her bed until the spread was bunched like a relief map.

"She's Sue-Ann's cousin. I'm sure she's very nice."

"Does she know how to play any games?"

"I would imagine she does." Liza carefully applied a second shade of eye shadow.

"I don't like her."

"Denny, you don't even know her. It's only for one night, anyway."

"Why do you have to go to the club tonight?" His voice shifted into a whine that scratched her already lacerated nerves.

"I told you before. I'll work Sunday nights for a while, just a little while, to save up the rest of the down payment on the house. Don't you want to buy our house so that Spotty can be with us all the time?"

"Yeah, but Mommy, why didn't we go see Spotty today? That dog really missed me today."

Be patient, Liza told herself. *Things will get better.* "Jeb is working today, sweetheart."

"He said we could come over anytime, even when he wasn't there. He said that."

Liza suspected that Denny sensed the problem between her and Jeb, but she didn't want to discuss her love life with her son. "I know he would let us go over without him, but we had too much to do today. Remember all the clothes that had to be washed? And we had to run the vacuum and clean the bathroom, too." She finished stroking on mascara and reached for her lipstick.

"I don't care about stupid old cleaning. I want to see my puppy. I want you to take me over there right now."

She turned, the lipstick tube in one hand. "Don't be this way, Denny. You know I can't take you now."

His brown eyes were dark with anger. "Then I'll call Jeb. I'll call him at the fire station."

"You'll do no such thing, young man. Jeb is working. He doesn't have time to talk to you now."

"Why are you so mean?" he demanded. "Why didn't you take me to see Spotty? I was home from school for two days, and I didn't get to see my dog once!"

"Can't you wait? Can't you have a little patience? I'm working as hard as I can to buy a house for us. Then you'll have Spotty every minute, but please stop carrying on about that dog!"

He jumped from the bed and stood before her, his small body rigid. "You're mean, Mommy. Mean and stupid."

She gasped. "Denny! I warned you not to talk that way ever again."

"I don't care. You are. Mean and stupid!" He ran from her room into his and slammed the door behind him.

Liza stormed after him. "That is enough, young man! There will be no television and no games for you tonight. I'll start your bath, and you can get ready for bed right this minute."

Denny scuffed his toe on the carpet and wouldn't look at her. "Don't care. Who wants to play with that stupid Denise, anyway?"

"Fine. Then get ready for your bath."

She finished putting on her makeup while Denny took his bath in record time and dashed back into his room. He was furious with her, but he'd get over it, she told herself. Next week he'd have Sue-Ann back. Liza hadn't realized that he was so attached to Sue-Ann.

Both she and Denny would have to make some sacrifices in order to get their house, she decided, but it would be worth the effort. Maybe when they had the house, she'd invite her parents over for a meal. She'd never done that, not even at Christmas or Denny's birthday, because her apartment hadn't seemed adequate for entertaining her parents.

A house, though, was a different matter. They could come for a Sunday dinner after she and Denny moved in, and she'd cook a roast. Maybe they'd begin a tradition of coming over every Sunday, or alternate between her house and her parents' house.

Liza smiled at the picture she'd created of her parents walking into the living room of her little house and exclaiming over the furniture, which of course would be new. The room would be filled with the combined scents of flowers arranged on a table and the just-bought smell of upholstery and carpeting. Then they'd sit down at her dining table to eat a tender cut of beef and perfectly cooked vegetables, all served on a new set of dishes. Maybe she'd open a bottle of wine, and her father could propose a toast acknowledging that she'd made the right choices in life, after all.

Her reverie was interrupted by the doorbell, and she hurried out to greet the new baby-sitter. She glanced at the wall clock in the living room and realized that she didn't have much time to brief the girl.

"You must be Denise," she said with a welcoming smile.

"That's me."

"Come in and I'll show you where everything is." Liza was glad Denise was a one-time situation. The girl was younger than Sue-Ann. She didn't look much over sixteen. Of course, Sue-Ann had been that age when Liza first hired her, but this girl seemed more juvenile, somehow. Maybe it was the gum or the untied shoes. "The phone's here," Liza said, "and all the emergency numbers are right beside it. That's my number at the club."

"Okay." Denise gave the list of numbers a cursory glance. "Does the TV work?"

"Yes. It's pretty simple." Liza showed her the knobs for on-off and contrast. "You shouldn't have a problem with Denny tonight. He's been instructed to go to bed early. He's, uh, been misbehaving."

Denise shrugged. "Fine."

"I'll at least introduce you to him, but I'm afraid he might not be terribly pleasant." Liza crossed the room and knocked on Denny's door.

After a few seconds Denny opened the door before racing back to hop onto his bed again and glare at them.

"Denny, this is Denise," Liza said. "I hadn't thought about it before, but you two have almost the same name."

Denny responded with a sullen stare. His Mickey Mouse pajama top was buttoned up wrong, and he sat cross-legged on his bed like an angry little frog.

"Denise will be in the living room watching television until I get home. Now climb under the covers."

Denny obeyed her but his expression didn't change.

"Good night, Denny," Liza said. She tried to kiss him, but he pulled away, so she turned out the light and left the room with Denise. "He's not always like this," she explained on the way out.

"It's okay." Denise seemed bored with the entire procedure.

Liza took her coat from the closet and put it on. "I'll be home by eleven."

"Fine." The girl nodded and turned on the television set. She was already curled up on the couch by the time Liza went out the door. Thank goodness this was only for one evening, Liza thought as she hurried down the hall. Next week she'd have Sue-Ann back.

From behind his bedroom door Denny listened as the television came on and the door closed. She'd really left him with this dumb girl he didn't know. His mommy didn't love him at all, or she wouldn't do this. If she loved him she'd have taken him over to see Spotty.

Jeb didn't love him, either. Jeb went to some party on Saturday instead of playing with him and the puppies. On Friday Jeb hadn't asked him once if his head was better. Not once. Jeb didn't care if his head was split wide open.

Denny was mad at them. Mad at them both. He opened his bedroom door slowly and peeked through the crack. There was that dumb old Denise, watching TV. She didn't care about him, either. Nobody did, except Spotty and Freckles, and he couldn't go over to Jeb's now. It was dark, and he couldn't find Jeb's house in the dark.

He watched Denise take something out of her purse. A cigarette. She lit it and tossed the cigarettes and matches on the table beside the couch. It looked like fun, Denny thought. He didn't know anybody who smoked, but Denise seemed to be having a really good time. Maybe he'd play a trick on dumb old Denise.

Slowly he edged out the door and tiptoed across the small space to the table. He was quiet as a mouse. Denise started laughing about the show on TV, and she didn't hear him take the cigarettes and matches. He'd really fool her and go into his mommy's room.

His heart was pounding as he tiptoed across to the other bedroom, where the bedside light was still on. He slipped inside and closed the door almost shut. Then he peeked into the living room again. Denise hadn't moved. She didn't care what he did.

Denny crawled up onto his mommy's bed. The covers smelled the way she did, like flowers. The smell reminded him that she didn't love him. She was mean and she didn't love him anymore. He dumped the cigarettes out like pickup sticks. Then he opened the matchbook.

CHAPTER SEVENTEEN

JEB WAS SITTING AT THE firehouse kitchen table eating beef stew prepared by Steve when the alarm came in. He threw down his spoon and leaped from the table with the rest of the men, not saying a word, but inside his head a voice screamed like a banshee. He knew that address as well as his own. The fire was in Liza's apartment building.

Steve caught the look on his face as they ran on to the apparatus floor and grabbed Jeb's arm. "What is it?"

"Liza's place." He shook his head in an effort to stop the wail of panic in his mind. He had a job to do.

"Maybe it's a false alarm."

"Called in? Not likely."

They looked at each other briefly, not saying what both of them were thinking. *The kid.*

As the ladder truck swung onto the street with sirens screeching, Jeb tried reasoning with his fear. It was Sunday night. Liza was home, and she'd get both of them out. It was early—too early for everyone to be in bed. Liza and Denny would be all right. They would be fine.

The air was still and cold, as if the pavement underneath them was made of dry ice. Anything that got in the way of the water tonight would freeze unless it was right on top of the fire itself. And there was a fire. First Jeb could smell the wood and paint burning, and then he could see it, smoke and flames lighting up a third floor window. Liza's bedroom window. He remembered sitting outside in his truck the day he'd waited for her at lunchtime, and he'd made a point of figuring out which window was hers.

The tenants were huddled on the sidewalk, and Jeb scanned the crowd for Liza and Denny. Their faces weren't among those turned upward to watch in fascinated horror as the fire grew brighter. *God, let them be at the grocery store, or taking in a movie,* he prayed. *Don't let them be in that building.*

The chief was there to meet him as Jeb leaped from the side of the truck, a halligan tool in one hand, his mask in the other.

"Only one tenant unaccounted for," the chief said. "A kid who lives in the apartment where the fire is."

Jeb's stomach began to churn. "I know them. What about his mother?"

"She's out for the evening. The baby-sitter is hysterical. Seems she couldn't find the kid and thought he'd run out here with everyone else."

"He started it!" cried a short, squat woman who ran over to them. Her face was mottled with anger and fear. "That Galloway kid started it, and now he's hiding in the bushes somewhere. Don't go in after that kid. He's not in there. He's run away because he started it!"

Jeb recognized the landlady's voice from their telephone conversations. "I'll check it out," he said to the chief and ignored the short woman shouting at him that he was crazy to go in after the little arsonist.

"Steve will vent the window from the outside," the chief said. "We'll keep looking out here, and I'll signal you on the radio if we find him."

"Same here," Jeb replied and headed for the front door of the apartment building. He pulled on his mask as he went and fought to concentrate on the job as if it were a routine assignment, as if he didn't love the little boy who could be trapped in the fire. He had to keep his head. Denny's life depended on it.

For some reason that he didn't understand Liza had broken her rule about four nights out in a row and had hired a baby-sitter tonight. Jeb easily imagined the scenario. Denny was frustrated at not seeing his puppy all weekend, and then his mother topped it off by going out tonight. Denny made his plea for attention in the only way he knew. It could be the last plea he'd ever make unless Jeb reached him in time.

Jeb forced himself to take the smoky stairs to the third floor at a pace that wouldn't exhaust his air supply. No telling how long his search would take, but at least he knew where to begin. All down the hall of the third floor doors were open, left wide in the residents' haste to flee the burning building. The air reverberated with the squawk of smoke alarms as gray clouds billowed into every apartment. Jeb crouched low, beneath the smoke, and closed each apartment door as he moved down the hall.

As he neared Liza's door he dropped to his knees and crawled under the layer of smoke into the living room. Through the dense haze he could see the flames consuming the furniture in her bedroom, the bed where they had made love. It didn't make sense. He'd expected Denny's room to be the source of the fire. The sound of breaking glass told him Steve was on the ladder outside the window. The smoke lifted just a little as it poured out the opening Steve had made.

He had to check Denny's room first; it was the logical place for Denny to hide. And kids would hide from a fire, dammit, sometimes after they'd been told how dangerous it was in fire prevention programs at school. But little kids got scared, and Denny would be scared for two reasons: the fire and the punishment for starting it.

He pushed his halligan tool under the bed. Nothing. The toy box was another favorite place for kids, but it was stuffed full of trucks and Fisher-Price toys. *Where are you, Denny?* Jeb burrowed into the closet next, flinging aside shoes and stuffed animals until he was satisfied Denny wasn't there.

The radio crackled, and the chief reported that the boy hadn't been found outside yet, but they would continue to search. Jeb felt panic building inside his chest. Was Denny in Liza's room with the fire? Was he—Jeb stopped his train of thought abruptly as he crawled toward the inferno of Liza's bedroom.

Jeb squirmed on his stomach through the doorway. The bed and nightstand were blazing. If Denny had gone under the bed... But he hadn't, Jeb told himself. Her closets were on the far side of the room from the bed. Maybe there.

He inched forward until he reached the bifold closet door. He pushed it back and burrowed into the darkness, squashing her shoes, shoving aside her dresses and slacks with his gloved hand as he tunneled toward the far end.

He thought he heard a whimper and then a cough. He moved forward and touched a leg that jerked away from him.

Denny screamed as Jeb grabbed for him.

"No! Don't eat me!" he cried, wriggling into the far corner of the closet. "No!" He coughed violently.

The overwhelming terror in Denny's scream told Jeb what the little boy believed had happened to him. An evil creature like those in his Saturday morning cartoons had slithered out of the fire and smoke to get him, to punish him for what he had done. In the dark closet Denny heard the deep, mechanical breath of the monster and dimly saw its hideous, snout-nosed face. Jeb reached for him again and he kicked, hard. Denny was fighting for his life.

Jeb unfastened his mask. "Don't be scared, Denny. It's Jeb." The acrid smoke hit his still-raw lungs, and the burning sensation made him want to stop breathing. He reached for Denny again and hauled the quivering boy close to his face. "It's me," he rasped.

Denny's eyes were like huge black coals. His white lips moved but no sound came out.

"Let's get out of here, sport." He took a moment to radio the chief. "Got him," he said when the chief answered. Then he reattached his mask and pulled one of Liza's skirts from its hanger to throw over Denny's head. The little boy clung to him now, wrapping his arms and legs so tight around his rescuer that Jeb had to loosen Denny's grip in order to move.

He put his back to the fire to shield Denny from the intense heat, and he felt the hair on the back of his neck singe where Denny had pulled the collar of his turnout askew. Sweat soaked his uniform as he crawled like a crab from the burning bedroom. Jeb kept them both inches from the floor until they were in the hallway. Then he moved to a crouching position, carrying Denny within the curved protection of his body down the hall and the stairs.

Once they were outside the engine company could put water on the fire, but Jeb knew that not much of Liza's material possessions would be saved. It didn't matter. He had Denny.

He staggered into the glare of the searchlights and heard a wild, inhuman cry of anguish that wrenched his gut. He turned toward the sound and saw her fighting like a tigress with the firemen restraining her from coming through the barricade to her son. But his job was to deliver Denny to the paramedics, not to her.

Denny was whimpering, and with one gloved hand Jeb pulled the skirt away from Denny's face. The cold night air entered Denny's lungs, and he coughed convulsively as Jeb carried him to the waiting stretcher. Before they arrived Denny vomited all over Jeb's turnout coat.

The paramedics pried Denny from his arms, and the boy began crying in loud, wracking sobs. Jeb unfastened his mask so he could talk to him. "It's okay, sport. You'll be fine, just fine. Let them give you some oxygen and cover you up, Denny. You'll be fine."

"Will he?" Liza's grip on his arm could be felt all the way through the heavy canvas of his turnout. "Jeb, will he?"

He put his gloved hand over hers. "Yes. He took in some smoke, but he didn't get burned. They'll keep him overnight for observation, probably."

She didn't reply but moved immediately to the stretcher. She glanced at the paramedic administering oxygen to Denny. "I'm riding to the hospital with you," she said. "I'm his mother."

"Then hop in, lady. We're about ready to roll."

Jeb stood for a minute and watched the ambulance drive away, its red dome light whirling. A short distance down the street the driver turned on the siren. Behind him the engine company was inside the building, putting water on the fire. He could hear the hiss of steam. Soon he and the others of Ladder Company Three would go back in and overhaul the walls and ceilings. They'd pry loose the burned wood and plaster to make certain no sparks remained that could start a second fire.

Eddie and Jack were directing a stream of water on an adjacent apartment building to guarantee that the fire wouldn't spread. Jeb thought of standing near the spray to wash the vomit from his coat, but it was too cold. He'd end up looking like Eddie, who was holding the nozzle. Already Eddie's helmet was covered with icicles, and his gloves were frozen solid. Jeb decided to clean up when he got back to the firehouse.

He glanced around at the mayhem—hoses littering the street like spaghetti, lights flashing, people in various stages of undress huddled together against the cold. At least nobody had been killed this time. He thought about Liza, and the way she'd screamed when he'd come out of the building carrying Denny. He thought of all the times he'd tried to tell her what could happen. *Would she listen now?*

NEARLY THREE HOURS LATER he sat in the firehouse kitchen drinking coffee with Steve. Neither of them was saying much. They couldn't talk about this fire the way they discussed most jobs. Jeb was too closely involved with this one.

Instead Steve picked a related subject. "When will those boys be sentenced, the ones who finally admitted to the Madison fire?"

"Next week, I think." Jeb sipped his coffee. "You know, before I met them I was ready to have them rot in jail forever, even if they are only sixteen. But now I wonder if there's something to save."

"Don't forget they killed a fireman. Worse than that, they went out and started another fire, when they knew the consequences."

"Yeah, but a guy hired them to torch the warehouse. That's the sentence I'm waiting for. He's as bad as a drug dealer, teaching kids to start fires for profit. At least they gave the police that slimeball's name. Now him I could do physical damage to if I had the chance."

"Yeah." Steve got up for a refill. "Me, too."

"He's being tried for first-degree murder, so that will get him a few years. I—"

Aaron poked his head into the kitchen. "Lady here to see you, Jeb."

Steve glanced around and raised an eyebrow at Jeb. "It's about time. You saved her kid's life, after all, and she took off for the hospital without a word."

"I understood that," Jeb said, getting up from the table. "She was totally involved in Denny and his welfare. Besides, we're not in this business to win medals."

"Damn, and I thought that was the whole idea." Steve grinned. "Well, go collect your gratitude, anyway, buddy."

Jeb walked out of the kitchen and saw her standing on the apparatus floor. The chief must have let her in. Then she'd come looking for him and bumped into Aaron on the way. Jeb walked toward her, his footsteps echoing on the cement floor.

She had on as much makeup as she wore when she performed, and it was hopelessly smudged around her eyes where she'd been crying. He wondered again where she'd been tonight when the fire broke out. She stood in her trench coat and clasped her hands in front of her like a supplicant.

"Hello, Liza," he said gently.

"I...I don't know how to say this," she began in a voice that was hoarse and weak. "I wouldn't listen to you. Because of that, I almost..." She closed her eyes and forged ahead with a bravery that astonished him. "I almost killed him, and maybe others, too."

He didn't touch her, afraid that he might disturb the delicate balance that kept her from becoming hysterical. She wouldn't want to break down here, in the middle of the firehouse. "This isn't the way I like to make a point," he said, shifting his weight and putting both hands in his pockets. "Believe me, I'd rather have been wrong about this."

"You weren't." She gazed at him steadily. "Denny's already admitted to playing with matches on my bed tonight."

"I know it's none of my business, but I thought you had something against baby-sitters on Sunday night."

She looked away. "The club is doing so well that Bill and Dulcie wanted to try adding another night of entertainment. I wasn't planning to do it very long, only until I got the money for the house...." She glanced up with a grim smile. "Now, of course, the landlady plans to sue me, Denny will require counseling, and I'll need new furniture. So much for my savings account. Not that it matters. Denny's alive. That's all I care about.''

"What about insurance?"

She shook her head. "I didn't bother with it. Thought it was a waste of money." She didn't flinch as she delivered her carefully chosen lines. "Some of us have to learn the hard way. I'm deeply sorry, Jeb."

God, she's brave, he thought. "You'll need a place to stay," he said. "At least for tonight."

She looked surprised. "Funny, but I hadn't even considered that. But I'm going back to the hospital. I'll be there tonight with Denny. Tomorrow I'll figure out something."

"You can stay at my place temporarily."

"No."

Her refusal cut deep. She would apologize, but she didn't have to like him for being right. He remembered reading somewhere that in Ancient Greece the bearer of bad news was killed. In this case, he'd been the bearer of bad news about her son, and it had killed her love for him. "Then what will you do?" he asked, still caring about her welfare, still loving her, despite everything.

"Stay in a hotel for a while, I guess."

"For God's sake, call your parents."

She gazed at him in disbelief. "I can't possibly do that. Do you think I want them to know that their grandson started a fire?"

"They'll find out, Liza, from the papers, probably." His control began to slip. He was going to say something he'd be sorry for later. He could feel it coming.

"Then let them find out by themselves. I'm not about

to rush to them and deliver Denny up like a lamb to slaughter.''

Once again, he spoke in a patient tone. He had a little forbearance left, but not much. ''I don't think it would be that way. Liza, it would be better if you told them and asked for help before they find out through the newspapers. That would really hurt them if they read it with their morning coffee.''

Her eyes narrowed. ''You never quit, do you? You can't resist meddling in my life for a second, can you? I came here to thank you for saving Denny's life, but you make that very difficult to do, Jeb.''

That was it. He'd had it. ''Dammit, Liza, haven't you learned anything at all? Haven't you blamed your parents long enough for a decision they thought was in your best interests at the time? Denny needs them now, and so do you, no matter how hotly you deny it!''

He noticed that her face had lost all color, but he couldn't stop himself. He'd kept his anger bottled up too long. ''Think about what happened tonight, and why it happened. Then tell me you can't go to your parents out of some stupid sense of pride. You once accused them of wanting to give him away. What are you trying to do, keep him wrapped up so tight, be so overprotective that he suffocates? Are you trying to kill that little boy, Liza?''

She weaved a little, and he poised himself to catch her if she should faint. She opened her mouth to answer him, but nothing came out.

''Call them, Liza. You've got to let them close to their grandson, for his sake and theirs. For yours, too! Don't keep yourself in this poisoned atmosphere.''

"But don't you see?" she whispered. "I'll be admitting to them that I've failed."

"You haven't failed. This isn't about failure. It's about mistakes, and growth. Call them."

Her lips quivered. "You don't know what you're asking."

"Maybe not, but you have courage. I've seen it. Use that courage to call them."

"I can't, Jeb. I just can't." She whirled and fled, running back the way she'd come, through the office and out into the night.

Jeb realized that every muscle in his body was tense, and he was breathing as if he'd just climbed four flights of stairs. She wasn't going to do it. She was brave, but not that brave. He wondered what sort of rigid expectations her parents had held up for her, that she was so deathly afraid of their disapproval.

Instinct told him that her parents wanted to make amends. He'd watched their faces during her first performance of the new show. They were totally absorbed in her, love and pride shining from their eyes. He'd seen that expression on his own parents' faces when he made the all-star team in Little League, and gave the class speech at high school graduation, and even when he walked into their house for the first time wearing his fire fighter's uniform.

Jeb knew love when he saw it. He knew yearning, too, and Liza's parents had both emotions written all over them that night at Rags and Riches. Liza wouldn't believe him, of course. She insisted on her own script, and it would take something major to change her mind. Maybe it was up to him to create something major.

His relationship with her was shot to hell. No doubt about that. She couldn't forgive him for being witness to her mistakes, and she'd been taught that mistakes weren't allowed. So what did he have to lose? He might as well put the final nail in his coffin and at least give her a chance to straighten out her life.

He walked into the main office and found a telephone book. After locating the number, he picked up the receiver of the desk phone and dialed. He waited impatiently until he got an answer, and then he cleared his throat. ''Mr. Galloway? Yes, I know it's late, and I'm sorry if I got you out of bed. Listen, you don't know me. My name is Jeb Stratton and I'm a friend of Liza's.'' He paused. ''Liza doesn't know I'm calling you, but something happened tonight, and I think you and your wife have a right to know about it.''

BY THE TIME SHE REACHED the hospital Liza had stopped shaking. Couldn't Jeb understand that her parents were the last people in the world she wanted to see now? There would be another scene, similar to the one that took place when she had announced her pregnancy and her decision to keep the baby. Her parents would want to assume all care of Denny. They might even take the matter to court and try to obtain custody.

The story of the fire would be in the paper, and she might have to face all those actions of her parents anyway, but why hasten the process by calling them now? That would only reveal her weakness and encourage them to be more forceful in their demands.

As Liza walked down the hall toward Denny's room someone called her name. She turned and saw Bill, Sharon and Dulcie getting up from the chairs in the waiting room, and her eyes filled with the tears she hadn't allowed herself in front of Jeb.

The three of them surrounded her, enfolding her in a nest of comfort that felt so good she started bawling like a baby.

"Everything's gonna be fine, honey," Dulcie crooned, rubbing Liza's back.

"We came as soon as we got the place emptied out," Bill added. "The nurse said you took a cab back to get your car. I wish we'd known. We could have done that for you."

"It doesn't matter." Liza found a tissue in her purse and blew her nose. "I...I had something I had to do on the way back, anyway."

Bill looked older, more careworn. "I feel so responsible, Liza. I'm the one who talked you into this Sunday night gig."

"It's not your fault, Bill. You had no idea Denny was so troubled."

"Oh, he'll be okay," Dulcie said, squeezing Liza's arm. "We'll cancel the Sunday night entertainment for a while, and you can spend more time with him. The club will be fine with three nights. We got a little greedy, I guess."

Liza swallowed. "I'm not sure that spending more time with me will help Denny." She surprised herself by admitting that, but Dulcie's attitude, which minimized Denny's problem, didn't sit right with Liza. Jeb's evaluation of the situation had been hard to accept, but had she listened to him earlier, none of this would have happened.

Still, she couldn't blame Dulcie and Bill for not seeing

things as they were. She hadn't allowed them to. Jeb was trained to look at Denny in a certain way; they weren't.

"Listen, we've talked it over, Bill and I," Sharon said, "and you and Denny are welcome to stay with us for as long as you need to get settled again."

"Or me," Dulcie added. "I've got room unless my son comes to visit, and I'll tell him to get lost for a while. I wouldn't mind doing that anyway, after the way he tried to sweet-talk me into early retirement."

"That's really generous of you, all of you." Liza gazed at them and realized she wouldn't feel comfortable sharing living quarters with Dulcie or Bill and Sharon. She simply didn't know them well enough. But the fact that they'd offered was wonderful. "I haven't decided what would be the best thing to do, and I don't want to move too quickly. But thank you so much for thinking of me."

All three of them, she realized, looked more relaxed. The offer had been made and kindly rejected. They didn't really want her problems, but they couldn't turn their backs on her, either. They were good people.

Liza touched Dulcie's arm. "And don't be too hard on your son. I'm sure he wanted what he thought was best for you. He was acting out of love."

"But couldn't he see that losing the club would kill me?"

"Maybe not," Liza said slowly, no longer thinking about Dulcie's son. Instead she was in the living room of her parents' home five long years ago. "Just because someone loves you doesn't mean they understand everything about you."

"Pretty heavy philosophy, there, Liza Gayle," Bill said playfully. "Think I could make a hit song out of it?"

Liza smiled at him. "I think you could make a hit song out of a grocery list."

"As long as I have you to help sing it. You're not going to let this thing with Denny stop you from performing, are you?"

Liza glanced at him. Of course he was worried about the future of the act. So were Sharon and Dulcie. Their first impulse in coming here tonight was to give her support, but they also needed to know that their newfound lease on life hadn't suddenly been canceled by a little boy with a book of matches.

"This would be kind of a bad time to take a break, with the customers coming in so regular, and all," Dulcie added.

"No, I don't plan to take a break," Liza said and could almost hear the sighs of relief. "That might encourage Denny to think that setting fires worked to keep me home. If I thought staying home would help Denny, I'd do it in a minute, but I can't believe that's the answer."

"That sounds like sensible talk to me, honey," Dulcie said.

"I'm surprised if I have anything sensible left in me. It's getting late, you guys. Why don't you go on home, and I'll go curl up in a chair in Denny's room. I'll call you tomorrow and let you know what's happening." She hugged each one of them. "And thank you for being such good friends."

"Anytime," Bill said. "And don't forget that we'd be glad to have you."

"I won't forget. Good-bye. You're all terrific."

And they were, Liza decided, watching them walk down the hall away from her. She vowed to become better friends with all three of them. She'd have lunch with Sharon and invite Dulcie over some evening. Dulcie had never met Denny. Dulcie would like her little apartment, and they could— Liza stopped imagining as she remembered. She had no apartment anymore. No clothes, no furniture, no piano. What was she going to do?

Quietly she entered Denny's room and settled herself into a chair to watch him sleep. The metal sides were up on the hospital bed, reminding her of the crib he used to have. Tears filled her eyes as she remembered Denny as a baby, round and always smiling. How had they come to this, that he had almost burned down an entire building because he was angry with her?

In the bed next to Denny's was a little boy who'd had his tonsils out. His side of the room was cluttered with stuffed animals and a bouquet of helium balloons. His parents had left for the night, secure in their son's knowledge of their love for him. All of Denny's stuffed animals were ruined, lying no doubt in piles of soggy debris from the fire he had caused.

The sliver of light from the door into the hallway widened, and she turned, expecting a nurse or doctor to come into the room. The two people standing there were silhouetted against the bright light, and Liza experienced a moment of unreality, as if she'd traveled backward in time to an era when these same two figures paused in her bedroom doorway every night to wish her sweet dreams.

She rubbed her eyes, confused by their sudden appearance. Perhaps she'd fallen asleep and the figures weren't real. Yet she spoke to them all the same. "Mom? Dad?"

CHAPTER EIGHTEEN

"SHH," LIZA'S MOTHER SAID. "Don't wake Denny."

Liza remembered the voice as if she'd heard it yesterday, that gentle, conspiratorial tone her mother had used so often years ago to whisper "don't wake your little sister," when Liza and Helen had shared a room. As the older one, Liza had been allowed later bedtimes and shorter naps. Once upon a time she'd felt privileged, special. No more.

"Come out in the hall where we can talk," her mother said softly.

Liza obeyed, still not sure whether she was awake or asleep. She blinked in the bright lights of the hallway. "How did you—"

"Never mind that now," her father said. "How's Denny?"

She looked up at him looming over her in the intimidating way he had ever since she could remember, and all her old fears returned. This was real, all right. After hearing all the facts, her parents might decide she was an unfit mother and take Denny away from her.

"He's just fine, Dad," she said tonelessly. She wondered how to fight them. Maybe after they'd left tonight she should take Denny out of the hospital and run away. They'd never find her. "He seems to be sleeping well."

Her father nodded, and the creases of concern on his forehead relaxed. "Good, good. He needs to sleep, poor little guy."

"We came as soon as we could," her mother said. "You look so tired, dear."

"I'm fine, Mom." She took a closer look at her usually well-groomed parents and was surprised at how disheveled they were. Her mother had no makeup on except a dash of lipstick, and her father's coat collar was sticking up on one side. He hadn't combed the longer strands of hair over his bald spot, and her mother's hair was flattened where she'd evidently been sleeping on it. They both looked as if they'd gotten out of bed, thrown on their clothes and raced over to the hospital.

"Let's go to the lounge," her father suggested, stepping between the two woman and putting a hand at each of their backs. "I'll get us some coffee."

"Coffee would be wonderful, Curtis. I'm not quite awake yet."

"Liza?"

"Yes, thanks." Liza decided not to be lulled by her parents' rumpled appearance. She'd still need her wits about her when she dealt with them tonight, and a dose of caffeine might help. She had a good idea how they'd found out that she was here, and she didn't like it, not one bit.

Her father started to walk away, but then he turned back. "Do you still like cream in your coffee, Liza?"

"No, I take it black now." She found satisfaction in being different from how he remembered her.

"Three black coffees, coming up."

Liza's mother watched him head off for the vending

machine. "He looks so in control of himself, but he nearly came apart when he heard about this. He was in tears."

"Tears?" Liza stared at her mother, who had never revealed any vulnerability, either hers or his. "I would have thought he'd stomp around the house and yell."

"No. A few years ago he might have, but—"

"Here you are, ladies. Good thing I majored in waiting tables while I was in college."

Liza felt an unwanted tug at her heart. She'd forgotten this little source of pride her father had in his serving expertise. In a ritual to impress his daughters he used to balance three or four plates at a time, and he'd always deliver the same tired old line. Liza used to groan when she heard it, but now it reminded her painfully of her childhood, when she had been loved. "Thanks, Dad."

She looked at him and tried to imagine him crying. She couldn't do it. Maybe her mother had mistaken allergies for tears. She sat down on a chair, leaving the couch, which was at right angles with it, for her parents.

"No, let's all sit here," her father suggested, taking her elbow.

Before she could protest, he had her boxed in between him and her mother. Obviously she had to stay on her guard. He was already starting to push her around, tears or no tears.

"So," he began in his typical businesslike manner, "how bad is the damage to your apartment?"

"First I think you'd better tell me who called you to-night. I think I know, but it's important to me to be sure."

Her father looked her straight in the eye. "Jeb Stratton, your fireman friend."

She clenched her hands around the Styrofoam coffee cup. "He's not my friend, and he had no right to do that."

Her parents exchanged glances as if they had expected her response. The look between them angered Liza even more. Was she so predictable? Had they discussed how to "manage" her after she got upset?

"Okay, I agree," her father said. "He didn't have that right."

Liza nearly spilled her coffee in her surprise. "You agree with me?"

"Yes, I do," he said quietly. "But I understand perfectly why he made that call, and I hope someday you'll forgive him for making it."

"I'm sure you do understand. You would have done the same thing in his place."

"Yes."

"You see? I—"

"And I would have been wrong," he added.

Liza stared at him in confusion.

"You see, Liza, sometimes people do the wrong things for the right reasons." Her father put his coffee cup on the low table in front of him and leaned toward her. "I'm convinced that man loves you very much."

The contents of Liza's coffee cup sloshed in her trembling hand, and she put the cup on the table before she spilled it all over herself. "I don't understand that kind of love."

"Don't you? What if Denny begged you to let him try hang gliding? Would you encourage him to try it?"

"Of course not."

"Why?"

"Because he's too young, and he'd surely be hurt,

maybe even killed. I have…" She paused and swallowed. "I have a responsibility to keep him safe." The knowledge of what had happened tonight had turned her statement into an accusation, and she waited for her father to chastise her for not keeping Denny safe.

He didn't. "Is it also because you love him?" he asked gently.

"Yes." Tears blurred her view of her father.

"Liza, Jeb Stratton called us because he wanted you to be safe. Safe with us, not in some hotel room alone."

"I…I can manage." The claim sounded ridiculous, even to her, but her father didn't attack her on that point, either.

"We know you can," he agreed. "And maybe…maybe you don't want to stay with us, because of…" He glanced away from her and swallowed.

Liza gazed at him in wonder as tears dripped down her cheeks. She'd never known him to hesitate or show intense emotion.

When he looked back at her his eyes were wet. "Liza, I hope you can forgive us, too, your mother and me, for telling you to…put Denny up for adoption."

A sob welled up inside her, and she put her hand to her mouth. After all these years.

Her mother placed a hand on her knee. "I know we've hurt you, sweetheart. We've hurt all of us." Her voice trembled. "We made a mistake. After living with you for twenty years we should have realized that you couldn't give away your own child. Lord knows we didn't want to lose a grandchild, either, but…" She made a small choking sound and turned away to fumble in her purse.

"But we thought," her father continued in a husky

voice while his wife dabbed at her eyes, "and we were wrong, dead wrong—we thought that it would be best for you to be free of the responsibilities of a child when you were still so young. We acted out of love."

Tears coursed down Liza's cheeks. "Maybe you were right. Look what's happened."

"Whatever's happened, we share the blame." He glanced at his wife and his voice shook. "But let's stop placing blame and start loving each other."

Liza's control dissolved. "I've…missed you so much," she cried, sobbing.

"We've missed you, too, sweetheart," her mother said, crying openly and pressing her damp cheek against Liza's.

"But it's over now," her father said. He gathered them both into one embrace. "We're going to be a family again."

"I can hardly wait to be a grandma," her mother said brokenly. "A real grandma who— Oh, dear, I promised myself I wouldn't be a leaky faucet about all this."

"It's okay, Mom," Liza said, laughing and crying at the same time. "We're only human around here."

THE NEXT MORNING LIZA sat in a chair beside Denny's bed while he ate his breakfast.

"This cereal isn't as good as yours, Mommy," he said, glancing shyly at her. He'd been very subdued ever since he'd woken up and had tried to say things that he thought would please her.

"I want you to eat it all, anyway, Denny."

"I will." He spooned more cereal into his mouth. "Can I go home today?"

"We'll see when the doctor gets here and checks you."

She shifted in her seat. Last night both she and Denny had been upset and hadn't talked about the fire except for his admission that he'd been playing with Denise's cigarettes and matches. Weeks ago Liza might have blamed Denise for what happened, but no more. The responsibility lay with her and with Denny, and they would face it together. Liza smiled. With the help of some friends.

"I hope I can go home," Denny said. "I don't like it here. It smells funny."

Liza decided the time had come to be straight with Denny. He couldn't be protected from the consequences of what he'd done. "We're not going back to the apartment, Denny. Everything we had there is...gone."

His eyes widened. "Gone?" he whispered. "Even my toys?"

"Yes."

"Even my fuzzy bear?"

"Yes."

"And my—" his chin trembled "—my Mickey Mouse quilt?"

"I'm afraid so, Denny." She pushed the breakfast table away so that she could sit on the bed and comfort him. "Fire is terrible. But it didn't take away the most important thing of all, thanks to Jeb. He saved you, and that's all I care about."

Denny climbed into her lap, and she held him tight. She could never repay Jeb for the gift of this little boy. Without Jeb she could be dealing with unspeakable tragedy this morning instead of holding her son.

"Mommy, will I ever have toys again?"

"Yes, but don't expect a chestful, all at once." She held him away from her and looked into his brown eyes, so much like hers. "A new toy, once in a while, will be given to a boy who is very, very good. Do you understand?"

Denny nodded solemnly.

"Things are going to be different—our life will be different. For a while we'll be living with Grandpa and Grandma."

"You like them now?"

Liza was shocked that he'd been so aware of her anger toward her parents. "Yes, I like them now. And I've always loved them, just as they've always loved me, and I will always love you."

"Even if I'm a bad boy?"

She didn't contradict him. "Yes, even then."

He heaved a long, shaky sigh of relief. "That's good."

She hugged him close. "Yes, it is."

FOR THE NEXT FEW DAYS Liza was busy with the endless details that follow any serious loss, but through all the necessary shopping and paperwork and newfound relationship with her parents ran a thread of longing for the man who had been the catalyst for all this change. Liza's feelings for Jeb were a jumble of passion and anger, resentment and regret. Each day brought a new sifting and sorting of her emotions for him.

If she was unsure of her own feelings, she imagined that he was equally confused. There had been no mistaking the fury in his last words to her. So much had passed between them that she wondered if it wouldn't be better to forget all about Jeb Stratton. And he might be thinking the same thing about her.

But she couldn't forget him. Every fire siren reminded

her of the danger he'd taken on willingly to save Denny, and the dangers he'd continue to face for others menaced by fire. She nearly went crazy wondering after each of his tours of duty if he'd escaped unscathed. She wished there could be some way to keep track of his welfare, to know at the beginning of each day that he was alive and well.

She figured out that the pain of not knowing, of being disconnected from him, had something to do with love. She was learning a lot about love these days and the power it had to melt years of misunderstanding. Could it also overcome the hurt that she and Jeb had inflicted on each other?

Liza was more than a little afraid of the answer, so she took the coward's way out and waited for a legitimate excuse to see Jeb. Even then she sent him a note rather than calling. She hadn't wanted to hear the rejection in his voice if he didn't want to see her.

His reply came in writing, as well. She read the short message dozens of times, fascinated by the neatly printed words, all in capital letters. She realized that she'd never had reason to see his handwriting, and yet she would have recognized his bold, precise personality in it. He would be home, he said in the note, on the morning that she indicated. He'd signed it ALWAYS, JEB.

She smiled at his choice of closings. Yes, he was always Jeb. Always strong, always bossy, always passionate and most of all, always in her thoughts. Would she have a chance to tell him so, or would they part with polite, empty phrases and never see each other again? After this last trip to his house, she would have no more excuses to contact him.

She thought a lot about what to wear. She would have

preferred something old, something ordinary, so as not to
signal that she placed importance on the meeting, but all
of her clothes were new. Finally she settled on jeans and
one of the oversize flannel shirts she'd bought on sale at
a discount store. Her original supply had come, one by
one, from her father's castoffs, but he'd told her recently
that he'd quit buying them when she left home because
they made him sad.

When Liza had bought a shirt for herself, she'd bought
several to give her father for Christmas. So many things
seemed obvious to her now—the coat she'd continued to
wear because it reminded her of her mother, the shirts that
were her favorites because they'd belonged to her dad. In
many small ways she'd tried to keep her parents near,
even as she had pushed them away.

On the morning she was to see Jeb, Liza drove Denny
to school without telling him of her plans. If she had confided in Denny, he would have insisted on skipping school
to go with her, and Liza wanted to be alone with Jeb. She
was frightened at the prospect of meeting him without the
protection of Denny's presence, but she knew that meeting alone was the only way true feelings would emerge.
She had to know the truth. Did he still love her?

The day was warm for the middle of November, and
Liza had to remind herself that the first snowfall and the
worst of an Illinois winter were still ahead of them. Instead it felt like spring.

She tried not to get her hopes up as she drove to Jeb's
house, but the warm weather and blue sky seemed like
good omens. The prospect of seeing him again after nearly
two weeks of no contact made her alternately giddy with
excitement and shake with dread. Would they fight? Or

worse yet, would they have nothing to say to each other? If he behaved with cool indifference, she wouldn't have the courage to tell him all the things she was feeling.

He answered the door in jeans and a sweatshirt with the fire department logo on the front. For a moment they stood looking at each other without speaking. She searched his expression for some hint of his reaction to her. Was that glitter in his blue eyes passion or anger? He didn't smile. Was that because he barely tolerated her presence or because he was completely absorbed in her?

"So you're ready for the puppy," he said, standing away from the door so that she could come in.

"Yes. We're staying with my parents until...until I get a place. They have a big yard."

He nodded and closed the door behind her. "I wondered if that was where you were. I checked the return address on your note with the telephone book."

She was encouraged by that small act of curiosity. "Denny seems very happy there. My mother's spoiling him rotten, baking cookies and taking him to the movies. Dad bought him a baseball mitt, and they play catch in the backyard every afternoon after work."

"That sounds nice, Liza." He put his hands in his pockets and watched her.

"It is nice." She stood there awkwardly, not knowing whether to take off her coat. "Where are the dogs?"

He tilted his head toward the back door. "In the yard. Want me to get Spotty so you can be on your way?"

"No! I mean...unless you have something that you have to—"

"All you said in the note was that you were coming for the dog. I figured—"

"What did you expect me to say?" She gulped and rushed on. "That I'm madly in love with you and can't get you out of my mind?"

Pain flashed momentarily in his blue eyes. "No, of course not."

Liza debated whether to respond to his words or the brief intense emotion she'd seen in his eyes. Then she remembered that today was her last chance. She was out of time. "I am, you know."

His careful mask of indifference slipped away, and he gazed at her intently. His voice softened. "Is that a fact?"

"Yes." Warmth surged through her. "And in spite of loving you I've behaved like a fool."

"True. And in spite of loving you I've behaved like a steamroller."

"True." She swallowed. "What do you think we should do about it?"

"We might give some thought to forgiving each other."

"I've already done that, Jeb. Days ago."

He raised an eyebrow. "Took you that long, huh?"

"Jeb…"

He grinned and held out his arms. "Come here, you crazy woman. We're wasting time."

They made love without pretense, without games. The knowledge they'd gained of each other's bodies mattered less than what they'd learned about each other's spirit. This time there was no leader, no follower, but two people journeying together down a single path.

As she moved beneath Jeb's heat and welcomed him inside her, she lost track of the boundaries between them. His breath became hers; his heartbeat became hers. At the flashpoint of their passion, when their cries of love mingled to a single note of ecstasy, she slipped inside his soul.

Afterward, he gazed into her eyes, and his voice was filled with awe. "I thought I knew what loving you was all about, but I didn't have a clue."

"How could you, with all those walls I'd built?"

He caressed her cheek. "The walls are down now."

"Thanks to you. My steamroller."

"I thought I cooked my goose forever when I called your father."

"It could have turned out pretty horrible, you know, if my parents had still been into the strong-arm stuff."

"I didn't sense that attitude in them, but I could have been wrong."

"Yes, you took a tremendous risk, Jeb."

"God." He touched his forehead to hers. "To think I could have lost you. I can't imagine it now."

"Don't try. It's all right. Everything is all right."

"I would say so."

"Jeb, my parents have been a tremendous help. My dad's talked Mrs. Applebaum into dropping her suit and helped me find a good counselor for Denny. Oh, and my mother, even though she hates dog hair, is the one who suggested that I get Denny's puppy now, because he really misses Spotty, and my folks have the room."

"Seems a shame to separate those two dogs," Jeb ventured.

"But that's what we always..." She narrowed her eyes suspiciously.

"No, we didn't." He grinned. "You did. My plan was to keep those puppies together, come hell or high water."

"Jeb Stratton, you've used those puppies all along, haven't you?"

"And they worked like a charm. Got you over here today, as a matter of fact. Now those dogs are so attached to each other, they should never be separated."

Her heart pounded as she looked at him. "What are you saying?"

"I wondered if I could still interest you in a house with a yard?"

"But—"

He raised up on one elbow. "I figure with what you have saved, and what I have saved, and some careful money management, we can swing it. As long as we don't go overboard on the honeymoon."

"You want to get married?"

"Why not?" He shrugged. "It beats separating the dogs."

"If that isn't the most romantic proposal I've ever heard!"

"What would you rather hear?" He spread one arm wide and chanted his next line. "Marry me, oh thou essence of womanhood."

"I would like to hear that very much."

"You just did."

"But you didn't really mean it."

He gazed down at her, and the teasing expression disappeared completely. "Yes, I did," he said gently. "Remember that little business about fire fighters? The more serious things get, the more they joke. I'm about as serious as I've ever been in my life, and I want like hell to be your husband, and I'm all out of funny lines. Please say yes."

"Yes."

"Just like that? You don't need time to think about it or anything?"

"Do you want me to take time to think about it?"

"Lord, no."

"Then kiss me, Fireman Jeb, before we waste another second of this wonderful life."

Silhouette Romance™

Escape to a place where a kiss is still a kiss...
Feel the breathless connection...
Fall in love as though it were
the very first time...
Experience the power of love!

Come to where favorite authors——such as
Diana Palmer, Stella Bagwell,
Marie Ferrarella and many more——
deliver heart-warming romance and genuine
emotion, time after time after time....

Silhouette Romance——
stories straight from the heart!

Silhouette®
Where love comes alive™

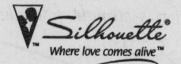

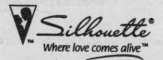

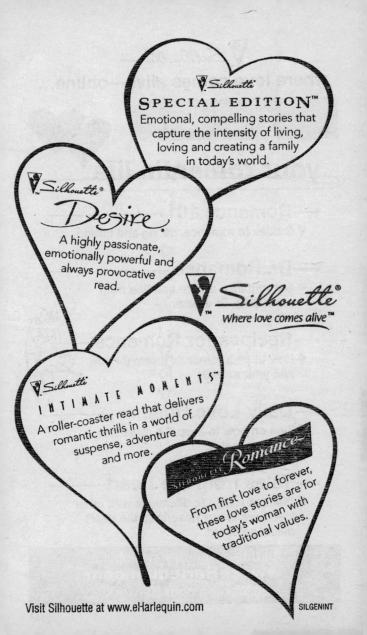

Silhouette® —

where love comes alive—online...

eHARLEQUIN.com

your romantic life

- **—Romance 101—**
  - ♥ Guides to romance, dating and flirting.

- **—Dr. Romance —**
  - ♥ Get romance advice and tips from our expert, Dr. Romance.

- **—Recipes for Romance—**
  - ♥ How to plan romantic meals for you and your sweetie.

- **—Daily Love Dose—**
  - ♥ Tips on how to keep the romance alive every day.

- **—Tales from the Heart—**
  - ♥ Discuss romantic dilemmas with other members in our Tales from the Heart message board.